DESERT PLACES

Kathryn Marshall

HARPER & ROW, PUBLISHERS
New York, Hagerstown
San Francisco, London

FIRST EDITION

Designed by Eve Callahan

Library of Congress Cataloging in Publication Data

Marshall, Kathryn.
  Desert places.

  I. Title.
PZ4.M3684De   [PS3563.A7222]   813'.5'4   77–3796
ISBN 0–06–012849–6

77 78 79 80 10 9 8 7 6 5 4 3 2 1

For Bob;
and for Richard Berg

With thanks to the Texas Institute
of Letters and the University of Texas

. . . the covertly hostile eyes of an alien who does not like the country in which he finds himself, does not understand the language nor wish to learn it, does not mean to live there and yet is helpless, unable to leave it at his will.

—Katherine Anne Porter,
Pale Horse, Pale Rider

1

BEATRICE LAWRENCE hated the sound of the telephone late at night. She hated it as she hated no other sound, unless it was the stabbing of boot heels on her polished hardwood floors or the sweep of the wind across the West Texas desert. The ringing of the telephone in the stillness of the house—especially when she was alone at night—always made her apprehensive. Getting out of bed, she felt her way across the room and found the light.

"Yes?"

The line clicked and began to buzz. She put the receiver down and stared at the surface of the desk, wondering why there was dust around the lamp base when the cleaning woman had been there just that afternoon. It occurred to Beatrice that she should have known better than to let her aunt send someone over—Louise had a habit of hiring women she felt sorry for, regardless of the kind of work they did. The clock at the end of the hall struck eleven. Beatrice continued to stand beside the desk, knowing that the phone would ring again. A moment later it did, but this time she let it ring six or seven times before she picked it up.

"Quinn? I know this is you. Did you call to let me know who you're screwing?"

There was no answer from the other end. Beatrice twisted her fingers more tightly around the receiver, hearing her voice steady itself so that it was almost impossibly calm.

"Is it the waitress who looks like Jayne Mansfield? The stripper

1

who followed you from Dallas last year? Or maybe it's the fifteen-year-old girl you were seen driving around with yesterday?"

She heard her husband cough into the phone. Too many cigarettes, she thought idly, holding the receiver away from her until the ragged noise had stopped. Then she heard his voice and put the receiver back to her ear.

"What did you say?"

"I said I forgot my keys. Leave the back door open."

He had been drinking, she could tell. Liquor gave his voice a peremptory quality, a note of blind impatience which always seemed to bring out in her the same series of responses. She watched herself fluctuate between anger and indifference, unable to feel anything but the rising tide of her contempt.

"You forget. The lock on the back door was smashed the other night."

For a long moment Quinn was silent. Then she heard him cough, away from the phone this time.

"Yeah. I forgot. See you later."

"Quinn?"

"Yeah?"

"There's nothing you can do to me any more. The nights may be long, but morning always comes."

She put the receiver down once more, hearing the sound of his coughing fade into the stillness of the house. Before, she would have screamed at him, played the scene out until the end, but now something inside refused to let her give him the satisfaction of knowing he had touched her. Maybe now he couldn't touch her, she thought. Maybe now there was no way for him to con her into caring, because it had just gone on too long. There had been too many nights when she had put the boys to bed at nine and then stayed up reading magazines, waiting for him to come home. Now, though, she was usually in bed by eleven, even though sleep didn't come until far into the night. Beatrice drummed her fingernails against the top of the desk, knowing that if the phone rang again she wasn't going to answer it.

A sound from upstairs startled her. Going over to the closet, she took out a robe and threw it on, and then she went into the hall. The pictures of her sons gazed back at her from behind the sheen of the glass: Tony laughing, with his hair falling down into his face; Lee, as always, too serious for his age. She stopped, one hand on the railing of the stairs. The pictures seemed to be receding away from her, becoming a series of memories which rose and fell with the years: Tony just after they had brought him home from the hospital, with Lee, age two, standing gravely beside the bed; Tony already talkative at two, Lee a quiet but unpredictable four; Tony just yesterday morning, chirping about his first few hours at kindergarten, Lee tied up in knots after one day in second grade. The sound came once again, and Beatrice hurried up the stairs. In the shadows of the hallway she could make out a small figure. It was Lee, standing just outside the door of his room.

"What's the matter? Can't you sleep?"

She saw him shake his head.

"Dreams again?"

He nodded. Beatrice went over to him, and he put his arms around her waist, pressing his face hard against her. She began to stroke his hair. He was frightened, his child's shoulders shaking with the violence of silent tears. She let her fingers travel down his face and neck, trying to quiet him a little before she put him back to bed.

"It's all right, darling. Come on, I'm here."

"I was scared," he said.

"I know. They're terrible, aren't they, those dreams?"

He nodded again, still clutching her. She reached for his hands and loosed their hold, feeling at the same time how cold they were.

"Where's Daddy? Is he still at the meeting?"

"Come on, Lee, let's go to bed."

"I don't want to go to school tomorrow. I don't like the second grade."

Beatrice wondered if Lee doubted yet the lies she told him about his father; Tony, she knew, was too young to suspect that Quinn's "meetings" lasted much too long. Switching out the hall light, Beatrice took her son's hand and led him into the darkness.

3

A bluish moon was visible from the bedroom window. She watched the clouds slide past it, momentarily darkening the street and lawn. The moon seemed to be hanging in the tops of the pines—she could make out Lee's profile, his face turned toward the sky, and she wondered what he was thinking. Was he wishing his father would come home? As they stepped into the bedroom she shut the door so that they wouldn't wake up Tony in the next room.

"I don't want to go to school tomorrow," Lee repeated, whispering.

"All right, darling," she whispered back.

They lay down on the narrow bed. Lee curled up against her, his head on her breast. Once again Beatrice began to stroke his hair, watching the way it caught the moon's light. After a moment Lee became very quiet. She could hear his breathing and feel the warmth of it every time he exhaled. The pines outside began to sway back and forth as a breeze blew in through the partially open window. Beatrice, thinking Lee was asleep, let her thoughts turn once more to Quinn. She wondered where he was and whether he was going to come home or even go to work in the morning. Her uncle, out of concern for her, had given Quinn a job in his lumberyard after he had been fired from odd jobs around town. Quinn rarely showed up for work on time, and there were days when he never went to work at all. Her uncle never said anything about it, but it embarrassed her. She knew how little her family thought of Quinn, knew that it was only her pride and stubbornness which kept them from saying anything about him —for seven years it had been this way, ever since she had gotten married. Suddenly she felt Lee shift his position so that his face was right next to hers.

"Mother?"

"What, darling?"

"I can't sleep."

"Try again. Here, put your head down."

She pressed his head back onto her breast. He threw one arm across her and buried his face in the folds of her robe, as close to her as he could get. Beatrice felt the soft hair sliding through her fingers and the weight of his warmth against her side. For a moment or two they stayed that way. Then Lee moved again.

"Mother?"

"Shh."

Once again she took his head and pressed it to her. Then she reached up and with one hand began to unbutton her robe. In the moonlight she could see the white rise of her breasts and next to them Lee's face.

"Shh," she whispered, still stroking the back of his head.

His dark hair fell over his eyes and spilled onto her as he lowered his lips to her nipple. She felt the wetness of his mouth, the pressure of his tongue; the arm that had been thrown across her moved so that one hand was resting on her other breast. He made a little noise, a kind of childish purring sound. She kept on touching his neck, his hair, and by the time she heard the downstairs clock strike one he was sleeping.

Moving Lee away from her as gently as she could, Beatrice got up and went downstairs. She was wondering if Quinn was going to come home so drunk she would have to lock herself in the guest room again. But she wasn't going to play the game any more, she had already decided that. Going into the bedroom, she sat down on the edge of the bed. A moment later she heard the sound of tires on the gravel of the driveway, and she stood up again, pulling her robe closer. At first she thought it was Quinn, until she realized that that wasn't the sound of his truck. It always wheezed and rattled when the ignition was turned off, and rather than leaving it parked beneath the window, Quinn would have pulled into the garage. Just as she was going to raise the blinds and look out, there was a knock at the kitchen door. She waited. Another knock. She felt herself go stiff with apprehension as she began to make her way down the hall. When her hand reached the light switch, she saw the red-bearded face of Buck Jonas on the other side of the glass panel. He was squinting, trying to shade his eyes from the glare.

"What's happened to him?" Beatrice asked as she led the way into the room.

When she turned to Buck again, he was looking directly at her.

5

In the bright light his face was harsh, severe. His bushy red hair stuck out from the sides of his skull, and his one good eye was set so deep in its socket that it was always difficult to tell what he was thinking. His other eye was glass. As Beatrice watched, Buck reached into his pocket and slowly—but with a slowness which nevertheless always seemed to suggest the potentiality of speed—pulled out a sliver of wood. Then, grimacing, he began to pick his teeth. Buck's habits, like many of her husband's, disgusted her; she waited for him to finish inspecting the end of the wood sliver before she repeated her question.

"They've hauled him to jail. Drunk driving this time."

She let out a breath, gesturing abruptly. Buck was still looking at her, and Beatrice couldn't help but wonder what he had done with whatever it was he had found between his teeth. Her aunt's cleaning woman might not have done a very good job, but it galled her to think Buck might have let something fall onto her kitchen floor.

"Well, at least it isn't rape again."

"You know as well as I do Quinn never raped that girl. She asked for it and you know it. Because Brenda Dew will do it—there ain't no one calls her Brenda Don't."

Beatrice bit her lower lip, saying nothing. Just the mention of that name made her angry, yet it wasn't so much anger as the humiliation of people's having known more about her private affairs than she would ever have wanted. The time Quinn had been arrested and charged with rape he had spent four hours yelling out the jail window that his wife "wouldn't give him the time of day, much less a piece of ass." Beatrice winced at the memory of it. She would never forget the curious, amused looks she had gotten at the Sheriff's office after that.

Buck backed away from her so that he was leaning against the refrigerator, and Beatrice saw his expression become more serious. He was going to lecture her, she thought. She had never gotten along with Buck Jonas, not only because he was her husband's friend but also because he never seemed to be content to leave their relationship at the level of a healthy dislike for one another. He was always trying to ignore the fact that his speech and

6

manners revolted her, and, worse than that, he insisted on taking her sons with him on fishing trips.

"Beatrice, you know why he called me instead of you, so you ought not to get so mad at him. He's sorry and you know it, else he would have waked you up to come down and get him out. The only reason I come over here was I knowed after I talked to him I didn't have the fifteen dollars on me."

"The Buick's in the shop."

"What?"

"Quinn dented the Buick the other night. That's why he didn't call me—he knew I wouldn't have any way to get down there."

"Well, come on, then. I'll take you."

Buck crammed his felt hat down on his mass of hair. With his arms upstretched, the shadow he cast reminded Beatrice of a giant bird; as his hands dropped back to his sides, dangling from the powerful, corded wrists out of sleeves that were too short, she regarded him and tried to make up her mind whether to say yes.

"I'll be ready in a minute. You can wait for me in the car."

She knew he would ignore her.

Going into the bedroom, Beatrice closed the door and began to unbutton her robe. The dress she had worn to the Women's League meeting that morning was still draped across a chair. She picked it up and was about to slip into it when she remembered how dirty the upholstery was in Buck's old Ford. But before she had a chance to decide on something else, she heard him knocking on the bedroom door.

"Yes?"

"I'll wait for you out in the car."

She was tempted to tell him he could wait anywhere he liked, preferably as far away from her as possible. Instead she stopped herself from replying and went over to the mirror. Her shoulder-length auburn hair was heavy and tangled, and, picking up a brush, she began to pull it through.

This time, she told herself, nothing was going to touch her. This time Quinn could say whatever he wanted, because he might as well be saying it to the wind.

Leaning forward to get a better look, Beatrice took the brush and arranged her hair so that it waved lightly across her forehead. Twenty-eight years old, she was thinking. Twenty-eight and still every bit as attractive as she had been the day she graduated from high school. Yet as she looked at herself she remembered something Quinn had said once about her eyes. Whenever she looked into a mirror, it seemed, she remembered it:

"Agate eyes. Like light-blue marbles someone has put in hot water, so that there are little cracks running all through them. The kind of eyes that when you stand in sunlight a person standing next to you can see right through."

She turned abruptly away from the mirror. Buck was waiting for her in his car.

"The boys going to be all right?"

"If we hurry. Quinn knows how I hate leaving them alone like this. Lee had another nightmare just tonight."

"He always was a kid for imagining things."

Buck backed the car down the driveway and out into the street. Most of the houses on the block were dark. Here and there a streetlamp burned, casting its oblique yellow glare onto the pavement. The September sky was brilliant with stars. Beatrice glanced out the window at the myriad tiny lights, wondering what had happened to the moon. She had seen it when she had been upstairs in Lee's bedroom, but now it seemed to have disappeared. As Buck drove along the main street Beatrice began to wonder if any of her friends were up, for she had the feeling that Quinn was going to be violent tonight and that it might be a relief to know she could call someone if she really had to. Yet except for an occasional light in a downstairs window or the flickering of a gas lamp, none of the impressive homes that lined the street in this section of town seemed to give any indication that their occupants were awake. Beatrice thought back to her conversation with Quinn as she looked out at the trees on the darkened expanses of lawn. No, she reflected, she didn't want to talk to anyone after all. It was better to keep everything to herself, as she had been doing for a long time now. A very long time, it seemed.

Buck was driving slowly. As they left the row of homes behind and approached the downtown area, her uncle's sawmill came into view. It was one of several that had originally been owned by her grandfather; Toombs Mill, tucked into a fold in the red land of East Texas, had always been a logging town. As a child Beatrice had listened to the idle talk of the old men who had sat around on upturned crates in front of the sawmills. One of the things they had claimed was that anyone who had spent his life in East Texas pine country had resin running in his veins. As she had grown older she had come to think it more likely that the resin was on the brain, and after spending three years away from Toombs Mill—two and a half at college and six months in the desert—she had lost all affection for the place where she had grown up; as the sawmill slipped past, Beatrice thought back to her childhood, memories of which always seemed to be per-meated with the odor of fresh-cut pine. She laughed softly to herself. Had the old men really had resin on the brain? Somehow, though, she supposed it was better to have resin on the brain than that infernal West Texas sand—Quinn's problem was that he had spent so much time in West Texas. He had grown up on an oil rig in the middle of the desert, and among the many ironies of his life was the fact that a quarter-century of sun had made him crazy but it hadn't dried him out: he had been drinking forever and would, she supposed, until the day he fell down dead.

"Did he wreck the truck?"

Buck looked at her as they passed beneath a streetlamp. For a moment one side of his face appeared stark, surreal, and his glass eye threw back the glare. Then the streetlamp was behind them and the car was dark again.

"He didn't say nothing about it."

Buck paused, and Beatrice heard him clear his throat. Already she knew what he was going to say.

"You don't have to tell me to go easy on him, Buck."

"I ain't honing to tell you how to run your affairs. But a man can't help it if he's got so much life in him it overflows at times. 'Course, one of Quinn's misfortunes is it overflows so much—women take to him like flowers to the sun."

"Yes. He's had a Violet, an Iris, and at least two Roses. And no telling how many time Miss Dew has fallen. On her back," she added, the bitterness rising to her voice. But she knew she had to check it, to keep all emotion down; this time, she reminded herself, he wasn't going to hurt her.

"You're a hard woman sometimes, Bea. Though maybe you're just full of shit."

"I don't need your pearls of wisdom, Buck Jonas."

Beatrice heard him laugh. She looked out for the moon again, wondering if Lee and Tony were all right; Lee didn't have nightmares often, but when he did they usually left him frightened for days.

"He's just a man," Buck went on. "And, like all men, there's some things he knows and some he don't. But he's past thirty now, on the way to seeing half his span. Pretty soon he's going to sit still long enough to understand the thing a man has to sit still awhile to understand."

"What's that?" she heard herself ask.

"Hisself."

"There isn't anything inside of Quinn." She paused. "That's why he drinks. Everyone in Toombs Mill knows it."

"Give a dog a bad name, folks are going to chunk rocks at him."

Beatrice looked over at Buck, wishing he would concentrate on driving and leave her private affairs alone. She resented his insistence on bombarding her with platitudes, but she knew it was useless to try and shut him up. For an instant it occurred to her that maybe there was some truth in what he had said; admitting that, though, would be admitting he was right about a lot of other things as well, and she wasn't going to grant him that. Because sometimes his good eye seemed to see right into her, and sometimes, strangely enough, it seemed to be his glass one. Buck had a way of looking at her with that eye that drove her wild, cocking the good eye to the side and letting the glass one stare straight ahead. She recalled the time Quinn had told her he was going to have a glass eye like Buck's put in, how she had nearly screamed him out of the house. That had been a long time before, though, back in the days when she had still been able to get mad enough to throw a set of heirloom china at his head; she turned toward the windows again, determined not to let Buck get the best of her.

"Besides," he went on, "if you really believed there was nothing on the inside of Quinn Lawrence, you wouldn't love him like you do."

"Maybe I don't love him," she answered sullenly.

"You love him, all right. And one day I'll get around to telling you why."

"I can hardly wait."

They pulled up in front of the jail and Beatrice got out.

"You going to make it home all right, you think?"

"I hope so. Sheriff always tows Quinn's truck back with him. I just hope he's sober enough to drive the old thing."

"You take care now," Buck said.

Beatrice watched him make a U turn, staring after the taillights until they had disappeared into the night.

As she went up the steps she stopped for a moment to collect herself. The jail had become familiar to her over the years. It was an old stone structure, though exactly how old she didn't know. Once she had asked Sheriff MacAffee if he recalled when her grandfather had had it built. He had glanced down before he answered her.

"I don't remember, Beatrice. But I do know this jail never held anyone by the name of Toombs."

Beatrice Toombs—that was who she had been before she had become Beatrice Lawrence, the only child of a woman with "sound common sense" and the man whose father had founded the town. Everyone in Toombs Mill had mourned the deaths of her parents, just as everyone had agreed it was a blessing they hadn't been alive to witness their daughter's marriage. But Beatrice remembered how she had returned Sheriff MacAffee's unblinking gaze and said to him, "You've known me all my life, long enough to know you shouldn't say things to me like that."

The matter had never come up between them again.

Beatrice pushed open the heavy doors and stepped into the bare, high-ceilinged room where a group of men sat around a television. She heard the pop of a beer can, and then a young man with hair cropped close to his head got up and came over to her.

"Where is Sheriff MacAffee, Claude Earl?"

11

"He went home, Mrs. Lawrence. Too much action on a Tuesday night."

The group of men around the television began to laugh. Beatrice waited for them to get quiet before she said anything.

"I came for my husband."

The young deputy fingered his beer can, nodding at her. He seemed to be slightly uneasy, but he smiled and offered to escort her down the hall.

"You don't need to show me. I've been down here often enough to know where you keep him."

As Beatrice turned to go the deputy said, "I think he was sicker than he was drunk, Mrs. Lawrence. Old Mac probably just picked him up out of meanness."

"What was he doing?"

"Oh, nothing much. Driving on the wrong side of the road or something. But, hell, there ain't ever anyone out after midnight anyhow."

Beatrice started down the hall, but the deputy stopped her again.

"Mrs. Lawrence?"

"Yes?"

"He's, uh—he's got someone with him."

She drew in a slow breath, feeling something inside her tighten into a knot. A moment passed in which she found herself staring down at a patch of paint that was peeling off the wall. The bare spot it was going to leave would probably stay there for years, she was thinking, and after a while no one would even notice it any more. Looking up into the deputy's face, she told him, "I bet you aren't old enough to be drinking that beer."

Then she turned, abruptly, and went down the hall.

The metal door leading to the row of cells was never kept locked. It opened noisily, and she found herself standing in front of her husband.

"Hello, honey."

Quinn tried to take her hand, but she was standing just out of his reach. As he let his outstretched arm fall back to his side and leaned forward against the bars, Beatrice looked silently at his high-boned face. He was a muscular man, just under six feet tall, and yet there was a surprising fluidity to his movements, for a certain sensual awareness seemed to mark every move Quinn made. Beatrice watched him reach up and push his dark hair back from his forehead.

"I got into some trouble."

"So I see."

"It was nice of you to come. Sheriff Mac don't run a Holiday Inn, even if he does charge fifteen dollars. You got some money on you?"

"The accommodations don't seem to bother *her*," Beatrice answered, gesturing toward the woman who was asleep on a mattress in the cell across the corridor.

Quinn smiled and reached through the bars again. Beatrice took a step backward this time, knowing when he looked at her like that there was more going on inside his mind than he was willing to let on. After seven years of battling the ebb tides of his moods, she had come to realize that his most affectionate expressions were masks for almost total absorption in himself. It was at these times, when he looked at her and his eyes seemed to be filled with a childlike need to be forgiven, that Beatrice trusted him least—and what he was asking for was her trust. Yes, she was thinking, Quinn could be quite a con man when he wanted to. She remembered the first time she had seen him, how she had been struck by the arrogance in his face. Only there had been something else there, too, a kind of reckless and irrepressible innocence which seemed to come, paradoxically, from his having seen too much too young. It was this quality in Quinn which for Beatrice was the most difficult to come to terms with, for the child, she knew, would do anything to get its way. She looked past him to the forgotten names and phrases scratched into the wall of the cell, and it occurred to her that of all the words of indictment and defiance, few had been read and even fewer had been heeded. She wondered whether any of them had been put there by her husband.

"I was just giving Brenda a ride home, honey."

"I wonder who was giving who a ride."

Quinn smiled again, screwing up his features in a mock-effort at thought.

"We-ell—"

That was when his expression changed. His face became dead serious, and as he looked at her she was amazed at the way he seemed to have been transformed. The playfulness was gone out of his eyes. It was as if, she thought, the inner structure of his face had collapsed, so that there was nothing to contain the intensity of his feelings.

"We have a lot to talk about, Beatrice. There are some things that have to be explained. I want to know what's been going on with you lately—you've got something on your mind and I know it. So why don't you just out with it and lay the shit on the table?"

His voice was heavy with whiskey, but he wasn't drunk enough for her to avoid answering him. In fact, despite his appearance, he seemed to be remarkably sober. Beatrice looked from her husband to the woman in the other cell, but Quinn's eyes wouldn't let her go. All of a sudden she was aware of a rising rage, a sense of the futile, timeless struggle to keep the self intact. The violence she felt inside would rip her to pieces if she didn't manage to get a hold on it, to force everything back down and show him only the cold face of her contempt. Because that was there, too, her utter scorn for his capacity for making a fool of himself, and yet there was more to it than that: he could penetrate her pride and make a fool of her. Beatrice knew she didn't have to answer him, but she would have to do something if she wasn't going to be forced into an admission which she wasn't prepared to make. It was uncanny, though, the way he could read her mind.

"I think you're the one who ought to do some explaining, Quinn."

"What do you mean? Listen, I might be a piss-poor husband, but at least I have some respect for myself as a human being. Not your kind of self-respect, because I don't believe you even under stand what it is. But I'm always straight with you, Beatrice. At least I've always been that."

He coughed, reaching into the pocket of his shirt for a pack of cigarettes.

"Got a match?"

She shook her head. Quinn kept his eyes on hers for a moment longer, and then he called out to the woman asleep in the other cell.

"Come on, Brenda, wake up. You ain't so drunk you can't find me a match."

Brenda Dew opened her eyes and looked at the opposite wall. "God."

"I need a match."

"I don't have a match."

"What happened to the ones you had out in the truck?"

"I don't have a match, I said."

Beatrice was leaning against the door that led to the main corridor. From the office she could hear the voices of the television and the intermittent sound of male laughter. Then Brenda Dew let out a shriek.

"Quinn, what's that bitch doing here? I thought you told me she'd left you!"

Beatrice watched her husband draw in on the cigarette as Brenda Dew got up and came over to the bars. Her make-up was badly streaked. One false eyelash was dangling at the corner of her left eye—the other lash was gone. Beatrice watched her reach up and peel the eyelash off.

"What did you come here for? Everybody knows you think you're too good for him. There's nobody in town who don't know what a tight-assed bitch you are. And maybe you don't know it, but you've got nothing to be so smug about. He don't give a damn any more whether you hold out on the goods or not."

Brenda looked at Quinn. Beatrice was waiting for him to say something in reply, something meant to goad Brenda into insulting her even more, but he didn't. He just stood there watching them, an amused, half-lit expression in his eyes.

"You cunt," Brenda said, turning back to her again. She was gripping the bars so tightly that the veins in her hands were standing out. "You hypocrite. What did you come here for, to flash that wedding ring in my face?"

"Flash it in your face—I ought to cram it up your ass."

15

Her voice came out low, so suddenly and so calmly that Beatrice could see the shock register on the other woman's features. Brenda let go of the bars and reached up to pat the ruins of her beehive.

All of a sudden Quinn said, "Let's get the hell home, honey."

"I ought to cram this piece of worthless metal up yours first, Quinn Lawrence."

"Beatrice—"

But she was already out the door. In the office again, the young deputy gave her a curious look.

"What's the matter, Mrs. Lawrence? Don't he want to leave?"

"No, at the last minute he decided he's so comfortable he wants to stay all night. Now if you'll tell me what the Sheriff did with the truck—"

She noticed then that one of the men had turned off the television. Except for the deputy's nervous shuffling as he shifted his weight back and forth, the room was completely quiet. Somewhere down the block a dog was barking, while just beyond the window the crickets kept up their cacophonous nighttime songs. Beatrice looked at the clock above the Sheriff's big wooden desk. It said two fifteen. That meant Lee and Tony had been home alone for almost an hour, and she felt a kind of panic at the thought of the darkened house. What if something had happened to them? What if Lee had woken up with another nightmare?

"It's down near the railroad yard," the deputy said. "Mac's tow chain busted yesterday."

Beatrice hardly heard him. For a moment she was aware of a vague fear somewhere inside, a kind of sickening certainty that something had happened to her sons.

"I can give you a lift home," the deputy went on.

"You stay here and mind the fort like you're paid to, Claude Earl. I'll give the little lady a ride home."

Beatrice glanced across the room to see a wiry, sharp-featured man looking oddly out of place in an expensive shirt and white patent-leather loafers. He was the only man in the office she had never seen before, and as she watched him reach for the set of

16

car keys on top of the television she knew instantly that she wasn't going to accept his offer.

"Well, ain't you going to introduce us?" he asked.

Before Beatrice could say anything, he was standing next to her.

"Meet Johnny Kingman's second cousin, Leon Pugh. You know Johnny over there, don't you?" the deputy asked. "And, Leon, this is Mrs. Lawrence."

"Thank you, Mr. Pugh," Beatrice murmured, managing to move away from him, "but I'd rather walk."

"Hell, ma'am, it's the middle of the night."

"Leon's from Oklahoma City," the deputy put in, as if that explained everything. Then, giving Beatrice an embarrassed glance, he tried again. "He came down here to see Johnny and celebrate his divorce—Leon's divorce, I mean. Anyway, that's how come all the beer tonight."

"You know, Claude Earl, they always told me to never trust a Cajun woman—"

"Them gator mamas will do it to you every time," a man whom Beatrice recognized as Johnny Kingman added from across the room. He crushed the beer can in his hand and tossed it toward the Sheriff's desk, where it hit and bounced onto the floor. "But you, Leon, not only did you end up with a Cajun—you had to go and get you one with red hair."

Leon Pugh guffawed and turned back to Beatrice. "I hope my offer didn't offend you."

"No, Mr. Pugh, not at all. Now about my husband—please tell the Sheriff I appreciate his concern but that I don't see the logic behind hauling men in for drinking *off* the job when he pays his deputy for drinking while he's *on*. Good night."

She heard Leon Pugh's raucous laughter as she left.

Outside, the street was completely empty. The downtown neon had blinked off, except for the dim letters which spelled out BUDWEISER in the window of the Corner Café. Beatrice didn't look forward to the half-hour's walk through the deserted streets, but she couldn't imagine calling anyone to come and pick her up

17

at such an hour. Her aunt and uncle would be asleep, and she didn't want to wake any of her friends to let them know she had had to go down to the jail again. They would find out anyway, she supposed, just as everybody in Toombs Mill found out everything. And they would wonder why this time she had let Quinn stay there all night.

2

BEATRICE AWOKE TO FIND the bed flooded with sun. The rays were dancing and shimmering before her half-opened eyes, and the world seemed to be alive with light. Blinking, she pushed back the covers and got out of bed. For a moment she had expected to turn over and find Quinn asleep beside her, but once she was fully awake she began to wonder why; even if Claude Earl had decided to let him out, he would have stayed the rest of the night with Brenda Dew. As she slipped into her robe and shook her heavy hair back from her face, she decided she wasn't going to think about what had gone on the night before. Her reaction to Quinn had been justified but pointless, and she had been foolish to leave Lee and Tony by themselves so long. Glancing at the clock, she realized she had an hour to get Tony ready for kindergarten. Lee, she remembered, didn't feel like going to school.

The night had left her tired. Yawning, Beatrice went over to the mirror. After inspecting the little creases around her eyes she drew her index finger lightly across her forehead. It was obvious to her that she was still a beautiful woman, though sometimes she found herself doubting what everyone else seemed to believe— that the years actually agreed with her, that they had evened out her features and given grace to her smile. Leaning toward the mirror, she looked more closely at what she took to be the effects of the preceding night. The skin beneath her eyes was tinged with blue, and there was a drawn look to her mouth. For a moment she felt a definite but undirected anger, anger at herself, at the town, at Quinn. Finally, trying not to think, she turned away from her reflection.

It was a little after eight. She made up her mind to hurry Tony off to kindergarten and then call her aunt and see if she wanted to go to the country club for lunch. Giving her hair a few quick brushes, Beatrice put on her house slippers and went out into the hall. Tony, as usual, was already up. She could hear the television in the living room and the sound of his bare feet slapping against the floor.

"What are you doing in there?" she called.

He was galloping around the room on an invisible pony, and she couldn't help but laugh at the sight of his intent face. She wasn't sure, though, if he was the cowboy or the pony, and when she realized that he wasn't sure either, she began laughing even harder.

"Come on, Tony-pony. It's time to saddle up for kindergarten."

He ran over to her and she bent to give him a hug. With his blue eyes and reddish hair, Tony seemed to be completely hers. Lee was the one who looked like his father. Unlike Tony, he had Quinn's Indian eyes, dark complexion, and brown-black hair, though he promised to be smaller than his father was. With Tony it was still hard to tell whether he would have his father's muscular build and broad shoulders. Nevertheless, Beatrice wanted both boys to excel in sports, even though Quinn protested at the thought of it.

It took her almost an hour to get Tony dressed and fed. He was so excited about his third day at kindergarten that he refused to stand still long enough for her to get his hair combed and his shirt buttoned, and she ended up having to chase him down the stairs with his shoes. The cereal was either too bland or too sugary, and the milk "tasted icky." Exasperated, Beatrice finally let him have a peanut-butter-and-jelly sandwich for breakfast. After he had eaten it she cornered him in the bathroom and wiped the jelly off his hands while Tony, protesting, tried to wiggle away from her.

By the time the minister's wife came by with her car full of kids, she was beginning to wonder whether the ordeal of getting him ready was worth the few free hours.

Beatrice stood on the porch and looked out across the rolling lawn. The summer had been a wet one. The back yard was a lush field of green, and along the walkway to the pines the flower beds were bright with color. She stepped down onto the grass to get a better look at them: the rows of pepper plants, the azaleas ensconced in dirt her aunt had brought up from Louisiana, the caladiums, the roses, the gardener's red zinnias which had come up purple. Above the tops of the pines the sun was still full with summer, but already its intensity was beginning to wane. Soon, she knew, the flowers would droop, the leaves would curl into themselves, and day by day the shadows of the trees would lengthen. For a moment she stood squinting up at the sun. Then she picked a bunch of roses from the climbing branches on the trellis and went back into the kitchen and found a vase. As she was filling it with water she heard Lee coming down the stairs.

"Good morning, darling." When he didn't answer, Beatrice turned around. "You didn't have any more dreams, did you?"

"They went away after you said I wouldn't have to go to school."

"I worried about you."

She went over to the table with the flowers. Lee was kneeling on the window bench. Sitting down next to him, she gave him a kiss.

"Aren't they pretty?" she asked.

Lee leaned across the table to put his nose to the flowers, and Beatrice threw her arms around him, pulling him toward her.

"I love you."

"I love you," he replied.

After a moment she let him go and went over to the stove to boil the milk for his hot chocolate. Her aunt, she hoped, wouldn't be busy that morning. If Louise could take her to pick up the Buick, they could meet for lunch at the country club and afterward she could stop by the grocer's.

"Lee, do me a favor and put some bread in the toaster. I'm going to call Louise and see if she wants to have an early lunch at the club."

"What about me?"

"You can play in the play yard while we have lunch. And you can get a hamburger at the snack bar—how does that sound, darling?"

Beatrice went into the bedroom and picked up the telephone. She would be scolded, she knew, for letting Lee stay home from school, but Beatrice had listened to Louise tell her she was spoiling him for as long as she could remember. At the other end of the line her aunt picked up the phone. The two of them talked briefly, and Beatrice went back into the kitchen.

"Go on upstairs and get dressed, Lee. Don't forget to wash the sleep out of your eyes this time."

"Hey, Daddy's home!"

Beatrice listened. Quinn's truck was turning into the driveway.

"Go on, Lee!"

He went reluctantly toward the stairs.

At the sound of Quinn's boot heels she felt herself go tense. The back door opened, but she kept stirring the milk on top of the stove. She heard him go over to the refrigerator. Then, without a word, he sat down at the table.

How, she wondered, could he just walk in like that? But before she had time to think, the milk began to steam, and she took it quickly off the fire. As she turned to reach for the cocoa, she saw that he had taken the milk carton out of the refrigerator and was drinking from it. Something exploded inside her. She ran and snatched the carton out of his hands.

"Do you have to do that!"

"It's almost empty," Quinn answered.

"That doesn't make any difference."

"No, what's inside doesn't make any difference to you at all. It's the way it looks that counts. Right, honey?"

"I refuse to have this argument with you, Quinn."

She watched him shrug, a stubborn, defiant grin beginning to spread across his face. Now, she knew, was the time to be calm.

22

Several moments passed. The clock struck nine at the far end of the hall. In the den the television was on, while outside on the telephone wires the doves were making their early-morning sounds. For a long time, it seemed, she looked down into her husband's face. She knew it hadn't always been this way with them. Yet it was hard to recall the time when there hadn't been a silence underlying all the words, a gap between what was said and what was intended so that for her the only safety lay in complete suspension of emotion. Beatrice closed her eyes. She was seeing Quinn as he had looked years before, remembering his laughter and the rippling of his body as he had bent toward her, shirtless, the first time they had touched.

Lee came into the kitchen just as Beatrice was going back to the stove.

"Daddy!" he cried, running to Quinn and then stopping beside the chair. It was obvious from Lee's face that he sensed something was wrong.

"Good morning, weevil. Hey, how come you're not in school?"

"Mother and Aunt Louise and me are going to the country club."

"He didn't sleep well last night," Beatrice put in.

She took the two cups of hot chocolate and set them on the table. Before she had a chance to sit down Quinn stood up and took her by the arm.

"I've told you about letting him stay home like this. Lee is seven years old, and you treat him like he still pisses in his pants. The kid's going to grow up as confused as you are—you want him to be a jock and yet you pamper him all to hell!"

"He had nightmares last night."

"Beatrice, you're ruining him."

"You sound like Louise!"

She heard her voice beginning to rise and jerked her arm out of Quinn's grasp.

"Well, maybe the old coon-assed broad knows more than I thought she did."

"How can you slander my relatives like that? After all they've done for you—"

23

"Slander? Who's slandering? I like your Uncle Milton fine, Beatrice. He's a bigot, a pussy-hound, and the crookedest businessman in town, but at least he'll admit it. Your aunt's another matter, though. Louise is such a hypocrite she can't even admit she farts—ask her sometime. I did once."

Beatrice pushed past him and went down the hall. In the alcove of the bay window the grand piano gave an added elegance to the gleaming floors and impeccable furnishings of the living room. Going over to it, she lifted the keyboard cover. For a moment she hesitated. Then she sat down and began to play a Chopin étude, concentrating on the rich intricacy of the notes. The music seemed to well out of the piano and rise to drift along the hall. She took a deep breath, letting the music carry her back to her girlhood when she had stood at the far end of the long room and listened to her mother playing Chopin. But at the sound of a slamming door she got up from the piano and went back into the kitchen. Lee was sitting on the window seat with a cup in one hand.

That was when she saw that Lee had pulled all the petals off the roses. The tablecloth was littered with deep red blots.

"Daddy's in the bedroom. He said for me to tell you to cut the goddamned noise so he can sleep."

Beatrice looked at him, saying nothing. He was sitting there sipping the hot chocolate, his face as closed and as expressionless as a doll's.

"I wouldn't mind having a cocktail first. Something cold would be lovely."

Louise took her by the arm and ushered her into the lounge, which was dimly lit and done in what Beatrice referred to as "country-club gothic." Though her aunt and most of the other women she knew agreed that the Hawaiian motif was "lovely," Beatrice thought everything about the place showed an embarrassing lack of taste. Taking off her sunglasses, she sat down across from her aunt in the corner booth.

"I think I'm going to have one of your lovely champagne

cocktails," she heard Louise saying to the waitress.

Beatrice glanced over at her. She was a well-preserved woman of fifty whose plump, powdered face revealed, among other things, a startling naïveté. Her silvering hair was set and sprayed so that it resembled some kind of helmet, and her clothes, as always, gave off a faint, too-sweet perfume.

"And you?" the waitress asked.

Beatrice looked up. Had she ever seen that girl with Quinn?

"I'll have a martini on the rocks. Extra dry, please, with a twist."

"You ought to have something nicer," Louise whispered.

"A martini will be fine."

What she really wanted was a double Jack Daniels', but she supposed a martini would have to do. As the waitress was walking away Beatrice looked at the girl's legs, thinking she herself would look better in that short costume. Then she felt Louise's hand on hers.

"You know, the thing I like best about the lounge is the waterfall. It's so peaceful."

"I think the money should have been spent on a painting or maybe even a few decent reproductions. Some Gauguins might have been nice."

"But, Bea, you know the Women's League brought in a bright young architect from Houston just especially to design that waterfall. And Houston, as everyone knows, is a lovely city."

"It's an architectural disaster area."

"But it has the Astrodome—"

"Which some people call the Half-assed-trodome."

"Beatrice, please."

A moment later the waitress was back with the drinks. Louise insisted they be put on her bill, but Beatrice shook her head.

"No, this is on me. Put it on mine—Mrs. Quinn Lawrence."

"He's been acting up recently, hasn't he?" Louise asked when they were alone again. "I can always tell, Bea, when Quinn's been acting up, because you let Lee stay home from school. You shouldn't do that, you know."

"Louise—"

She picked up her glass, noticing it was garnished with an olive instead of a lemon twist. Annoyed, she called the waitress back over to the table.

"I ordered my martini with a twist."

"Would you like me to bring you one on a napkin?"

"I'd like you to bring me another martini."

When the girl had returned with the drink Beatrice leaned back into the booth's naugahyde depths, hoping her aunt wouldn't say anything else about Quinn. But Louise was concentrating on the bubbles in her cocktail. Relieved, Beatrice began to scan the faces of the people in the lounge, realizing without surprise that she recognized every one of them. Members of the Women's League were always at the country club for lunch, and the more successful businessmen and professionals made regular noontime appearances. Beatrice waved at Ron Prather, who had recently come back from Harvard with a law degree and an absurd New England accent, and then she acknowledged Eliot Cramer's smile. Eliot was the husband of a woman whom Beatrice had known and disliked since grade school, but as Ann Cramer's mother had been her mother's closest friend, it was impossible for Beatrice to avoid her. And then, just as she was getting ready to ask her aunt how the champagne cocktail was, she saw a man she didn't know coming in their direction.

"Who's that?" Louise whispered.

Suddenly Beatrice recognized him. It was Leon Pugh.

"Mind if I join you, Mrs. Lawrence? You do remember me—the name's Leon Pugh. We met last night."

Beatrice asked herself why she hadn't recognized him sooner. Something in his manner was unmistakable, she decided as she nodded in answer to his question. There was a glaring vulgarity about him, even with the expensive clothes. He set his drink down on the table, and Beatrice held out her hand.

"Yes, Mr. Pugh. I remember you."

"I've always been told I'm a hard man to forget."

He laughed and looked straight at her. Beatrice took another sip of her martini, wondering how he had gotten into the club.

"Well, won't you sit down, Mr. Pugh? I'm Beatrice's aunt,

Mrs. Milton. I don't believe I've ever seen you around Toombs Mill. Of course, we aren't a metropolis, but then again we aren't—"

"I'm from Oklahoma City, ma'am," he put in, sitting down next to Beatrice.

He had positioned himself close to her, too close, she thought as she saw him slip one hand beneath the table. Her aunt, though, seemed not to have noticed.

"Yep," Leon Pugh went on, "I was born an Okie and I guess I'll always be one. And you know what, Mrs. Milton?" He leaned forward then, as if to tell them something personal. "I'm a divorced man."

"What?"

Leon Pugh began to laugh. He had moved over even closer to Beatrice so that he was sitting right next to her. All of a sudden his hand was on her leg. A rush of anger went through her, and then, slowly, she willed herself to relax. It was obvious that what she should do was reach down discreetly and let him know she had no intention of allowing his hand to stay there, but she didn't. Instead she turned to him and said, "I suppose your wife left you?"

"Beatrice!"

Her aunt set her drink down so abruptly it almost spilled in her lap.

Leon Pugh let his hand slide down to her knee. Beatrice could feel his moist palm through her nylons as his fingers found the hem of her dress and then her slip and inched their way beneath them. Raising her glass to her lips, she looked over the rim at her aunt, who was mopping up a little pool of champagne with a cocktail napkin.

"It's all right, Mrs. Milton," Leon Pugh went on. "What I was trying to say was I'm down here on vacation. You know how divorces are. They sap all your energy so that afterward you need to hole up for a while to get it back."

"I'm afraid neither my aunt nor I has had that experience, Mr. Pugh."

"Leon. And may I call you Bea?"

She set down her drink. "Beatrice. You see, we're both married women, and neither of us has ever had any reason to consider divorce. Louise has four grandchildren and I have two children. And my aunt—my aunt is even lucky enough to have a husband."

She smiled, and he let out a laugh which seemed to indicate that he thought she had just let him in on something. But the moment he began to slide his hand along the inside of her thigh, she crossed her legs, at the same time reaching into her purse for a cigarette. She knew he would feel obligated to offer her a light, and she wondered how he was going to manage it with one hand trapped between her thighs. As she took the book of matches from the ash tray she glanced at him, enjoying his moment of awkwardness.

"Please don't trouble yourself," she said, pressing her thighs together.

Caught off guard, Leon Pugh tried to protest, but Beatrice went ahead and lit the cigarette herself. As she exhaled and watched the smoke waft upward, she began, very slowly, to un-cross her legs. A moment later she felt him rub his palm against her nylons. His hand, she noticed, was damper than before.

Louise finished mopping up the spilled champagne. "There. How silly of me—you would have thought I'd had too much to drink, wouldn't you, Mr. Pugh? Now tell me, what sort of business are you in?"

Beatrice watched him pick up the swizzle stick which had been in her martini and, grasping it in the fingers of his free hand, begin to clean his thumbnail. The other hand was inching along her thigh again, but this time she did nothing to discourage him.

"Pest control. I own and operate Oklahoma City's largest exterminating outfit. Last year we fumigated over fifty thousand homes and offices in the Oklahoma City area, killing an untold number of termites, silverfish, earwigs, and other household pests. Of course," he added, letting his fingers move along her nylons to her bare skin and then sliding them up to the edge of her panties, "we don't claim to have gotten all them little buggers, but you have to admit we gave them one hell of a fight."

"No doubt you did," Beatrice murmured. Finishing her martini, she looked over at her aunt in hope that she might be ready to go.

"It sounds like you have a successful business," Louise said.

"More than successful, ma'am. We've redefined the concept of pest control."

Beatrice felt herself begin to panic when she realized his hand was between her legs. She felt the pressure of his palm and the insistence of his fingers and then, after a moment's hesitation, she let her thighs move slowly apart. His fingers slipped beneath the elastic of her panties. When she finally crossed her legs again, she felt as though she was going to scream—it seemed impossible she was really doing this. Then she noticed Leon Pugh was still cleaning his thumbnail with the swizzle stick, and her anger gave way to contempt.

"Louise, would you like to go into the dining room now? I'm sure Mr. Pugh is bored with our conversation."

Beatrice put out the cigarette, feeling her own wetness against her skin as Leon Pugh withdrew his hand and laid it on her thigh. She had made it evident he wasn't welcome to have lunch with them, but she wasn't entirely certain he would pay attention to the hint. As Louise excused herself to see if there was a table available, Beatrice turned to him and said, "I'm sorry we can't ask you to join us."

He waited until her aunt was out of hearing, and then he leaned toward her, so close she could feel his breath on her face and smell the mingled odors of mouthwash and whiskey. Reaching down, she took his hand from her leg. Her nervousness didn't show, but she was anxious to get away.

"I've got a room at the Holiday Inn. Meet me there in an hour."

Beatrice straightened the hem of her skirt, feeling her stomach begin to tighten. How, she wondered, was she going to refuse him? And then by virtue of panic's peculiar logic she realized that it didn't really matter what she did. Nothing this man could do meant anything to her—he was nothing, hardly even a name.

"Well, little lady?"

She picked up her sunglasses and put them in her purse and

then, taking the pen from the tip tray, she signed the check. He was waiting for an answer—the name of a motel came to her, and she scribbled it on a cocktail napkin. Beneath it, in small handwriting, she wrote down a date and time.

"I'm leaving town tomorrow—"

"Oh, really—"

"But I might be able to stay—"

Beatrice snapped her purse shut. When he didn't stand up for her to get out of the booth, she slid around to the other side of the table.

"This will cost you, you know."

The words came out with that edge of practiced calm which she knew revealed nothing. He had a curious look on his face as she stood up.

"All right," he said after a silent moment had passed during which Beatrice had been listening to the liquored laughter of the men at the bar. Then she saw him reach into his coat and pull out a roll of bills. Grinning, he laid one on the table. "A hundred bucks."

He was looking at her expectantly. She glanced down at the table before she raised her eyes to his face again.

"It will cost you twice that, Mr. Pugh."

"Well, who would have thought you were such a little business-woman? All right. Friday at two o'clock."

Beatrice turned and walked quickly through the bar. She had a feeling she was going to be sick, so instead of going immediately to join her aunt she pushed open the door of the ladies' room. Inside, the noise of the air-conditioning filled her ears and the odor of disinfectant burned her nostrils. She sat down in front of the mirror with her face in her hands, feeling her whole body go tense. Outwardly, she knew, nothing had betrayed her, but inside she wasn't sure what was happening. As she raised her head to look into the mirror she felt a tremor of something which she could only identify as satisfaction.

Because suddenly it was in her power to obliterate the pain of seven years.

That afternoon when she got home from the club Quinn was still sleeping. After supper he was gone for several hours, and the next night he didn't come home at all, so that by the time Friday came she was more determined than she had been before. As she dressed for her meeting with Leon Pugh she thought back over the disappointments her marriage had brought her, reminding herself of all the bitterness and all the endless nights. Not that she was without apprehension, and she knew she wasn't without guilt. But she kept telling herself that she was justified in making Quinn suffer as she herself had. And, besides, it really didn't matter—there was so little left between them any more.

At one forty-five on Friday Louise came by to stay with Lee and Tony. Beatrice, having told Louise she was going shopping, drove to the Violet Crown Motel. Leon Pugh had wanted her to drive ten miles d↓n the interstate to the Holiday Inn, but she had a sudden impulse to meet him at the place which everyone in Toombs Mill knew rented, on request, by the hour. Beatrice wasn't sure why she wanted it this way, except that she imagined Quinn often took his women there. And anyway, she told herself, she had wanted to see the inside of one of those rooms ever since she had been a girl. The motel was on the edge of town, next to the water tank and the railroad yard. It was a grim-looking structure with its sagging sign and its flower beds overgrown with weeds. As she turned into the parking lot she saw a new yellow Thunderbird with Oklahoma license plates and was instantly certain that it belonged to Leon Pugh. Determined not to let her nervousness show, Beatrice got out of the car. The motel had a dead look about it. Except for number ten, all the doors were closed. Breathing deeply, she walked past the rows of rooms until she reached the open door.

"Hello, little lady."

Leon Pugh was standing in front of the desk with a bottle of bourbon and an ice bucket. As she closed the door, he flashed her a grin.

"Could I fix you up? It's awful warm outside." When she hesitated he went on, "You do drink bourbon, don't you? I noticed you drinking a martini the other day. Me, I'm usually a tequila man, only today I thought I'd bring out the sweeter stuff."

"I drink bourbon if it's good bourbon," Beatrice answered. "But no thanks. I'm just fine."

She sat down in the room's only chair and looked around her, wondering if Quinn had ever been here. The carpeting was frayed and faded. Across from the bed was a mirror; Beatrice let her eyes wander from it to the bed again. It seemed impossible that in just a matter of minutes she would be lying there with the man who stood before her. She put the thought out of her mind, watching as Leon Pugh uncapped the bottle. Then, to relieve the tension, she said, "I suppose the air-conditioning isn't working? In these older motels it never seems to work."

He stopped pouring and glanced up at her. "I hate to say this, but you sure picked a low-class place."

"I thought it would be more—more convenient."

Leon Pugh recapped the bottle and dropped some ice in his glass. Then he took off his coat and tossed it toward the top of the television, where it stayed briefly before slipping to the floor. Without bothering to pick it up he went over to the bed. The next moment he was stretched out with the glass of bourbon balanced on his stomach.

"You know, my room at the Holiday Inn faces onto the swimming pool. I can open my door and damn near fall right in."

"I'm sure you can. So your stay in Toombs Mill has been pleasant?"

"It's been fine. Real fine." He took a long drink, and then he ran his tongue across his upper lip, a little nervously, she thought. "Sure you don't want something to cool you off?"

"Oh, no. I'm fine," she said, reaching up to loosen the scarf around her neck. The room was stuffy, even with the windows open.

"All right. If you say so."

She wondered what she was expected to do. He was watching her, gauging her every move. Reaching up again, Beatrice took off her scarf and began to tie knots in one end of it. She could feel her palms perspiring.

All of a sudden he grabbed his glass and sat up. "You know, I didn't really think you'd come."

"Didn't you?"

"Nope," he said, shaking his head. Then, setting his drink on the nightstand, he leaned back again. "The best whore I was ever with was in Korea."

"Oh, you were in Korea? So was my husband."

"Is that right? Yeah, she sure was something. She knew every trick in the goddamned book. Everything. Never saw anything like her before or since."

Leon Pugh looked over at her. She was twisting the scarf between her fingers, pulling the knots tighter.

"What's the matter, you nervous?"

"Not at all," she answered lightly. "Give me a drink, please. I've changed my mind."

"What? I thought— Sure."

Beatrice watched as he went over to the dresser and poured some bourbon over a glass of ice cubes. He was an ugly man, she thought. There was something unpleasant in his expressions, something furtive about the eyes. When she thanked him for the drink he said, "My pleasure, little lady."

A few minutes passed. Leon Pugh rambled on about the Korean prostitute while Beatrice sipped her drink, saying nothing. The scarf was still in her hand. From time to time she gave it a twist, not daring to let her mind roam ahead to the moment when conversation would give out. The nervousness rose to her throat. She found herself wondering what she should do next.

"The money, Mr. Pugh."

Her voice seemed to be terribly controlled. As she watched him pick up his coat and take two one-hundred-dollar bills out of his wallet she realized that she *was* in control. The thought struck her so clearly and yet so unexpectedly that she almost laughed out loud.

"Thank you," she heard herself murmur as she stuck the bills inside her purse. "And could I have another drink?"

33

She didn't care that she was drinking much too fast. As he refilled her glass she began to unbutton her blouse, taking her time with it, letting herself enjoy the bourbon's effects. A pleasant bodily awareness had replaced her apprehension. She felt light, almost giddy. Letting out a little laugh, she reached up and smoothed her fingers across her hair. Through her open blouse she knew he could see the parting of her breasts.

"Everything in the book, you said?"

When he didn't answer, Beatrice let her blouse slip from her shoulders. Taking another sip of bourbon, she draped her blouse over the back of the chair and began to unfasten the hooks on her skirt. When she stood up the skirt fell lightly to the floor. She bent to pick it up, knowing he was watching her.

"Yes," she heard him answer.

Beatrice touched her hair again. Her body, it seemed, had never been more her own. Never had she felt so sure of herself, so certain that every impulse was right. Going over to the bed, she sat down next to him. The scarf, she noticed, was still in her hand, but as she began to peel her stockings from her legs she let it float to the floor. When she had taken off everything but her panties she rubbed up against him, feeling his erection pressing against the fabric of his slacks.

"Shit," he said hoarsely.

She took off his shoes and socks and then reached for the buttons of his shirt. He whispered something and grabbed at her breasts, but she stopped his hand. For a moment he stared at her. Then he lay still and let her unzip him.

"Relax," she whispered back.

She touched him and he breathed in sharply.

"Goddamn it, I *can't* relax."

Laughing at him, she spread her thighs. He groaned, watching as she slipped out of her panties. And then she felt the full weight of his body against hers, and the smell of him seemed to envelop her. Closing her eyes, she tried not to think. Yet she kept on seeing Quinn. How long had it been since he had touched her? How long had it been? Leon Pugh was panting. She glanced at his face as he writhed against her, noticing how red it was and how it was contorted with the effort of his body. Then, with a shock, Beatrice realized she could see his backside in the mirror, and she felt a ridiculous urge to tell him so. Instead she reached down and took the scarf in one hand, with the other grabbing his buttocks. When his movements became frantic she thrust the knotted end of the scarf inside him and gave it a violent jerk. A tremor ran through his limbs, as though every muscle was contracting. At last, crying out, he collapsed on top of her.

Beatrice wasn't sure how long they stayed that way. She was still staring over his shoulder at the mirror, her mind completely blank, when someone in the next room began to play a saxophone. Its low, plaintive sound seemed to reawaken something inside her. Pushing Leon Pugh away, she got up and began to dress. He slowly pulled himself to a sitting position, one hand lingering at his crotch.

"Goddamn," he said, a puzzled expression beginning to spread across his face. "I don't know what you did, but I shot my wad three times—bam bam bam—just like that. I thought it was going to take my balls off, but I'll be damned if that isn't some trick. Some trick, all right."

Beatrice didn't answer. Keeping her back to him, she dressed as quickly as she could.

"Hey, wait a minute, you aren't going yet, are you? What's the matter—didn't you get your fun?"

She picked up her purse and headed for the door. When her hand touched the knob she stopped. A wave of revulsion had re-ignited her contempt for him.

"You're a fool if you don't realize how you disgust me. All the money in the world couldn't get me to walk back across this room. You're crude, you're stupid, you lack all traces of finesse. You express yourself like an adolescent, and you don't have the slightest idea of what good manners are. As far as I can tell, there's nothing about you that could possibly appeal to a woman, unless she's a woman who has a particular liking for dull animals—and in that case she'd do better with a donkey. A donkey, at least, is adequately equipped. So in short, Mr. Pugh," she added as she stepped out the door, "I find you incapable of intelligent conversation and a lousy fuck. Thank you for the drink. Good afternoon."

Beatrice had known Quinn would find out. She had known it before she ever talked to Buck. The comings and goings at the Violet Crown Motel were common knowledge in Toombs Mill, so it was almost certain word would get around. And, anyway, she knew that even if no one had seen her, Leon Pugh was sure to talk.

It was around five thirty one afternoon not quite two weeks later when Buck knocked on the door. Beatrice had just put Lee's and Tony's dinner in the oven and was on the phone with the chairman of the PTA, trying to straighten out some last-minute difficulties. When she heard someone at the kitchen door she put down the phone, annoyed.

"Oh, it's you," she said when she saw who it was. "You're going to have to wait a minute."

She finished talking and went back into the kitchen. Buck was still standing beside the door.

"I'm coming right to the point, Beatrice. I know Johnny Kingman likes to shoot off his mouth. I also know his cousin is a shit-eating Okie jackass. So me, I believe what them two are saying about you is a lie, and I aim to be the first to tell Quinn so. Otherwise he's liable to hear it from someone else. And if he hears it from someone else he's certain to get hisself in trouble."

"And what if what you heard isn't a lie?"

Beatrice felt her breath beginning to come faster as she watched the effect of her words on Buck's usually impassive face.

"Then I don't know what's going to happen to him," he answered uncertainly.

"What do you mean? Do you think he'll go after Leon Pugh with a shotgun?"

"Oh, I reckon he'll do that in any case. But no, that's not what I'm getting at. It goes a sight deeper." Buck crossed one arm on top of the other and rested his back against the refrigerator. "You know, you treat that man like he was a secondhand corncob. Quinn would die for you, Beatrice."

"Are you trying to tell me Quinn is going to kill himself when he finds out?"

There was an edge of sarcasm to her words. She looked directly at Buck, a smile flickering across her lips; irritated as she was, she couldn't help but feel a certain amusement at what struck her as a melodramatic account of her husband's feelings. Going over to the oven, she opened it and checked the casserole. Then, glancing up, she said, "I have a PTA meeting to go to at seven thirty, so I really don't have time to talk."

"No," Buck went on, as though he hadn't heard her. "A man like Quinn wouldn't do hisself in unless he believed there was nothing but a whole lot of yesterdays. I mean, sure Quinn drinks too much. Sure he has too many women. But there's something else there, too, Beatrice. There's a part of him that loves you and refuses to believe that someday he won't be able to set things right."

As Buck fell silent Beatrice heard the hall clock strike the hour. She went to the doorway and called Lee and Tony, and then she turned off the oven and carried the casserole to the table.

"Would you please leave now? It's getting late."

Buck's big jaws worked slowly, grinding his teeth together. Then, without a word, he turned to go.

She had hardly gotten her sons settled at the table before she heard the sound of Quinn's truck. Going into the bedroom, Beatrice opened the closet and took out the dress she was planning to wear. Her fingers trailed across a spot on the collar as she heard Quinn coming down the hall. When the door opened, she continued to concentrate on the spot, and then, glancing up, she went over to the dresser.

Quinn's face had told her all she needed to know.

"I suppose you want me to tell you whether it's true or not. All right: it's true. I had sex with another man. I didn't want it, I didn't enjoy it—in fact, it was no different than it is with you. So I spent an afternoon with a stranger in a motel room. Is that enough, or shall I say more? No? Then please leave me alone. I have to dress for the PTA."

She picked up the hairbrush, looking at him in the mirror. He was leaning against the door, a stunned expression on his face. As she pulled the brush through her hair Beatrice wondered what he was thinking, whether he realized that it was over between them —for she had deliberately and willfully violated whatever it was that had remained.

"For money?" she heard him ask.

"For money."

The next moment Quinn was standing just behind her. She could read the anger on his taut, indrawn lips.

"Do you remember what I've always said about your eyes? That they remind me of agates. That they're cold and bloodless, like glass."

He put his hands on her shoulders. She turned away from the mirror, feeling his hard fingers wrap around her throat.

"Leave me alone." Her voice was husky. Never had she hated him more.

Yet as his hands dropped away from her, her hatred seemed to dissolve. She found herself barren, emotionless, not even surprised that there was no satisfaction in knowing she had hurt him.

He crossed the room to sit beside the windows. As he slumped down into a chair Beatrice looked at the face that had always been so rugged and so arrogant, so full of an irrepressible self-assurance and a terrible, maddening pride, and it seemed she hardly recognized him.

"Do you know how I've loved you, Quinn? I've loved you since the day I first saw you, the day you came up to me on the street in downtown Dallas and asked if I knew where you could get a decent cup of coffee. I'd never seen a man like you. We ended up in a restaurant and you told me you'd just gotten out of prison. When I asked you what for, you said, 'I drove a forklift out a second-story window.' Of course I didn't believe you. You laughed when I told you so, and then you said, 'Well, maybe that wasn't me. Maybe that was someone else.' And after that I fell in love with you. There was something about you, a kind of

38

recklessness that seemed to me to represent everything I could never be. And for seven years I've let you live your life the way you've wanted to. For seven years I've done nothing to keep you from your women, your filthy creatures who have no conception of self-worth. I've waited and I've raised our sons, enduring every sort of degradation until my insides have revolted at the memories. I've been a fool in the eyes of my family, and yet I've held up under the knowledge of it. I've defended you, even though you've flaunted your contempt for everything I believe in. And it's all been out of love. I've loved you, Quinn. Only now there's a lifeless taste to it all. On my best days—on my best days I can hate you."

The words seemed to spill out because she was at a loss to do anything but let them. Yet they had a rehearsed, mechanical ring, she knew. For a while Quinn sat staring out the window at the long, sloping diagonals of light which cut across the shadows. Beatrice stood beside him, looking down at his dark head.

"No, Beatrice, everything has happened just as you planned it. You've wanted to be a martyr all your life."

There was no amusement, no trace of irony in his voice; when he turned toward her she saw how the lines in his forehead seemed to have deepened. There was a weariness about him which struck her as strange. She had never seen it, nor had she imagined it to be possible.

"No," he went on, "there ain't a thing that hasn't happened like you planned it. I was willing to do anything for you—to put on new clothes, to change my manners, my way of talking. Those are things that can be done, exterior things, things easy and meaningless enough in themselves. Maybe it's true that I'm a self-made son-of-a-bitch. Maybe it's true I would have gone to hell in a hack a lot faster if I hadn't married you. But it's also true that for a while I did everything you asked me. You probably don't remember, though—you have this habit of forgetting things you don't want to think about. You've always been that way, and I guess you always will be. You're never going to change, I see that now, except to harden. Only your hardness isn't going to be what you think it is. It won't protect you, Beatrice, because that kind of hardness is only a brittle, fragile shell. It doesn't let in anything, not even light, so that you can't see, you can't judge. The world takes on a kind of sameness, and you exhaust yourself by trying to fight off everything. And then one day the shell cracks. It just breaks apart."

He turned toward the windows again, leaning back in the chair. Beatrice had begun to notice his speech pattern changing, something which happened whenever he was deeply immersed in himself.

"No, you wanted to make me different at the very center. I was even willing to let you do that until I realized you were twisting me and I couldn't take the pain. I gave up the only life I knew and I damn near gave up my sanity just so you could be here where you said you belonged. But that was all right, too. I didn't belong here, but I was willing to see if I could change. Only you suddenly became cold to me. You mocked me. You let me know how worthless I was in your eyes. And why? Because I'd done what you refused to do—I'd opened myself up, I'd thrown off my shell. I'd loved you, Beatrice. But you didn't know how to love. So what was left to me but to gather together the remains of my pride? What was left but the women and the booze, because I couldn't leave you—because my insane love for you wouldn't let me? Do you remember the nights I came to you and you locked the bedroom door in my face? Or the nights you didn't lock it, but only out of contempt? Jesus Christ, you've even learned to make your juices serve the workings of that steel trap you call your mind. No, you never went out and got laid before, did you? Your record is spotless, right?

"I'm a hard man to starve, but you've damn near done it. This time, Beatrice, you're right about something—there's no life here any more. So I'm leaving."

She felt a need to protect herself, to humiliate him in some way. Beneath her robe she was naked. Reaching up, she undid the buttons and let the robe slip to the floor.

"Please don't come near me any more," she said as she walked over to the closet. "This is my house. They're my sons. Now would you mind leaving? I told you before I have to get dressed."

40

Before she knew it Quinn's arms were gripping her. She began to scream as he carried her across the room. He pinned her wrists behind her and pushed her onto the bed, and for the space of a single instant she was terrified he would kill her. As his mouth came down hard on hers he forced her legs apart. Then he was inside her, and she felt as though he would suffocate her, break her with the violence of his embrace. As she tried to push him away she felt a strange exhilaration, as though she was standing on the edge of a cliff and forcing herself to look down. She wanted so much to prove to him that she wasn't afraid, that even when he was physically violent there was no way he could dominate her. Yet her body seemed to be defying her, for she felt herself responding. As he drove deeper inside her she kicked at him, cursing, glad that in the deepening shadows her expressions were obscured. Because she knew that if he could read her face he would know how much she wanted him to stay with her.

IT WAS DECEMBER in Dallas. Rita Cobb stood by the windows, looking out at the wintry sky. Leaves were blowing against the panes, gnarled, bitten leaves that seemed to come from nowhere. She watched a flurry of them fly upward, trying to discern their individual shapes before the wind scattered them across the schoolyard.

A big one, yellowish at the center, was clinging to a pane directly in front of her. As she reached out to trace it, it began crawling downward. A moment passed in which the leaf seemed to be balancing on the ledge at the bottom of the window, and then, before she had a chance to put her finger to the icy glass, the leaf swooped up, its colored center momentarily bright against the sky. The next instant it was gone. Beyond the windows there was only the gray expanse of winter.

The clock above the blackboard said three forty-five. Rita heard its dry clicking, the sound it always made when it struck the quarter-hour, only in the emptiness of the classroom the noise startled her. Most of the time she hardly noticed it; keeping a group of adolescents quiet and attentive was something she had never done particularly well, and now, after several years of trying, she found it difficult to conceive of a classroom in which she could hear the hands of a clock click the quarter-hour. The sound dissolved into the silence of the building, and Rita laughed nervously to herself. It crossed her mind that she wasn't meant to be a teacher. The thought occurred to her every time she walked into a classroom, and yet she knew for certain she wasn't meant to be a wife.

Another leaf pressed against the pane and she moved closer to the window. One corner of the leaf rose and fell with the wind, and it seemed to Rita that it was a living thing. Then this one, too, swirled away from her, disappearing into the leaf storm bursting upward from the ground. No, she thought, she had never regretted leaving Adam. But Quinn—there was an element of regret in her memories of the past four years. The constant sense of waiting for him seemed to pervade the very air she took in, so that she lived always in its ambience, its shadow. Looking up again, Rita saw the hand of the clock approach the twelve. Four years, she was thinking. Four years this Christmas. Then, letting go a wisp of hair she had twisted around her finger, she turned toward the books and papers on her desk.

Rita hated the stacks of adolescent scrawl, hated classifying the various degrees of failure and writing the neat red capitals next to the hundred and fifty names. Some of the longest nights she could remember had been spent beside her fireplace with piles of papers in her lap. Though when Quinn used to come and see her more often, the nights hadn't seemed so long—the thought came to her as she picked up the compositions. Tonight, she supposed, she would drag a new log in from the porch and see how many papers she could grade before she was tempted to throw them all into the fire.

The janitor was coming down the hall, his mop making a soft, deceptive sound in the stillness of the building. Rita scooped her books together and put them in a leather satchel. As she stuck the papers inside on top of the books, she let her mind jump ahead to the great quiet of the winter evening in which the only sounds would be the crackle of the fire and the turning of pages as she flipped through her students' work. It occurred to her that with a new log and some sherry the night might be almost pleasant, and if the moon was white and full she would go for a late walk and watch the winter sky dissolve and reassemble as clouds slid across the moon's path. The janitor was almost at her room. She finished putting her pens and pencils in the satchel, shut the clasp, and started for the door. A wad of paper by the wastebasket caught her attention. She bent down and picked it up, reading on its crumpled surface "Miss Cobb is horny." And beneath it, in another hand, "I'll bet she's never been popped."

Rita tossed the note into the wastebasket and stepped out into the hall.

Someone said her name. She turned to see the janitor leaning on the handle of his mop in the recess of the doorway to the next room.

"Working late today, Miss Cobb?"

"No, not really." She didn't know what else to say. "It's cold in here."

"Norther blowing in."

"I think it's here already."

The janitor looked away from her. Then he took up his mop again and began moving slowly down the corridor. When he had gone a few steps he stopped and turned around.

"No," he said. "I think it'll be blowing in tonight."

"You may be right," she answered.

The sound of the mop lingered in her ears after he had turned the corner. She shifted her satchel to the other shoulder and went on toward the front of the building. Her footsteps seemed too loud. Their echo made her feel the silence around her, made her aware of the solitary hours to come. Before, nights like tonight had simply been the spaces between other nights, the nights when Quinn would call to say he was in town. She had been perfectly content then to spend time alone, because that time had never seemed to mark the bounds of her existence. But for months now —it had been September when she had last seen him—nights like the one to come had been all there was. They had been no different from the days, which were taken up with all sorts of banal things—the pens and pencils of waking life, the questions never answered, the sheets of wadded paper like the one she had picked up just now. It was all the same to her: none of it really mattered.

It wasn't as if she demanded anything of Quinn, she told

44

herself. It wasn't as if she expected fidelity or a promise that he finalize his four-year separation from his wife. But she had expected he would keep in touch with her, not just disappear altogether from her life.

She pushed open the old-fashioned doors and stepped onto the porch. Under the bare oaks the leaves were stirring again. For a moment she simply stood and stared out across the colorless winter grass, and then she began to follow the sidewalk around to the other side of the building. The cement here was cracked and uneven, and she had to pay attention so as not to miss her step. Nevertheless, shifting her satchel again, she broke into a run just as the sun came out from behind a crescent of cloud. Rita glanced up at it, hoping it would stay despite the wanness of its light.

Where the schoolyard ended, the houses began. Most of them were old, formerly elegant homes that had been divided into apartments when east Dallas had come to be hemmed in by businesses and freeways. The one she lived in was only a few blocks from the school. She reached home in ten minutes, pushed open the beveled-glass door, and went down the hall to number three.

The building was quiet. Setting down her satchel, she made her way through a maze of furniture. Though the rooms weren't large, Rita had managed to assemble a collection of oversized Victorian pieces, things which she sometimes thought of as a set of props, a set of gestures. It wasn't the things themselves that caused her to regard them in this way, but rather the knowledge that they were meant in some way to define—even to create—her. Yet she was at a loss to say exactly what it was she hoped they would define or create. The only objects in the apartment which she felt really touched on her at all were the shelves and shelves of books. She put her hand out in passing, letting her fingers trail along them as she headed for the back door. For a moment she simply stood there shivering, and then she opened the door and dragged a split log inside. When she had gotten it into the living room she noticed that one side was damp, but she thrust it into the fireplace anyway. The flames took a long time to catch. Finally the log shifted. She watched it begin to burn, and then she took off her coat and put a match to the space heater.

Outside, the sun's hues were deepening. Rita went over to the window and watched as a bar of yellow gathered itself into a ray and fell slowly through the masses of cloud. Maybe, she thought, there would be a sunset after all. Maybe the norther wouldn't blow in and tomorrow would surprise her with signs of an early spring. She could remember once, as a child, having stood among a cluster of elms and stared off across a park, watching the colonies of birds coming home for the season. Maybe she would be able to go out in the yard in the morning and see the ripple and flurry of the birds returning and know that the ice in the shadows was gone. Yet something in the unexpected sun told her that tomorrow would be just like today, but colder. She turned the heater up. Then she took a decanter of sherry from the mantel. After she had poured herself a glass she sat down on the sofa directly in front of the fire.

A moment later she noticed the log wasn't burning evenly. The flames had sunk so low she could hardly see them any more, so, getting up again, she moved closer and began to inspect the log. Its bark was still damp in places. Too tired to coax it, Rita grabbed the poker and stirred the ashes until the fire winked slowly out. It no longer mattered, she was thinking. She wasn't going to grade the compositions anyway. The glass of sherry went down easily, leaving her warm inside. After a moment she got up and poured herself another one.

Rita looked down into the glass, swirling the sherry a little. The light from the window was still bright enough for her to make out the liquor's amber color. As she took another sip she felt its warmth flowing all through her body. She closed her eyes, feeling a myriad of languid sensations and recalling moments suspended like hairs or bits of spider's web in the comings and goings of memory: summer lightning in a sky convulsed with rain, and the droning of the drops on stucco; the infinite slowness with which two people could recede into one another; the extravagance of desire when the body's fires were the only warmth against the damp; the sweet curiosity of the dark. The sofa seemed to enclose her. She found her mind adrift, her body almost dreaming, and then she was setting the sherry glass on the floor and sinking back into the cushions with one hand resting inside the folds of her blouse. Very lightly she began to stroke her breasts. The skin was delicate, velvety, responsive to the touch. She let her fingers trail across the nipples, feeling them lift themselves against the fabric of her underclothes, contracting like petals until they seemed to be the locus of all physical sensation. For a long time she touched herself. The tide of her own caresses carried her deeper into the past, and yet the contact of self on self could ease the pain no more than could the passionate contrivances of memory. Her blouse made a soft sound as she slid her hand out, buttoning it once more. On the floor beside her the glass was empty. She went over to the cabinet again; the room, it seemed, had grown a little warmer.

She could remember it all so clearly. The wind was sweeping across the desert, stirring the dust into miniature white whirl-winds. Behind the gas station the land sloped upward for a hun-dred yards, culminating in a knoll which, except for a few crippled mesquite trees, seemed to be devoid of vegetation. The gas station itself was a squat stucco structure with two old-fashioned pumps out front and a pile of rotting tires just beyond the garage. Rita recalled that as they were pulling up beneath the awning it had occurred to her that the place was deserted; later on, of course, she would realize Quinn had been watching them all along. She would even see him in her mind's eye as he stood at the top of the knoll, waiting for them to come to a stop before he started down the slope.

As they got out of the car, she noticed that the door of the gas station was banging against the wall and that the windows were dark and dusty. Adam brushed by her, going to stand next to the gas pumps with one hand resting protectively on the hood of the car. Something blew against his leg, and Rita followed his eyes as he looked down. A tumbleweed. He bent toward it, but it flew out of his reach and attached itself to a pump, where it stayed until the wind hurled it into the pile of rotting tires. Adam got back into the car. A moment later he got out again.

"Cold," Rita said as he approached her.

"Real cold," he answered.

She followed him around to the side of the building, where there was nothing but an assortment of oil drums and the corroded skeletons of what looked like drilling machinery. The stalks of giant thistles were poking upward through the remains of the wheels and shafts. She stared at the thistles as they swayed but never snapped, for the protruding jags of metal kept them from the full violence of the wind. When she turned toward Adam again, she saw him kick a piece of chrome plating across the ten feet of dirt between them and the side of the building. Then he looked down at his shoes. They were covered with white dust. Across the toe of one was a long, irregular scar. A moment later they went back around to the gas pumps and Adam was caught full in the face by a cyclone of candy wrappers. He flailed at them, and then he stood looking down at the hood of the car; the wind's invisible fingers were clawing at the paint. He turned and walked toward the open recess of the building, where the door on its loose hinges was still banging back and forth.

That was when Quinn had stepped outside. Dressed in a worn jacket and a pair of dusty Levi's, he could have been an attendant at any number of gas stations in West Texas. Yet something about his face had struck Rita the moment she had seen him. The abrupt angle of his cheekbones, the fine, continuous line of his brow, the nose which looked as though it had been broken one time too many, the thin but expressive lips—there was something classically right about his features, and yet at the same time they were flawed. A ruined patrician face, she remembered thinking. A marble mask that had been smashed and only imperfectly pieced back together.

"Hey! You run this place?" Adam shouted.

For an instant Quinn scrutinized them. Then he turned and led the way inside. With the door shut the room was only dimly lighted, for where the windows weren't painted they were blinded by layers of dust.

"You run this place?" Adam repeated, looking unceremoniously around.

"Sometimes. When there's anything to run."

The answer was markedly abrupt, as if beneath his words he was laughing. Rita wondered if Adam had noticed it. Realizing he hadn't, she began to look more closely at Quinn.

"I didn't think anyone was here. How about filling my car with ethyl and taking a look at my oil while my wife and I stretch our legs a little? And check the tires and get the windshield. This desert driving is murder on a car."

Adam sniffed, half turning. The wind blew against the side of the building, so that he didn't seem to hear Quinn when he said, "No gas."

Rita noticed Quinn was watching her. She let her eyes rest on his, and then, without saying anything, she looked away again.

"Always this windy?" Adam went on.

"No. Just ninety-nine percent of the time. I ain't got any gas, mister. You'll have to drive on another twenty miles. There's a Conoco just off the highway."

"Will it be open today?" Rita asked, raising her eyes to his again. There was something hard and yet undeniably sensual about his features. She remembered wondering if he had spent all his life in the desert.

"I don't know why not."

"We've passed a lot of places that haven't been."

He smiled at her then. "Merry Christmas. I'd forgotten."

"No gas, you say? Aw, come on, you've got to know where we can get some gas. My wife and I have to make Carlsbad before midnight."

"Well, it ain't going to be midnight tonight," Quinn said. He went over to the cash register and turned the key in the lock. The drawer sprang open with a tinny sound. "Not if you're thinking on getting gas here, it ain't. Like I said, your best bet is to go on up the road."

"That's twenty miles! I've been on empty since before I pulled into this hole!"

"Well, it looks like you're going to be on empty when you pull out, too."

He leaned his elbows on the cash register and looked at Adam. With one hand he reached down and slammed the cash drawer shut. He had a dime in his palm. Walking past them, he went over to the hot-drink machine and slipped the dime into the slot. Rita watched him punch the soup button. The machine whirred faintly.

"So what am I supposed to do, spend the rest of the day and the night in this place? Come on, you must have some gas."

"Sorry, mister."

"Son-of-a-bitch!"

The wind blew against the side of the building, drowning Adam's words. Quinn sat down on the edge of the desk. Once again Rita felt his eyes flickering across her face.

"You and your wife are welcome to stay. I've got a man coming early tomorrow with some gas."

"Isn't there a hotel or motel nearby? I thought I saw some signs about—"

"Calvary's twenty-one miles from here."

Rita moved closer to her husband and put one hand on his arm. "Adam, I think we should wait until tomorrow. We really can't do anything else."

"And spend the night here? But I told Mother—"

"We can call her. Do you have a phone?"

The wind rose and settled. Quinn crumpled the paper cup and tossed it into a trash can. Then he moved toward a partially open door that led to the rooms at the back of the station.

"No phone. But I've got a couple bottles of whiskey."

"This place is a dump," Adam said.

Later on he said it again. It had just gotten dark and the three of them were sitting at a table in the back, finishing a supper which Quinn—whose name she had finally learned—had prepared in the makeshift kitchen. The main room was barely large enough for the table, a sofa, and a stack of crates that served as both stools and shelves, and beyond the kitchen Rita could see a tiny bedroom. The stucco walls had once been white, but with

50

the passage of time the color had changed to gray. There was nothing to mitigate the starkness of the walls except a shotgun on a rack above the sofa; from time to time Rita glanced at her surroundings, conscious of the rise and fall of the wind and the glare from the bulb suspended above the table which fell with equal harshness on Quinn's and her husband's faces.

"This place is a dump. I mean, how do you live out here? Miles from anything that could be called civilization, with the god-damned wind blowing all the time. How in hell do you stand it? It would drive me crazy."

Adam reached for the bottle of whiskey and poured himself another shot. He had been drinking steadily for several hours, while Quinn, Rita realized, was taking his time. Quinn had been listening to Adam's loud, increasingly obnoxious monologues with a self-absorbed expression on his face, as if he hardly heard him. Adam was making her uncomfortable, though. Every time he opened his mouth to rail on about his business or his politics or his football-playing days she was reminded that her marriage had always been a fruitless, quietly miserable attempt.

When Adam had emptied his glass again, he leaned his elbows on the table and gestured drunkenly toward Quinn.

"Say, Quinn, what do you really do for a living?"

In the glare from overhead Quinn's dark eyes seemed unnaturally bright. Rita watched as he glanced up at her husband, whose fleshy features were drawn together in a squint.

"I'm derrick man on an oil rig."

"What?"

Quinn began to laugh. Leaning back in his chair, he reached into his pocket for a match. As the flame flared and he took the cigarette from his lips, he said, "Derrick man. Ever been to a drilling tract?"

"We drove past some," Rita replied.

For a moment no one said anything. Rita heard a car out on the highway. A coyote howled somewhere. When the car had passed and the animal had fallen silent, all she could hear was the wind. Then Quinn asked her if she had noticed the derricks.

"Hell, I've seen a derrick before," Adam answered for her.

51

"Anybody knows what an oil rig looks like."

"Then I guess I don't need to do much explaining," Quinn said with a note of amusement in his voice.

"I don't know anything about them," Rita said.

Adam reached for the bottle again, looking at her sullenly. "You know you're not interested in hearing about oil rigs."

"Maybe I am. Maybe they interest me more than you know."

"Hell, all you care about is books. A goddamned bookworm, that's what I've got for a wife."

Rita didn't answer. She turned to Quinn, but he was keeping his distance from their disagreement. Then, unexpectedly, he began to talk again.

"It's not a bad job if you don't mind being alone with an eighty-foot drop of darkness all around you. For twenty-five or thirty miles around you can see the lights of towns, and you can see the cars out on the highway ten miles away. You've got to like working at night, though—daytimes are hell. There's something about the desert sun that causes a kind of inversion of your responses, so that after you live out here awhile you only come alive at night."

"Desert animals are nocturnal, aren't they?" Rita asked, feeling ridiculously like a schoolteacher but conscious of a desire to draw him out.

"Sure."

"Well, it might be a rough life, Quinn, but I bet it's not as rough as pro ball. I had the chance to make a career of it when I got out of college—you have to be damned tough to play professionally, you know. I was one of the meanest defensive ends in the southwest conference. They even used to have a nickname for me."

"I bet it was Steamroller, wasn't it?" Quinn said.

Adam filled his glass again. His drunken outbursts didn't embarrass Rita; she felt such a sense of detachment from him that she often wondered if there was anything he could do which could really elicit a response from her. Yet Adam did make her uncomfortable enough to wish he would either stop drinking or finish

52

off the bottle and go to sleep. The wind was shaking the building. Quinn got up and adjusted the gas heater, and then he went into the other room and came back with a deck of cards. For another hour Rita watched the two men play gin rummy—Adam drunkenly, Quinn with that self-contained, amused look on his face—and finally, when she had gotten tired of looking on, she took a book of poetry out of her purse and went over to the sofa.

It was around ten o'clock when Adam announced he was ready to quit. Rita watched him push his chair back. He stood up uncertainly and made his way across the room.

"I'm afraid we're inconveniencing you," Rita said as she put a hand out to steady her husband.

Quinn picked up the empty bottle and set it on top of the stack of crates. "Inconveniencing me? No. I'd rather sleep on the couch anyway—the bed sags in the middle. And sorry, but the bellboy is on vacation and the room-service waiter quit last night. Though if you need anything, let me know."

"Just as long as the bed doesn't squeak," Adam said, putting his arm around Rita. "We wouldn't want to keep you up all night." She began to pull away from him, and he grabbed her by the waist. "Well, Quinn, we'll see you in the morning. I can tell my wife's ready to hit the sack!"

Thinking back, Rita realized how easy it had been. Adam had fallen asleep before he had even gotten out of his clothes. When he had begun to snore she had taken down her hair and brushed it until it hung straight and shiny down her back. Then, wearing only a nightgown, she had stepped into the other room. Quinn was standing next to the sofa, his back to her. When he turned around she saw he had her book in his hand.

"How was the bed?"

"I hope we haven't put you out," she said, aware of his amusement when she didn't respond to the question. She noticed, too, how curiously he was looking at her, as if he hadn't quite made up his mind what to think.

"No problem. You read a lot?"

"As my husband says, I'm a goddamned bookworm." She went

53

over to the sofa and lifted the book out of his hands.

"The Roethke poem, the one you were reading—I dog-eared the corner for you."

Rita was startled when she heard him pronounce the name correctly. But she didn't mention it. Instead she flipped through the book and then set it on the stack of crates.

"I teach English. But even if I didn't, I'd read all the time. I enjoy it, especially poetry."

"You teach poetry?"

"I teach a little of everything. When I get back from the holidays my students will be plowing through Shakespeare. Tell me, what would you think of a man who willed his second-best bed to his wife?"

"I'd congratulate him on the originality of the insult. But what did she do—cheat on him once too often or just stop making home deliveries?"

Rita began to laugh. "Nobody knows. And nobody knows who Shakespeare willed his best bed to, either."

"That's easy. If it wasn't his wife it had to be some broad he was screwing on the side."

Though she was laughing, she was wary, wondering at what she saw in his eyes. In the next room Adam's snores were audible even above the wind. She took another step toward Quinn and he put his arms around her waist. As he bent toward her she felt her lips part, and then she opened herself wide to him. He pulled her down onto the sofa. The next instant she was aware of her softness, her own strange, inert weight dissolving into nothing beneath the hard and unfamiliar heaviness of his body. His neck and chest smelled of tobacco, and his breath on her face was hot. Though the springs of the sofa were bulging against her back, after she began moving with him she no longer noticed them. All she could feel was the sheer power of his body and the mute, live nerve of wanting that kept her holding on.

So she had separated from Adam the winter she had met Quinn. The months had gone by and their divorce had come through, but Quinn had never answered any of the letters she had sent. More than once, she recalled, she had made up her mind to stop writing; the letters seemed to be no more than ink spots on a sheet of yellow paper, they conveyed nothing, were incapable of translating her feelings into words. But she wrote them anyway. And then one day, several months after that night in the desert, she got a call from him. He was in Dallas and he wanted to see her. They spent a weekend together then. After that she didn't hear from him until July, when he showed up at her front door one morning. He was on his way back from East Texas, and he had his son with him, a dark-eyed seven-year-old who looked almost exactly like his father. The three of them drove to the desert together, and Rita spent two weeks with Quinn and Lee in the stucco building beside the highway. Often during those weeks they camped out on the mesas, where Quinn taught them both to listen for animal sounds and to identify the stars. Rita could recall one brilliant July night when the campfire had burned down to an orange eye. Lee had already crawled into his sleeping bag. She and Quinn were sitting apart from him, gazing up at the high, diamond light.

"I never camped out before I met you, Quinn. I'm surprised I like it, in a way. It's not the sort of thing I usually enjoy."

She tilted her head back, tracing the arc of the sky. Then she looked at him. He was out of her reach, on the other side of the fire, but in the glow from the stars his features were distinctly visible.

"There's something about the desert that diffuses the stars' light," he said. "Each grain of sand acts as a mirror, so that at times the light can appear to be coming from everywhere at once —just look down there. I can remember a cousin of mine who claimed he could read the numbers off a dollar bill even on a moonless night. Like tonight."

Several moments went by. Rita felt a slight wind flickering across her face, and she began to wonder what it would be like to spend the rest of her life on the desert.

"The people who have lived out here a long time are inward people," Quinn said when she told him what she was thinking.

"There's something about this place that withers men just like it withers mesquite trees. Both seem to shrink as they get older, growing more and more toward their own centers so that with age they become twisted and hard."

"I think I'd like living here. Not by myself, of course."

"No," he told her, stretching out so that he was lying flat in front of the fire. "You don't want to stay. I saw a woman almost ruined here by sheer monotony and blasted hope."

"What do you mean?"

"My wife. I saw what this place did to her. Day after day, week after week, I watched her waiting, only she never knew for what. And then one day her face set in that mask of waiting and she didn't recognize me any more."

"What do you mean? Did she go crazy?"

"Crazy? No. She just stopped loving me."

"But that wouldn't happen to me."

"No, that wouldn't happen to you. You're a different breed of female. Beatrice is as hard-edged, as well defined as a piece of quartz. The desert only drove her more into herself. But you it would leave a bundle of raw nerve ends. A kind of hysteria would take over you, and you wouldn't know where to turn. After a while you'd hardly be able to function. Beatrice functions too well, so well that often she doesn't feel a thing but blind necessity. You're a much more sensitive woman."

"More sensitive? How so?"

"You're alive to changes. The seasons, the passage of time—in the desert, time doesn't mean much, and there aren't seasons so much as absolute extremes of heat and cold, sun and cloud, wind and stillness. Nothing seems to change. You'd live here in a static corner of the earth where the only measure of anything would be your own imagination. No, Rita, you need to live some-place where you can look out your window and see something different from one day to the next. You need the flow of life—my wife doesn't. She seems to get along very well by shutting out everything."

Quinn said the last few words with a barely perceptible touch of irony. Rita was quiet, waiting for him to say more. But he was looking into the eye of the fire with an expression on his face which was foreign to her, and she didn't know how to respond to him.

The two weeks passed quickly. In the daytime, when Quinn wasn't working in the gas station or driving Lee around the oil fields, he and Rita simply sat and talked. His fascination with the desert was strange to her, but after the first few days she began to get up at dawn and take long walks across the sand. Sometimes Lee went with her. He seemed to like being by himself, and on their walks he rarely talked except to point things out to her. Most of the time he amused himself playing solitary games on the pile of rotting tires, and whenever a car would pull into the station he would dart out to jump up and down on the bell hose. Then, without a word, he would disappear. Rita found him to be a strangely affectionate child. Toward the end of her stay, when he had gotten used to her being there, he began collecting rocks, insects, and the bright-colored cactus flowers and setting them where she would be sure to find them. As July wore on and she knew that soon she would have to go, she realized she would miss Lee as well as Quinn. His shy, serious face would stay with her, she was sure of it.

The first week of August she and Lee repacked their suitcases and Quinn put them in the back of the truck. The sun was just going down as they pulled out onto the highway. Rita watched the sky deepen and the horizon become less distinct. Finally everything went dark. A few stars lighted the sky. Looking out at them, she thought back over the time she had spent with Quinn. The two weeks had gone by quickly, but even so she felt she was taking more than memory away with her. It was as if something of him had stayed inside her, something as barren and yet as brutally alive as the land itself, something as watchful as whatever it was that lit his eyes, and equally filled with laughter. So the lights of little towns had slipped past her in the night, the road had unfolded northeastward, and before she had realized it the desert was a hundred, two hundred, and finally two hundred and fifty miles behind her.

The old house was quiet; the sherry decanter was empty. For

a long moment Rita gazed at the clock above the mantel, realizing that for hours she had been falling in and out of sleep. As she got up from the sofa to check the lock on the front door, it occurred to her that maybe she was in the wake of a love which had never existed and of which even the lingering illusion was unreal.

THE FOLLOWING MORNING was a Saturday. Rita was awakened early by her nextdoor neighbor's canary, and after she had lain in bed for a while she went into the kitchen and made a pot of tea. When it was ready she took her cup into the living room. Then she began to scan the rows of books, occasionally taking one from the shelf, flipping through it, and putting it back in place. Today it seemed as if nothing would satisfy her; she sipped her tea, reminding herself of the walk she hadn't taken the night before.

The morning was cold but clear. Beyond the windows a watery sunshine was touching the yard with light. As she stood among her books, her bric-a-brac, and her clutter of antique furniture, she realized she didn't want to spend another Saturday indoors. A walk was just what she needed. She took her cup and went back into the kitchen. Across the hall the canary was singing again, only this time Harriet, her neighbor, was whistling along off-key. Soon Rita heard the bird begin to squawk as Harriet opened her door and went heavily down the hall. She let out a breath of relief then, grateful for the temporary silence.

After she had rinsed her cup she stood for a moment admiring its delicate colors before she dried it and put it on the shelf next to the others. There was something reassuring about the objects that she lived with, though it was her books—and only her books —which gave weight to her life. The other things seemed to give it something different, something which she could only describe as a kind of borrowed charm. Borrowed because there was an artificiality, an element of posing, about them. Rita didn't like to think of herself as a deliberate person, and on the whole she didn't believe she was, yet what disturbed her was the idea that everything about her emulated old-maidishness. At times she saw herself posing as an old maid in order to overcome her dread of—in spirit if not in fact—actually becoming one. She hung the dish towel on its hook, telling herself that today there were other things she could more realistically be concerned about. As she was setting the teapot on the back of the stove she remembered the compositions she had yet to grade. Tomorrow, she decided. Today she was going over to Turtle Creek and wander around the park.

She went into the bathroom and turned the water on in the tub. Then she went back into the living room, where she curled up on the sofa. The stacks of ungraded papers were in front of her on the coffee table. She let her eyes rest on them briefly before she stuffed them into her satchel, not wanting to be reminded that today was going to be one of those restless, impossible days. Today, she knew, she was going to be existing on the periphery of things unless she could shake off the mood which had come over her the previous afternoon. Going into the bathroom again, she turned the water on full force. Then she slipped out of the long nightgown and let her fingers trail down her belly. Above the tub the curtains were wide open. She could see the trees and the sunny, uncertain winter sky, and then, letting her imagination wander, she saw a man's face peering in at her. It was one of her favorite fantasies, the man with the unwavering eyes who stood at the window when she undressed for her bath. The steam rose and the glass became more clouded; at last the man went away. Rita pinned her hair on top of her head and stepped into the tub.

When she got out she dressed quickly, putting on loose slacks, her most comfortable pair of shoes, and a heavy sweater that smelled faintly of mothballs. Outside, the air was still and cold, and there were patches of ice along the sidewalk that the sun hadn't yet melted. All up and down the street the old houses seemed to have resigned themselves to winter. The wooden gables and stone facades had an appropriately faded look, as though, she thought, in anticipation of a long wait before warm weather. As Rita was bending down to toss the newspapers onto the porch her braid, which had been only loosely pinned, swung around into her face. She reached up to push it away from her, and at that moment she saw a familiar truck pulling into the driveway.

Something gave way inside her. What she felt wasn't relief or happiness so much as a perfect certainty that her own small, circumambient world was complete again, and she ran across the yard. As Quinn got out of the truck, she simply looked at him, almost without any need to touch.

He was smiling, as she had known he would be. And though it was a smile which told her nothing, she had expected that of him, too.

"Why so long this time?"

He shrugged and reached out for her. "The things of life— trying to keep your debts from eating you alive, making sure your kids haven't forgotten you and that the price of whiskey isn't going up. So how have you been, schoolteacher?"

Rita took his arm and led him up the steps. As she opened the front door her neighbor, Harriet, came down the hall.

"Did we disturb you, Rita? Pagliacci was singing up a storm this morning. I hope we weren't too loud. Well, I'll let you go on now. You and your visitor seem anxious to be alone."

"Who's that?" Quinn asked as they stepped into the apartment. "And who the hell is Pagliacci? Sounds like something you'd put tomato sauce on."

Rita began to laugh. "Pagliacci is a clown in an Italian opera. He's also Harriet's canary. But never mind about clowns and canaries—I'm glad to see you, Quinn."

He took off his jacket and sat down in one of the overstuffed armchairs. Rita watched him light a cigarette, noticing that his hair was a little longer than she remembered but that otherwise he didn't look different. His expressions still amazed her, because they seemed to reveal such an impossible combination of qualities. And his eyes, she thought, were unchanged—dark, almost pupil-less.

"You don't look as though three months have done you any harm," she said playfully and yet with a touch of dryness. "The least you could have done is gotten a haircut or maybe shown up with a magnificent scar. Just so I'd know you've been alive." Rita looked at him more closely, wondering what was going through his mind. "I've missed you."

Quinn stood up, stretching. Then he came across the room to where she was still standing by the door.

"Sometimes I wonder why I want to spend so much time by myself," he said.

He bent to kiss her. She closed her eyes, giving in to the warmth and the pressure of his arms.

"Are you tired?" she asked at last.

"Yeah. It's a long drive."

"Do you want breakfast? Coffee?"

"Later."

"All right—later."

She went with him into the bedroom. As they took off their clothes she looked at him across a gap of space and silence. Never had she wanted a man so much, and yet somehow she was content just feeling his arms around her. Once again she looked into his face, trying to understand what it was about his eyes—often she thought she saw in their depths a kind of light, a pathway through the darkness. Yet she knew there was always the chance that everything was of her own making, that the pathway ended in a cul-de-sac and the light was nothing but a reflector at the end of a long, blind alley.

After they made love they lay next to each other without talking. Then Rita lifted her head from his chest, kissing him lightly.

"Would you like some breakfast now?"

Quinn reached for his cigarettes, which had fallen to the floor. Rita brushed her hair away from her face. Giving him another kiss, she got out of bed and began to dress.

"Are you staying long?"

"I can't. I told my boys I'd be there tonight."

"Oh," she answered, trying not to let disappointment take over her. "But you'll stay longer when you come back through?"

"Maybe. I don't know."

She watched the smoke from his cigarette float up toward the ceiling, where the light from the high windows was clear and bright.

"My kids—I'll be glad to see them." Quinn set his cigarette down and crossed his arms. She had noticed before that talking about his children seemed to make him draw inward, even to embarrass him a little. "I'm taking Lee back with me for the holidays. Tony—Tony's a different kind of kid. He don't like spending time out there. Lee's more like me than Tony is—but you saw him once. He must have been almost eight then. Yeah, I remember that summer," Quinn went on, more to himself now than to her. "That was three and a half years ago, wasn't it? Maybe I'll see if I can get his mother to let me have him longer this summer. He's a quiet kid, kind of keeps to himself. Damn smart, too, even if she is trying to make him into a jock. Hey, I'll show you the new pictures I have of them. Give me my pants, will you?"

Rita picked up his Levi's and sat down with them on the bed.

"You're right," she said when he handed her the photographs. "Tony doesn't look like you at all. He must look like his mother."

Quinn mashed out his cigarette. Then, without looking up, he said, "Bea's got darker hair. Kind of reddish in the sun. But look at Lee."

"Yes, he looks like I remember him. He has your hair and eyes, though I imagine," she added teasingly, "that he'll be prettier than you are. Your nose isn't on straight, you know."

"Let him get his nose broken as many times as I have and he might learn to keep it out of other people's business. It took me twenty years to learn, though. I had a bad habit of chasing after married wives."

"Married wives?"

Quinn stood up and began to pull on his pants. "Yeah. There are two kinds of wives, married and unmarried. Just like there are two kinds of women."

"Yes, I remember what you told me once. There are barmaids

and there are schoolteachers. I guess it's perfectly obvious what I am, isn't it?"

"Shit," Quinn said, laughing a little. "It's never obvious. Women always have a way of seeming to be something else. There are a lot of schoolteachers who act like barmaids—it don't take long to figure the schoolteachers out, though. It's the barmaids you have to be careful of."

Rita went into the kitchen then. She knew without a doubt that he had been thinking of his wife.

For a minute she simply stood beside the stove, wondering what it would take to make the feeling of superfluousness go away. The last thing she wanted was to retreat into herself, and yet she didn't know how vulnerable she was willing to let herself be.

"Hey!" Quinn called out from the living room. "You have more goddamned books than you did the last time I was here!"

He came into the kitchen. She knew he recognized the expression on her face, because he put his arms around her and dropped the teasing tone of voice. Yet she pushed away from him and went over to the refrigerator.

"Your books say a lot about you. Only there are other things that say more. To me, at least."

"Like what?" she asked.

He leaned against the counter while she tried to concentrate on the omelet she was making. Though she felt an overwhelming need to touch him now, she couldn't let herself. And though she was afraid of what he had to say, she was curious to hear it.

"It's not in your talk. And it's not in the way you dress. You're not beautiful, you're not even very pretty, and yet you're the most sensual woman I've ever been around. It's the way you move. You remember the Roethke poem—'She moves in circles and her circles move'? That's you, Rita. There's nothing awkward or forced about you when you walk, you sit, you curl up on the bed. Because, unlike most women, you aren't trying to be sexy."

There was a silence between them. She set the table, made coffee, and took a pan of muffins from the oven. Then, motioning for him to sit down, she slid the omelet onto a plate. Quinn continued to lean against the counter, watching her with his arms folded across his chest.

"Do you want breakfast or not?"

"Yeah."

He followed her to the table. After they had begun to eat he continued talking in the same, almost subdued, tone of voice.

"I read a lot when I was in prison. For two years I read everything I could get my hands on. You'd be surprised at some of the books I managed to get through."

"But afterward you stopped?"

"Yeah. There were too many other things I wanted to do."

"Like what?"

"Like find out how to live in a world run by narrow bigots."

"And do you think you've succeeded?"

"No. I don't see how a sane man can succeed."

Rita toyed with one of the thin, painted cups. "Why were you in prison, Quinn? You've never told me that."

"It was a long time ago. And it ain't important—or maybe I ought to say it *isn't* important, English teacher." He looked at her, half smiling. "I can say it right when I want to, you know."

"I know." She picked up her fork and then set it down again. "But it doesn't really matter."

"Not to you. You don't live by arbitrary rules. But to a lot of people it does matter. Most of the world lives by rules, and if you want to get along you have to learn to live by them, too. And you can't question them. You can't ask how come they only benefit the people who make them or why they never reflect anything worth living for. It's questions like that that get you sent to jail."

"I suppose it doesn't hurt to just ask, does it?"

"When you're young you're never satisfied to just ask. You've got to try and do something about it all. But when you're old— well, that's another story." He laughed shortly. "Yeah, and I'm almost thirty-eight."

"That's getting there," she mused, and this time he didn't answer.

They made love again before the morning was over. Afterward

65

Rita suggested they go out for a walk, but Quinn shook his head.

"All right, then. I know you have to leave." She moved away from him to the other side of the bed. Then, almost involuntarily, she reached out and touched his arm. "But you might finish telling me what you were thinking awhile ago."

"About what?"

"About me."

A moment passed. She kept her eyes fixed on his face, prepared for anything except a shrug of blank indifference. Yet when the sadness came over her she wasn't prepared for that; if only he would call out to her, she thought. If only he would ask her to help save him from ruin and loneliness, from the gaunt, eroded country which fascinated him so.

"The way you move says something about the kind of woman you are. You're fluid, receptive, always in motion. You seem to thrive on change—on life, in a word. You aren't a person who lives by static formulas, and so you aren't always in conflict with the things around you. Do you remember what I said once about the desert—how the absence of change there would drive a person like you to the brink of hysteria? I still believe what I told you that night. You're a sensual woman, Rita. Without a continual inflow you'd find yourself wanting to scream every minute of the day."

"That sounds like *you*, Quinn."

He looked at her, surprised. "Yeah. You might be right."

"Maybe we're more alike than you think."

"Maybe. But I'll fall harder. I've believed in too many things too long."

Rita didn't know how long she sat on the bed after Quinn had gone. Hours went by, but she kept on trying to sort out what he had said to her. In a way he had been right. But somehow she knew he had been talking only about himself, about someone who was a product not so much of a past as of a landscape, of a way of being which was much more elemental than her own. It was as if he was transformed by his own glittering, shimmering quality into no more than a mirage when he tried to look into himself.

Or as if, when he looked at other people, he was blinded by the reflection.

Unless, she thought, it was all in her own way of seeing him.

THAT MORNING Lee smelled the caliche dust in the air and knew he wasn't at home. Opening his eyes, he turned them upward in time to see a spider swing down from the ceiling on its almost invisible wiring. Silvery, spinning, the strand caught the light and vanished; Lee looked for the spider, but it, too, was gone.

Out on the highway a car was passing. The wild dogs his father fed in the mornings were barking behind the tire pile, and the sound of an oil drum's being rolled across the pavement meant he was up already. Lee leaned on one elbow and looked around the room. Through the doorway, in the other room, his father's bed was empty. He kicked the covers back, yawned again, and stood up. The sun hadn't quite made it out from behind the mesas, and Lee could see that there was a haze in the sky. The mountains in the distance were just becoming visible. He could see them, jagged, through what was still left of the night. As he was pulling on his tennis shoes he looked through the window again and saw his father getting into the truck.

"Wait for me! Hey, I thought you said you were quitting today."

"Hurry it up!" Quinn yelled back at him. "I've got some last-minute business to take care of over there, and then I'm heading on into town!"

He finished tying his shoes and scrambled outside. His father was waiting for him. The back of the truck was filled with empty oil drums, and Lee turned around to look at them as they pulled out onto the highway. Quinn operated what he called a "sometimes gas station." The sign out front read: SOMETIMES I'M OPEN AND SOMETIMES I AIN'T, and when travelers stopped to fill up or to buy the ancient tins of food which had all but mummified in the desert air, they often asked his father how he made a living. Lee, watching them, would think about what they didn't know: that his father worked in the oil fields most of the year. The pay was good, there were plenty of men to drink with, and though Quinn had never told him so, Lee knew that the relentless machinery held a strange fascination for him. There were times, Lee knew, when his father would stand at the top of the drilling rig and look out over the land, hating it for its barrenness. In his mind's eye Lee could see him squinting into the painful brilliance of the sand as he listened to the machinery with a sense of their complicity.

But there were other times—he knew this, too—when it was the iron his father hated, times when the rig would seem not an accomplice so much as an enemy, destroyer of a land all the more awesome because of the demands it made on men. Those were the times when he climbed down from the rig and didn't go back again. Then would follow the weeks when he would stay around the gas station doing odd jobs, watching the highway, and playing solitaire when he got tired of pumping gas.

The oil fields were just up the highway. Lee remembered them from the times he had been to visit his father, for every time he came, it seemed, his father drove him around and showed him all the machinery the drilling process required. The rig with its unwieldy apparatus was more interesting to Lee than anything he knew of, and whenever his father pointed something out to him he always memorized its name. "Christmas trees," "Hughes' bit," "horses' heads"—the names seemed to spill off his father's tongue as easily as the words of a song, and there was nothing as exciting for him as watching the incessant activity around the wells.

To get to the oil fields they had to turn off the highway onto a sandy road. His father was driving slowly, and it seemed to Lee to be taking a very long time. He listened to the rattle of the empty oil drums. The sound wasn't unpleasant, and after a few minutes it became a kind of low, unbroken droning which nearly put him back to sleep. He rubbed his eyes. The morning was just beginning to get hot.

"I've got to see if Humble wants any of their oil drums back," his father said.

They passed the gate and drove onto the tract. Lee saw his father wave at a one-armed man carrying a ledger beneath his stub.

"Who's that?"

"Jimmy Jimenez. You've never seen a man with worse luck in your life."

"What happened to his arm?"

His father pulled up next to the other mud-spattered pick-ups. The roar of the diesel engines filled Lee's ears. He could smell the rotten-egg odor he knew to be hydrogen sulfide, and though he had smelled it before they had gotten inside the gate it was stronger now, pervading every inch of air.

"What did you say?" his father asked, raising his voice above the noise.

Next to them a huge flatbed truck was backed up to the platform. A gang of roustabouts was unloading lengths of pipe, their hard hats glinting in the early sun.

"His arm!" Lee shouted back.

"He fell seventy feet and caught it on a beam—had to hold on almost half an hour before anyone could get to him! Some weevil hadn't secured the building platform, and the thing fell right out from under him."

Lee knew that a weevil was a greenhorn on a drilling project, and just understanding what his father was talking about gave him a feeling of satisfaction. One thing he never wanted to be was a weevil. He hoped that in another five summers—by the time he was sixteen—he would be able to go to work on a drilling rig and know enough not to make any mistakes. His father had all kinds of stories about accidents caused by weevils. "When you're loading a pipe onto a rack," his father had told him, "you don't ever want to put a weevil on the tail end. You see this finger here? We

70

put a weevil on the tail once and he didn't hoist in sync. The pipe came down and nearly crushed my goddamned hand."

They got out of the truck and Lee followed behind his father, trying to stay out of the way of the gangs of roustabouts carrying tools, pipes, and heavy lengths of chain. Someone shouted his father's name, and Quinn turned to wave at a man squatting next to an immense system of valves projecting from the well.

"You lazy mother!" the man shouted. "Where the—"

And then they were out of hearing. As they climbed the steps to the doghouse a man in a white shirt whom Lee knew to be the tool-pusher crossed the platform and took his turn swearing at Quinn.

Quinn scowled and elbowed past him. "Come on," he said, turning around to Lee. "This greasy bastard's got nothing to say to me."

Lee felt ridiculously out of place in the presence of all these men. His father was talking with another white-shirt; left momentarily to himself, Lee sat down near the edge of the platform, leaned his head back, and squinted up at the derrick. It was equivalent in height to a nine- or ten-story building, a slim, graceful structure which, from this angle at least, seemed hardly sturdy enough to carry the weight of the traveling block. Above him, halfway up the derrick, he could see the platform where he knew his father usually kept watch, and at the very top he could see the crown block with its narrow catwalk.

The sun, it seemed, was everywhere. There wasn't a grain of sand or a speck of caliche dust which didn't mirror it back into the cloudless sky. Lee looked out beyond the drilling area across the expanse of desert. He could make out clumps of mesquite and salt cedar, the mesquite hardly more than brush. The salt cedar was also stunted, not like the cedar he had seen near Austin on the far edge of the Edwards Plateau or the cedar that grew near home, in the red dirt of East Texas. Here it was hardly full enough to shield a lizard from the sun. He put his sleeve to his forehead and blotted the drops of sweat. The air was heavy with hydrogen sulfide, and not a breath of wind was blowing.

"Let's head on into town!"

Lee turned around and saw his father going down the steps. He got up and ran after him, almost tripping over a coil of cable in his hurry to catch up.

"Didn't they want the drums? Say, you quit, didn't you?"

They were pulling out of the parking area. His father waved once more at the one-armed man and then stepped on the accelerator as they drove through the gate.

"You know why he limps? Because the year before he lost his arm he damn near lost his leg!"

Lee looked over at his father. "You quit?"

"Yeah. It's time to lie back and let the world go on chasing its tail. Just lie back and glide along—me and the buzzards, both of us gliding on air. I've always thought that if I could be reincarnated I'd come back as a buzzard. Nobody hates them or envies them. A buzzard doesn't have to worry about women, he can sleep standing up, and he can eat just about anything!"

"A buzzard?" Lee repeated, laughing.

Across from him his father was leaning easily back into the seat. One arm was out the window, and Lee noticed that his shirt was torn at the elbow where the cloth had finally worn through. The shreds were flapping in the air—Lee looked at the other elbow and saw it, too, was torn, and he felt a kind of secret satisfaction. He looked down at his own Levi's to remind himself how dirty they were, and then he reached up to touch his hair. It hadn't been combed since his mother had done it on the day his father had come for him two weeks before.

"He ain't going to a funeral, Beatrice," his father had said when he had seen him with his hair combed and his tennis shoes washed.

And his mother had answered, "I've told you I'm not going to have my son look like an oil worker's child."

There had been a tense silence. His father's face was touched with the shadow of anger. His mother's face seemed hard, not a face he recognized at all. Lee watched, breathless, as his parents confronted each other. Then his father began to laugh.

"Beatrice, you're still as beautiful as you always were. But I wouldn't touch you with a ninety-foot drill shaft."

72

She lifted her chin a little. Lee watched her nostrils flare, reminding him of a sleek-headed mare who sees the trainer approaching with the bit. He felt her hand on his shoulder and marveled at how cool it was. As long as he could remember, her hands on his body had been cool.

"My son isn't going to look like an oil worker's child," she repeated.

"He's my son, too, you know."

"Oh, really?"

There was an iciness to his mother's words which Lee could feel all the way through him. It seemed to penetrate to his very bones and leave him not cold but numb, and terribly afraid. His mother's hand tightened on his shoulder. He wanted to wrench away from her and run to his father, but he couldn't. He felt that he didn't exist, that there was nothing between his parents but empty, gaping space, that it wasn't him they were fighting over. It was someone else, some*thing* else—an absence, a faceless, nameless thing. And then his father took three steps forward and looked down into his mother's face. His mother looked back at him, and Lee could feel her hatred.

As they were leaving the house he turned and saw his mother standing on the front porch. The morning light didn't betray her. She looked much younger than thirty-two, and the dark red of her robe accentuated her hair, which was a rich auburn and wavy down to her shoulders. Lee knew the smell of her hair. It was a strange mixture, but mostly the scent of talcum powder; sometimes at night he would lie in bed and think about that smell, trying to find the right words to describe it. Yes, he thought, his mother was beautiful. And then, when they were almost at the end of the sidewalk, he heard her call out.

"Quinn! Come back a minute. I want to talk to you."

"Get in the truck," his father said to him. "I'll be back in a minute."

So he waited. The minutes stretched on to a quarter of an hour. Overhead on the telephone wire a dove was making its soft morning sounds. Lee listened, closing his eyes and leaning back against the seat. He wondered how long it would be before the four

73

hundred miles began, before he and his father would start the drive that would take them almost all the way across the state, from the eastern boundary to the trans-Pecos desert. Finally the front door opened and his father came out to the truck. His face was tense. Lee could see that something his mother had said had made him very angry.

Quinn glanced at him and let out a laugh, a self-absorbed, almost scornful sound. He started the truck and they sped along the street. Lee watched the green lawns and neat houses go by, not knowing what to say to his father. Quinn reached out and flipped on the radio.

"The bitch."

Lee didn't answer.

That had been two weeks earlier. He had spent half his allotted month with his father now; every morning he had woken up and counted the days, checking them off reluctantly in his mind and trying to envision the remaining time stretching ahead indefinitely. The empty oil drums in the back were still rattling, their low, soothing sound broken only by the passing of an occasional car. He looked over at his father. His hat was pushed back on his head. It had been weeks since his last haircut, and his hair was beginning to curl up on his neck, just beneath the hat brim. But Lee liked the way he looked. When his father's hair was long he looked more like the quarter-Indian he was.

As Lee gazed at Quinn he found himself thinking back to the time he had first realized that his father had Indian blood.

"Really?" he had asked. "You mean you're really Indian, and so me and Tony are Indian, too?"

"That's right," his father had said. "Didn't I ever tell you about my side of the family? My great-grandfather was a full-blooded Comanche who got married to his cousin. After the wedding he found out that this cousin was also his aunt, but it was too late to do anything about it. So their son, my grandfather, ended up being great-uncle to his own parents. Well, my grandfather got married three times, each time to a white woman, and each time he had a daughter. The third daughter, Anna Maria Raintree, was my mother, and she got married to Travis Lawrence, who was half jackal and half snake. They had one son who was an idiot, one who was mostly snake, and one who they never could tell if he was an Indian or a jackal. The fourth son was me, but by that time they realized the odds were against them, so they traded me to a Mexican for two bushels of jalapeños and a mule. It wasn't such a bad trade, I guess. The jalapeños killed my father, and my mother ran off with the mule. But to this day nobody's ever been able to figure out what I turned out to be."

Lee remembered how his father had laughed as he had told the story. Now, though, he was hardly talking, and he certainly wasn't in any mood to laugh. He was just watching the road unfold beneath the wheels, from time to time looking up into the rearview mirror. Finally, when they had gone a few miles up the highway from the oil fields, Quinn reached across Lee into the glove compartment and pulled out an unopened pint of whiskey. Lee watched him break the seal and unscrew the cap with the bottle between his thighs. Then he tilted it, took a long drink, and stuck it back into the glove compartment.

"Say, Lee. Take a look in the rear-view mirror."

Lee leaned forward and gave the mirror a twist. The sun was misty orange above the mesas, its light made translucent by a thin film of cloud.

"It was orange last night, too," he said.

"Sandstorm," his father answered.

Quinn reached for the glove compartment again. Lee watched the sun for another moment, and then he turned the mirror back toward his father.

They didn't talk much the rest of the way into town. Lee watched the clumps of scrub go by, following with his eyes the occasional surprised jack rabbits and staring at the clusters of buildings in the shadows of lazy windmills. Lee wondered, as he did each time he came to visit his father, how people could survive in West Texas. Except for buzzards and jack rabbits, the only living things seemed to be the pump jacks, and they were always moving, day after day, year after year, so that after a while you forgot about them. Like big black grasshoppers, Lee thought, things out of dreams. Unless they caught fire, and then from miles away you could see the smoke and smell oil heavy on the air. It always occurred to him how different West Texas was from East. For Lee it was like going to another planet, a place where there weren't pine forests and rivers but only scrub and dry arroyos. Here the rains were infrequent but treacherous—electrical storms which turned the sky the color of metal and then disappeared, suddenly, leaving everything as it was before. And there were sandstorms, especially in summer.

Lee looked out the window at the sky. "How long? Before midday?"

"This evening," his father said, his eyes on the road. "It'll be blowing in from the west."

"How can you tell?"

"I can tell."

Quinn uncapped the bottle and tilted it again. A car was coming toward them on the other side of the white line. Lee strained to make out the license plate.

"California."

When his father didn't answer, he turned around and watched the car fade into the distance. The sun was brighter than before. It was glancing off the tops of the oil drums, casting shadows around the tools and the mound of greasy rags. Lee was up on his knees looking out the rear window, and when he turned around again he nearly knocked his head on the shotgun in the rack. He sat back down, smelling the odor of gun oil. Just the night before, he had watched his father clean the gun. The smell of the oil had stayed with him all night, it seemed, because he remembered waking up in the dark and not being able to forget the smell which had been there just before his father had turned out the light. And then, this morning, there had been the smell of dust.

They were almost at the turn-off to the town. Lee looked ahead and saw a long building with a sign in front which read SUNDOWN MOTEL. He knew it was new, because he remembered it from the Christmas before, when the building hadn't been finished. As they came closer he leaned out the window to get a better look before his father turned the truck off the highway. There weren't any cars in front. The only sign of life around the motel was a

76

yellow dog on the pavement of the adjoining gas station. The gas station, too, was new, though it didn't seem to be doing much business, and neither did the coffee shop. Quinn slowed for the turn-off and guided the truck off the highway onto the blacktop. The road was full of potholes; the rattling of the oil drums became tinny, uneven.

A few minutes later Lee glanced over at his father again. The whiskey had given him a faraway look, an expression which wasn't unfamiliar to Lee. It was the same expression he had had on his face the last few nights when they had sat outside after supper, Lee watching the lights approaching on the highway, his father staring off into the dark. It was a strange look, a dreamy look, as though he was being caught off guard. Only it seemed to Lee that it wasn't dreamy in the way most people can look dreamy, but different somehow, as though his father wasn't dreaming so much as he was already recollecting the present—the sun glittering on the sand, the mountains rising purple in the distance, himself driving the pick-up with the pint of whiskey between his knees. It was as though, for Quinn, everything was rushing to become memory, as though the moment had been sucked into the future and he was looking back on this morning from somewhere else.

The town of Calvary was just ahead. It was little more than a wind-swept cluster of stucco and wooden buildings. The false fronts of most of them were stark and sagging, though not, it seemed, so much from the elements themselves as from a kind of timeless futility, a pact sworn between man, wind, and sand only to be violated over and over again. As they passed a row of shacks on the outskirts, Quinn slowed down. Tilting the bottle again, he turned toward the window and honked the horn with his free hand. A group of Mexican children was playing by the roadside, and when they heard the horn they stood up and began to shout. A woman came around the side of one of the houses. She waved at the truck, and Quinn waved back as he leaned out the window and said something to the children which Lee couldn't understand. They began to laugh, and one of them threw a dirt clod at the oil drums.

"Crazy kids," Quinn said. "I've been friends with them ever

since I caught them trying to hotwire the truck—damn smart little bastards, too. I used to visit her on Saturdays, and one afternoon I heard someone starting up the truck. I ran outside in my underwear and kicked their tails, but we had a good laugh over it afterwards. Damn smart little bastards."

The faraway look was momentarily replaced by a smile. Lee watched his father tilt the bottle once more before he screwed the cap on again and stuck it back into the glove compartment.

"We're coming into town," Quinn said. "You hungry?"

"I could use some pancakes."

"Use some pancakes? What the hell you planning to do with them?"

"Eat'm!"

"Eat'm!" his father repeated. "I thought maybe you had something else in mind."

"Like what?"

"Oh, hell—nothing. A fat pancake would taste pretty good, you're right. With just a little pat of butter. And a whole lot of that sweet, sticky syrup—hot."

Lee smiled, but he couldn't bring himself to laugh. He knew his father was kidding with him, and it pleased him, though it also made him uncomfortable. The easy bantering, the smiles that passed between them, the vaguely sexual references which pervaded his father's talk—all of this he missed at home. Listening to his father made him feel almost adult, as though something forbidden and secret was being shared between them. Yet his father's talk disturbed him at the same time that it made him smile, for always in the backwash of his awareness was his mother. Her hands were cool and gentle and her talcum-smelling hair gave off memories of mornings a long time in his past. There was a softness about her, a loveliness which he couldn't put into words and yet which he knew instinctively had nothing to do with what his father was talking about. The vague stirrings inside him had nothing to do with his mother. Her hands, her face, her hair—they were a universe of their own, and yet when his father talked to him as he was doing now, Lee was aware of a shadow of something. It was a kind of shame, a memory which wouldn't quite come into focus. And so when Quinn laughed again, Lee smiled, but this time he turned his eyes to the window and concentrated on the town.

They passed another row of tin-roofed houses, a laundromat, and a defunct movie theater. Farther on, the blacktop became gravel, and then the gravel became pavement again, not as full of potholes as the road leading from the highway but in an almost equally bad state of repair. The truck bumped along, the oil drums clattering in the back. Finally they reached the main street, where the pavement was wider. Lee hadn't seen Calvary in over six months, but it was no different than he remembered. Here the old men didn't gather in front of the sawmills as they did at home, but rather in front of the depot, where the rusty rails ran from nowhere to nowhere and faded into the distance at some point out in the desert. Most of these men, he knew, had spent their lives on drilling rigs, having made their way out to the oil fields in the twenties and thirties. Some of them, his father had told him, had been ranch hands, and some had even worked in the cotton fields after irrigation and chemical farming had come to West Texas. All of them were hard-looking old men, graying phantoms with bony, joyless faces. Lee stared at them, but they didn't seem to see him when he passed.

It was when they were driving by the grocery store that Lee saw the old man sweeping the steps. He had on a butcher's apron over a pair of Levi's, and he was wearing bright-colored, obviously hand-tooled boots.

"Did you see those boots?" Lee asked his father.

"Sure. You want some?"

"Some what?"

"Boots!"

"I don't know."

"Well, you *better* know. You're not going to be kicking any shit in tennis shoes."

Lee smiled again.

"Yeah, we'll get you some regular kickers. But right now it's time for breakfast. You go on over to the café and order. Bill down at the Conoco's got a lug wrench that belongs to me, and if I don't

79

get it back from the bastard I may never see it again. So go on now. I'll be there in a shake."

Lee opened the door and stepped out into the street. The truck spun out and he was left by himself with the still-early sun dappling the buildings, not yet a dusty sun, though it was already hot. A car passed and the driver, a teen-age girl, waved. Lee waved back, not certain whether he had seen her before. He supposed it didn't matter, though. West Texans weren't that much different from people in Toombs Mill, though they had a drawn look about them, less mobile features and oddly glassy eyes, as though the war with the elements had visibly hardened their faces. He wondered again about the girl, whether she had known he was Quinn Lawrence's son. Then, shrugging, he crossed the street and went into the café.

"Coffee?" the woman behind the counter called out as he was sitting down at a table near the window. From there he could look out and see the Conoco down the block.

"Coffee over here?"

"What?"

He looked toward the counter. The waitress was a tall, wiry woman with a worn face and hair the color of his mother's, only it looked as if it had been dyed. Lee watched her moving across the room with a glass of water and a menu in one hand, two plates of chicken-fried steak balanced on each arm. She set the plates down in front of a group of men at the table next to him. They were young men, oil workers, he thought, noticing their muscular forearms and darkened fingernails. He watched one of them put out his cigarette and reach for his fork in a single motion, hearing at the same time the waitress's rasping laugh.

"Start shoveling," she said.

One of the men reached out to grab her, but she laughed again and stepped over to Lee's table.

"How are you this morning?" she said, thrusting a menu into his hand. He realized then that she hadn't been talking to him when she had asked about the coffee.

"All right. And my father's coming—"

"Two of you?"

80

"Yes, ma'am. And coffee."

"For you or him?"

He looked up at the painted face with its lines of irritation or maybe boredom around the mouth. At home he never drank coffee. His mother wouldn't let him. Ordering coffee now was more a measure of how far he was from home than a wanting. The waitress was looking at him, one eyebrow raised.

"For me. But he'll want coffee when he gets here. And I don't have to look at the menu. I already know what I want."

"Doreen!"

At the back of the café a man was waving. The waitress spun around, smiled, and then wiggled her hips a little as she turned back to Lee. He looked over at the group of men at the table next to him, and then he looked at the waitress again.

"Come on, sweetie. I don't have all morning."

"Pancakes. With lots of butter."

"You mean a short stack?"

He was staring at her hair, wondering if it was gray beneath the dye and trying to imagine how she looked at night when she wiped her eyebrows off.

"I guess so."

She turned and brushed by the table next to him. This time Lee couldn't help but notice the way her hips were moving, knowing that the men had noticed it, too.

"She's not bad for an old broad," one of them said, turning toward his table. "Hey, you eating breakfast all by yourself?"

"Yes," Lee answered, embarrassed that they had seen him staring at the waitress. Then: "I mean no, my father's coming."

"What's his name?" the man said.

Lee looked at him as he sat hunched over the steak, his fork moving quickly from plate to mouth, his jaw not stopping chewing even when he talked. He was a muscular man with a small blue tattoo on his right forearm.

"Quinn Lawrence," Lee told him.

"Yep, I know him," the man said, tilting his head back and taking a final gulp of coffee. "Works for Humble, don't he? Say, Virgil, wasn't he the one who put out that electrical fire about a month ago? Is he a big man, sonny, looks kind of Indian? See, Virgil, I told you so. He put that fire out single-handed, and drunker than a dog, too."

"Give me enough beer and I can piss hell to ashes," the one named Virgil said as he reached into his pocket and pulled out a bill. "Come on, let's go."

"Come on, Billy Dean," one of the other men said. "I ain't spending my Saturday morning in the same place I spent my Friday night."

The man with the blue tattoo smiled at Lee and stood up with the others. "Yeah," he said. "Drunker than a dog and done it almost single-handed."

"Leave Doreen some silver, Billy Dean."

Lee heard the sound of change hitting the vinyl top of the table and felt someone punch him on the arm. When he looked up, the men were gone. He thought about what the man with the blue tattoo had said, a little ashamed of himself for having felt so shy around them. When the man had started talking to him, he had looked down, pretending to be studying the menu, but he hadn't wanted anything else. Something about them had made him want to recede into himself, to gather his thoughts together and hide in a dark corner, looking out and listening without anyone's seeing him.

The waitress set the plate of pancakes in front of him, her arm seeming to appear from nowhere to lift the menu out of his hands.

"Well, is he coming?"

Lee looked from her face to the window. "I don't know," he said.

He noticed then that she hadn't brought the coffee. For a moment he felt just the slightest stab of rage. For a moment— just a moment—he wanted to jump up from the table and grab her by the hair and demand to know why she hadn't brought the coffee. And why did she have that hair, that dyed copper hair, and why was she looking at him like that through her mask of paint and pencil?

"My father's going to pay for it," he told her.

"I'll believe it when I see it," she said.

The warmth from the pancakes was drifting upward into his face, and he could smell the butter now. The waitress had turned away from him and was clearing the table where the men had been sitting, humming to herself. Lee reached for the syrup. The pancakes weren't as good as the ones he was used to at home, but he was hungry and they were hot. He finished them in a hurry, pushing the plate to the other side of the table. The sun was well above the roofs of the buildings now, coming through the window brilliant and metallic, illuminating the tiny specks of silver embedded in the vinyl of the tabletop. For a moment he leaned his head back against the cool, still-shaded seat. Then, rubbing his eyes, he turned to the window.

His father was coming down the street. Lee watched his boots strike against the pavement, hearing in his mind the sound they made. It was an abrupt sound, a sound he heard, it seemed, even in his dreams or at least at the moment of waking when he knew his father had long been up and was outside getting ready to leave. The wind, just a little wind, hardly more than a ground breeze to touch the tops of the bunchgrass, was causing the newspaper in his hand to ripple. He watched as his father came through the doorway, folding the newspaper and smacking it against the counter as he passed.

"Have you eaten already, or didn't you order yet?"

"I just finished. I would have ordered something for you, but—"

"Never mind. I'll just have coffee."

As Quinn sat down the woman came over to the table. Putting one hand on the back of the seat and the other on her hip, she said, "Hello, Quinn."

Someone had just put a dime in the jukebox, and a steely, plaintive sound seemed to be everywhere in the room.

"Two coffees," his father said. "Black."

Lee looked up at him gratefully as the waitress walked away.

"Did you get your lug wrench back?"

"What? No, the bastard loaned it out."

Quinn was turning through the newspaper. Suddenly he set it down on the table and looked directly at Lee. Just as he was about to say something the woman returned with the coffee. Lee noticed again the distracted, strangely distant expression on his father's face, and he felt a surge of anger at the woman for having come between them. A few moments passed. Lee remembered what the tattooed man had said and was on the verge of asking him if it was true when his father said:

"Let's head out for California this morning."

"What?" Lee heard himself reply.

Quinn put down the spoon he had been using to stir his coffee. Lee listened to its dull tinkling, not taking his eyes from his father's face.

"California? Why do you want to go to California?"

"What was the license plate you read off to me awhile ago?"

"California," he answered, still not comprehending.

"Well, hell, we might as well be in California as Texas. This is my time off, and I don't get to see you every day. What do you say, Lee—you ready for a little traveling?"

"I don't know," Lee answered, toying with his cup.

The sun coming through the panes was collecting in stagnant pools now around the empty plate. Lee reached out and shifted its position slightly, moving it into the shadows.

"I don't know," he said again. And then: "Sure, I'd like to go to California!"

Of course he wanted to go. For years now, it seemed, he had heard about Disneyland. Wasn't all of California Disneyland, or was that just something he had believed long ago when he had been younger? He felt a thrill of excitement, a desire to jump up and hug his father.

"But what about Tony? His feelings will be hurt if I get to go and he doesn't."

"He's too little," Quinn answered. "He don't even spend summers with me yet."

Lee's eyes met his father's, still without comprehending. Quinn took a drink of coffee and wiped his mouth with his hand.

"Nope, Tony's too little," he went on. "When he gets to be eleven I'll take him to California, too. Come on, finish your coffee. We ought to get out of here this morning, before the sandstorm blows in."

The song from the jukebox was still in Lee's ears as they left the café. Above the buildings huge, vague clouds were surging over the desert, cumulus clouds which seemed to have faded without having lost their monstrous appearance, a strangely immobile, almost transnatural quality which always made Lee wonder if the horizon was real. He gazed up at them as he climbed into the truck, wondering if there were clouds like that in California.

"Let's go," his father said.

The truck began to bump along the street again. The clatter of the oil drums was the only sound Lee could distinguish in the windless calm. Soon the weathered storefronts, the low squares of stucco in front of which Mexican children were playing in the dirt, the anonymous sheet-metal warehouses rusting beside the railroad tracks—all of this, the town which was so different from the one in which Lee lived and which was yet, because he associated it with his father, strangely, achingly familiar—all of this was behind him. His father had already turned onto the highway, and they were headed west, away from the sun. For a moment he wondered why they hadn't gone back to pick up some clothes and get rid of the load of oil drums, but somehow those things didn't matter. All he could think about was being with his father, just the two of them, and they were going someplace he had always wanted to go.

Beyond the window the derricks were skeletal, elemental against the sky. Lee could see the roustabouts working in the shadow of the steel girders, their hard hats deflecting the sun onto the sand, which in turn sent it streaking up into the clouds again. He could see the spindly greasewood as well as clumps of bear grass, so sharp it would cut your legs to pieces if you didn't wear boots or heavy denim. And everywhere were the pump jacks, moving, always moving, the word LUFKIN on the eyebeams going up and down. In the distance, on a deserted strip of road, a big car was shooting across the sand. Lee watched it swerve and fishtail among the clumps of scrub, finally making a turn at what looked to be a ninety-degree angle and then picking up speed again as it hurtled toward the highway. A little farther on the car pulled out in front of them, and Lee saw it was a cinnamon-colored Mercury with a pompadoured old man at the wheel. The chrome gleamed in the unrelenting morning light. Then the car was out of sight, leaving a cyclone of dust behind.

Quinn wasn't talking much. The bottle was between his knees again, and every now and then Lee would look over and see him tilt it to his lips. There was a tightness around his father's mouth which Lee couldn't quite feel comfortable about, and his gaze was narrowed, as though he was looking into the sun. But he wasn't. The sun was still at their backs, and Lee knew it would be that way for at least three hours. He turned away from his father and stared out toward the mesas rising to the right of them in the distance. Overhead buzzards were circling leisurely above the sand. Their flight had a disarming laziness about it, the black, oily bellies seeming to be suspended, floating. Yet Lee knew they could swoop down out of the sky with the suddenness of death itself, and he tried to force his mind away from them.

The sound of the radio startled him. He turned away from the window and looked back toward his father.

"See if you can get El Paso."

The radio crackled and blared as he turned the dial. Snatches of accordion music, broken bits of newscasts, the raucous notes of a steel guitar—Lee kept on fooling with the dial until he saw his father nod. Then he leaned back and listened to an insistent female voice sing a love song.

The air was still and very hot. His Levi's were beginning to stick to the seat where he was sweating behind the knees. Leaning the upper half of his body out the window, he closed his eyes, hoping the wind created by the truck would give him some relief. As he bounced down a moment later, he nearly hit his head again on the shotgun in the rack. His father glanced over at him.

"Serves you right."

Quinn laughed then, more to himself than at Lee. It was a low laugh, almost drowned out by the noise of the truck, but Lee

86

heard it and reddened a little. For some reason he was beginning to feel uncomfortable with his father, though whether it was the heat or the drinking or just a vague desire to know what was on his mind Lee wasn't sure. And then he found himself doing what he had been wanting to do ever since they had left the café— asking his father whether or not what the man with the blue tattoo had told him was true.

Quinn took a while to answer.

"Yeah," he said at last. "That's the way it was."

Lee wanted him to say more, but he had fallen silent. All the rest of the way into El Paso neither one of them said a word.

LEE STOOD ON THE CORNER just beyond the traffic, looking up the hill at the row of old homes and wondering if San Francisco looked anything at all like this. The wide, sloping streets reminded him of pictures he had seen at school. But then, looking back toward the railroad tracks, he saw the crowded industrial district and the slums sweltering in the summer heat, and his fantasy of San Francisco vanished. El Paso was a long way from San Francisco, he was thinking as he began to walk back toward the tracks. The sun reflecting off the tin roofs of the warehouses was causing the sidewalk to blur before his eyes, and for a moment he enjoyed a dizzy, unreal sensation, like walking underwater. He laughed a little as he squinted into the glare. The smells of dust and limestone were all around him now, and as he passed a long, boxlike building he could smell the noxious odor of fiber glass. It burned his nose and caused his eyes to tear. No longer laughing, he began to run.

Away from the blocks of factories again, Lee slowed his pace and slipped easily into the Saturday crowd. He was on a busy street in a section of the city which seemed to be entirely Mexican. Women with sacks of groceries brushed by him; dark-haired children shrieked and laughed; fruit vendors called out to him in musical English. He had the sense of being in a dream world, a bright-colored place where people moved endlessly by him, going nowhere in the sun. But soon he saw his father's truck parked far down the street on the opposite side. He walked toward it, the faded blue coming nearer and nearer, and then he saw the bar nearby. It had been over an hour since his father had told him to take a walk and then disappeared inside. Lee hurried on toward the open door of the bar. Just as he reached it two men stumbled out, muttered something in Spanish, and pushed by him. Lee stepped to the side to let them pass, hearing the laughter they left behind them mingling with the music from inside.

The second time he approached the door more cautiously, sticking his head in and blinking as the darkened interior met his eyes. The place was nearly empty. The bartender looked up as he stepped through the door, and when the man said nothing Lee took another step. Inside the air was cooler, smelling of whiskey and stale beer, with the odor of chili coming from somewhere in the back. Lee rubbed his eyes, the glare from the street still blinding him. Then, blinking, he saw his father. Quinn was sitting by himself in a corner with his back to the door.

"Dad!" he called, moving toward the table.

Lee could tell that Quinn had had a lot to drink. His gestures were slow and heavy, and his words seemed to be coming from somewhere else. Lee sat down opposite him and started to ask if he was ready to go, but Quinn held up one hand in a signal for silence.

"There are a lot of things I never told you," he said after a moment had passed.

Lee looked at him uncomfortably, wondering what he was going to say. His father finished the last of his whiskey. There were three glasses, all empty, on the table, and Lee pushed them to one side. The table was sticky where they had been, and it gave off an unpleasantly sweet, dank smell. Lee glanced at the light coming through the open door. He felt almost chilly now. The bartender went over to the jukebox and a low Spanish voice began to sing; Lee, looking at his father, remembered the nights the two of them had spent sitting on the steps behind the gas station, watching the moon rise slow and silver and listening to the same voice sing the same Spanish song. On those nights Quinn had sat with his back leaned against the step above, smoking cigarettes, talking, drinking quietly and looking past the bottle toward the stars. It didn't seem to Lee that they had talked much on those nights, but on one of them, he recalled, his father had said the same words in that same faraway tone of voice—"There are a lot of things I never told you—" and then he had begun to tell him about women, about their bodies, their secret parts. Finally, laughing, he had said that that was all there was to know about women. But usually on those nights they hadn't talked. What stayed in Lee's mind most clearly were his father's face silhouetted in the moonlight, the feel of the wind rippling low against the bunchgrass, and the shapes of cactus outlined against the sky. There had been the sound of coyotes on the sand hills, the snorting of javelinas, the occasional passing of a car out on the highway, the creaking of the steps as his father shifted his weight. It had seemed to Lee then that he understood his father's drinking. He had felt almost in tune with the silences which came over him, the silences that made him wonder just what was going on inside him . . . so that now, looking at him across the table, he wondered what he was going to say.

But Quinn didn't say anything. He just sat quietly, staring down at the empty glasses. When a few moments had gone by he looked up at Lee.

"Come on."

Lee pushed back his chair and stood up with him. The Spanish song was playing for the second time as they went out into the street. The heat descended on him again, more intense, it seemed, than before.

"It's an oven," Lee said.

"It's hell," was his father's answer.

As he was about to open the door of the truck Quinn stopped abruptly and stared at him. Lee stopped, too, puzzled.

"What's wrong?"

"Come on, let's go buy you some boots."

The words came slowly. Lee was looking at him with one hand shading his eyes so that he could see the expression on his face.

"What? You mean—"

"The number-one saddlery in El Paso is just around the corner.

We're going to get you some boots, like I told you. Come on."

Lee followed his father down the sidewalk to a solitary wooden building. As they pushed open the door he breathed in the odor of neat's-foot oil and noticed how cramped things were inside. The man behind the counter was gnomish and wrinkled, with a face and scalp which were almost entirely without hair.

"Afternoon," he said as they came in.

"Afternoon. You're Maurice Best, ain't you?"

"Well, I ain't his brother."

"Didn't take you for him," Quinn answered. "Say, I'm looking for a pair of boots for my son here. Got anything offhand to fit him?"

Maurice Best looked Lee straight in the face. Then he looked down at his tennis shoes.

"A three and a half? Four?"

Lee nodded, amazed that the old man had been able to guess his size. He watched as he ducked into a back room.

"We're getting you some good ones. Real, hand-tooled leather —that all right with you?"

"Sure!"

His voice sounded unnaturally loud in the tiny shop. Embarrassed, he turned away from his father and began to inspect a row of boots on a shelf behind the counter. They all seemed to have been custom-made, and some of them were very fancy. The saddles hanging from the rafters also seemed to have been carefully crafted. Lee wished he could see into the back room or maybe even watch the old man at work. The cramped place with its leathery smell was fascinating to him. He had never seen boots or saddles which were so sturdy and yet so intricately designed.

"I'll get some fancy ones, won't I? Say, what do you think is keeping him back there?"

His father shrugged, smiling at him across the room. Impatient, Lee leaned across the counter and tried to get a glimpse into the back. Finally the old man appeared again, a brown-wrapped parcel in his hands. He watched as Maurice Best took a pair of beautiful boots out of the paper and set them on the

91

counter. For an eternity, it seemed, Lee stared at them.

"Go ahead and try them on," his father said.

He reached for them. The old man motioned toward a stool. Lee pulled off his tennis shoes and put on the boots. Then he walked from one side of the shop to the other while his father and the old man looked at one another as if the two of them were sharing some secret.

"They fit, Dad!"

"How much?" he heard his father ask.

"Sixty."

Suddenly Lee was afraid the boots would have to go back into their brown wrapping, back into the old man's hands, back into the room through the door of which he couldn't see, onto a shelf in a corner until someone else came along with enough money to buy them. Then he saw that Quinn had laid a handful of bills out on the counter.

"Dad—"

"Thanks, Mr. Best. Maybe we'll see you again when his feet get bigger."

When they were almost out of the shop Lee put his hand on his father's arm.

"Dad?"

"What's the matter?"

"I don't want to wear them. I—I want to save them, wrap them up till we get to California."

"If that's what you want."

"Yeah—"

"I'll wait for you outside. Go on in and ask him to wrap them up again."

Maurice Best didn't say a word as he handed Lee the brown paper and helped him pull off the boots. He wrapped them carefully while Lee put on his tennis shoes. Then, tying the parcel with a piece of twine, he gave Lee a wink.

"I made them for a midget," he said, stroking his hairless chin. "He was with a traveling sideshow."

"How come he didn't come back for them?"

"I don't know. I never got the chance to ask."

Lee took the boots and the old man winked again. This time Lee winked back at him, and then, suddenly, he smiled.

Later on that afternoon Lee would ask himself if he had ever really believed he would see California. He would wonder why he had believed his father, and it would be hard to keep back the tears.

But now they were still headed west. El Paso had just slipped into the distant haze, a mingling of dust and factory fumes which lay on the air as motionless as the heat. When Lee turned around to look behind him he could hardly see the city at all. Surrounded by mountains of rock rising up out of the monotony of the desert, El Paso was gone, swallowed up, it seemed to Lee. He put out his hand and caressed the brown-wrapped parcel on the seat between him and his father. Sixty-dollar boots, he was thinking. Hand-tooled, sixty-dollar boots. And then once more he was overcome with excitement, imagining himself standing at the entrance to Disneyland with his new boots on his feet.

He was jarred abruptly out of his thoughts by the notes of a steel guitar. His father had turned the radio on again. He hardly seemed to be hearing it, though; it was as if, for Quinn, the sound was merely something to fill the gaps between tilts of the nearly empty bottle. For a moment Lee stared hard at him. His features were set, almost clenched. With each drink his father took, Lee could see him receding further and further behind this mask, this stony other self which was terrifyingly undefined, which showed anger and despair and a lot of other things besides, but which was foreign, unknown to Lee. It seemed vacant, hollow, merely an outer form. And then it dawned on him that what he was seeing wasn't a mask, that he was frightened because he was actually seeing his father for the first time.

Quinn finished the whiskey and tossed the bottle over the top of the truck. Lee saw the jerk of his shoulder and a moment later he caught a glimpse of the bottle as it shattered against a background of yucca and rock. They were going faster now. The surface of the highway had changed once they had crossed the New Mexico line, and the even clatter of the oil drums had become a loud rattling. One of them had fallen over and was rolling from side to side in the bed of the truck. Lee put his hands over his ears. The noise, he was sure, would drive him crazy if he had to listen to it much longer.

"Hey, Dad."

His father didn't seem to have heard him. He raised his voice.

"Dad!"

"What is it!"

Even above the banging of the oil drums and the discordance of the steel guitar Lee could hear the annoyance in his father's voice. He reached out, instinctively almost, and touched the brown-wrapped parcel, wondering how this could be the same man who had bought him his boots. The complicity in his father's voice when he had spoken to the old man, the way the old man had winked as he was leaving, his face knowing, his eyes telling of the many times he had been through that scene before—Lee had taken it all to mean that there was something between himself and his father that neither of them had ever been able to put into words. It was something that the old man had recognized, something that bound them together more securely than he had ever been bound to his mother through the flesh. But no, he thought, maybe he had been wrong. Maybe he had been imagining everything, for now there was no acknowledgment in his father's eyes. There was only that hard, focused gaze, that glassy stare which frightened Lee and seemed to fix him to the seat.

"What!" his father said again.

"The oil drums—can't you hear them?"

His father turned his eyes back to the road. Lee felt the truck beginning to slow down. A moment later they came to a stop on the sandy shoulder.

"Come on."

"Huh?"

"Get out."

Lee opened the door of the truck and followed him around to the back. Quinn climbed over the tailgate and stood the oil drum on end again, and then he sat down on it with his hands on his knees, staring drunkenly at Lee.

"It'll never stop. It'll never stop because man is self-destructive. He'll destroy himself and the earth at the same time. Natural-born destroyers, all of us. Now, can you tell me why that is?"

His words came slowly, slurred with the false pensiveness that liquor sometimes brings, and Lee didn't know how to answer him. The sun was hot. Lee could feel himself sweating all over, could see the dampness on his father's face beneath the hat.

"Sometimes I ask myself how come the wind, the sand, the stars? How come people are all the time begging and sorrowing? I don't know why, but I know we can be overcome with this earth and with the people on it, and it has something to do with beauty and with some kind of spirit."

His voice faltered once more. He was swaying back and forth on the oil drum, and Lee was afraid he was going to topple over.

"Dad—"

"Shut up," his father said.

Lee stared at him, not understanding.

"You think I'm some kind of hardrock hero, don't you?"

Lee didn't answer.

His father began to laugh. "Yeah, this land burns hard. It burns the color from cloth and paint. It burns the water from the creek beds. It burns the love out of people, because love is a soft thing, made of pretty colors. And so people retaliate. They take it out on whatever's closest at hand—themselves, the earth that made them, other people. And, hell, it's the same everywhere. It's not just West Texas.

"Though I got to admit there's something about this place that pledges you to loneliness. You sweat and hate, and hate and sweat, and you come to know for certain there's no City of God in the hereafter. There's nothing, you learn that fast. Though sometimes the sun follows you with a blinding shaft, no matter which way you turn, and you can almost believe His eye is on you. But if it is, it's on you for retribution, and what He's telling you is your bones'll be licked clean by flame. It doesn't happen often, though; most of the time spirit's a matter of the individual, and it's a rare occasion when it has anything to do with God. Because it's you who puts the beauty and spirit in the desert. In itself it's nothing,

95

and if there's beauty and spirit here it's because the desert has forced you to finish its beginnings. It's the same with a great poem, I guess. You have to bring the love to it and then find the reward without much help.

"Like I said, though, it's not just the desert. People are the same everywhere. They don't know how to see."

Lee watched Quinn climb down from the truck. He began walking across the sand, making his way among the rocks and clumps of cactus. Lee could see the pattern the sweat had made on the back of his shirt; as he stared at his father staggering across the windless, glittering sand he felt such a hurt that he could hardly keep from calling out to him. But he didn't. He stood tight-lipped and silent, feeling as though he was going to crack open inside. A moment later he began walking after his father. Quinn took a few more steps and then stopped and turned around.

"Shit," he said uncertainly.

Lee didn't answer. He was staring at his father's face.

"Shit," Quinn said again.

"Let's go back to the truck."

Lee moved toward him until he could have reached out and touched his shoulder. Quinn stepped backward, swayed, and almost fell, but Lee caught him. For a moment the whole weight of his father's body rested against his chest.

"Come on, Dad, let's go back to the truck."

Quinn let him take his arm and they started toward the highway. When they reached the truck he pushed Lee away from him and got in on the driver's side, but almost immediately he slumped forward against the wheel. The horn began to sound. Lee, opening the door on the passenger side, was about to climb in when suddenly Quinn jumped out again.

"Let's go, Dad. You said we were going to make it to California by the day after tomorrow."

"I've changed my mind. We ain't going to California."

Quinn reached into the truck and a moment later Lee saw the keys flying through the air. He squinted after them, but it was impossible to see where they had landed. The rage inside demanded he should say it now—*now*—tell his father how he hated him for making himself so much less than he was. Yet he couldn't do it.

"I'll go find the keys," Lee said at last.

It was only after several minutes of intense searching that the keys turned up. They were half buried in the sand at the base of a yucca, and Lee almost missed them. Finally, when he had them in his hand, he started once more for the truck. His father said nothing when he held them out to him, but he took them. They both got in. Lee slammed the door and sat gazing at the mirage at the end of the long, unbroken perspective of the highway.

"In love with the same damn broad for going on twelve years," Quinn said after a few moments had passed. "And every time I give a little, I put my balls in a meat-grinder—now tell me what a hardrock hero I am."

Lee didn't answer. Quinn stared at the keys for a while before he put them in the ignition. The engine started. Lee closed his eyes, feeling the truck swerve sharply as his father made a U turn and they began to head back the way they had come.

The sandstorm had taken all day to blow in.

As they approached Calvary, Lee could see the water tank with its faded lettering outlined against the sky, and he felt a rush of weariness, as though the elemental unrest was descending into the very core of him. It would be a while yet before the storm actually began. But he wished it would hurry, for he longed for it to obliterate everything the day had brought: all expectation, all memory, all his puzzlement and all his hurt. If that happened, he might be able to forget the hatred he had felt as he had watched his father stagger along the highway somewhere in the badlands of southern New Mexico. And he wanted very much to forget.

When Quinn slowed down just before the turn-off to the town, Lee was so deep in his own thoughts that he hardly noticed. It wasn't until his father had turned the truck into the parking lot of the Sundown Motel that he realized they wouldn't be going directly back. He sat up straight then, looking toward the motel and wondering what his father had in mind.

"We're going to stay the night," Quinn said when they had come to a stop in front of the office.

It was the first time he had spoken since he had turned the truck around, twenty miles back on the other side of El Paso. Lee looked over at him, unable to discern what was behind his words and too exhausted from the long ride to do anything but nod in reply.

"The sandstorm," Quinn went on. "I don't want to get caught, even if it is only another few miles. And, anyway, I've got to be in town early tomorrow to get that lug wrench back."

Lee watched him get out of the truck and go inside. He was glad his father hadn't had anything to drink on the way back, because he liked Quinn much better when he was sober. As he disappeared through the door of the motel office Lee leaned his arms on the window and put his chin down on them. The color of the sky was deepening, and yet the shadows didn't seem to be getting longer. They were disappearing, Lee noticed, as a thin rim of pink became visible in the western sky. It was as if he could actually see the day give way as the front moved toward him, its eerie light lifting like a curtain across the darkening path of the sun. Already the wind had begun. There was a heaviness in the air which he could smell now, and he recognized it as the odor of night not yet fallen, a night which promised to be thick with the isolation of the land. For soon, he knew, the sun would begin to look like a mud ball on the horizon. The sand would begin to glow in shades of orange and brown, and every particle would become a mirror, so that the light would be hazy and diffuse. It would be difficult to distinguish color. Objects would fade and disappear. Finally the clouds would constrict and there would be a stillness beneath the wind, a stillness so profound you couldn't help but feel that at any moment the storm might lift and suddenly, unexpectedly, you would find yourself on the very edge of the world. Lee raised his head and watched the wind scatter sand across the pavement. A car passed, its windshield-wipers on. The dog he had noticed earlier in the day was sitting on the porch in front of the motel office, looking out at the parking lot, which was empty except for the truck. Lee rolled up the window as the sand began to sting his face. A moment later his father stepped outside. He stood directly in the wind and looked out across the land, and then, clapping his hat to his head, he got inside the truck.

"We're down at the far end," he said to Lee. "Yeah, it looks like all hell is breaking loose."

His father pulled the truck up in front of the last of the long row of doors. Lee got out and followed him as he hurried to the shelter of the roof's overhang and then waited as Quinn fumbled with the key. He ducked his head down into his collar, wishing his father would hurry up and open the door. The key didn't seem to fit. Lee looked from the doorknob down to his feet. He could make out the word WELCOME in rubber letters on the mat. Then Quinn gave the knob another twist and leaned his shoulder against the door. It flew open, and the wind swept into the room, a room which looked like every other motel room Lee had seen in his life. There was one double bed with a melon-colored spread, a television, a desk, and a pair of lamps with bases in the shape of covered wagons. Above the nightstand was a green plaster-of-paris cactus. Lee watched his father sit down on the edge of the bed and then lie back against the pillows without taking his boots off. His feet, he noticed, reached all the way to the end.

"Well, it's as good a place as any."

"I guess so."

"TV and everything. Hey, how about running out to the truck for me and making sure the windows are tight."

He didn't want to go outside again, because he could hear the intensity of the wind as it sent grains of sand against the motel windows. In the last five minutes the storm had grown worse. Lee listened to the rattling of the door, wondering if the flimsy building could withstand winds of up to eighty miles an hour. He looked from his father's face to the window opposite, watching as Quinn got up and turned on the air-conditioning before stretching out once more on the bed. But a moment later he was running out to the truck, wanting only to get back inside as fast as he could. He jerked open the door and rolled up the window on the driver's side, and then he slammed the door and ran.

In the room once more, he stood at the window watching the sky thicken into night. The red-brown glow had faded, and the world outside was almost black. His father was still lying on the bed, directly beneath the fluorescent ceiling light, which was shining down on his sunburned face. At that moment Lee began to wish he was at home. What, he wondered, was his mother doing now? It would be just after supper, and all up and down the streets the porch lights would be blinking on. People would be coming outside to sit on the steps in the soft East Texas night. Maybe it was raining and the mingled odors of grass and honeysuckle were rising from the earth; his mother would be sitting with his brother in the kitchen, watching the dark settle in. Now she would be pushing her heavy hair back from her face, and a breath of talcum powder would be drifting through the room. . . .

"Here's some money. Go get yourself something to eat."

Lee watched his father reach into his wallet and take out a twenty-dollar bill.

"Take it. It's yours. Buy whatever you want—hell, buy a steak if you want to. Buy two of them. The coffee shop is open."

"I don't—"

"Go on! Get out!"

Lee didn't know what to say. He was hungry, but he was hurt by the tone of his father's voice. For a moment he stood shifting his weight from one foot to the other. Then he took the money, opened the door, and stepped out into the storm. Yet he knew when he began running that he wasn't going in the direction of the coffee shop. He didn't know where he was going, didn't know what the sound of his own running meant; all he knew was that he didn't want to go any place where he would have to talk to someone and risk having all his confused feelings burst out for some stranger to see. He headed away from the light, but the storm, at its height now, forced him to run for shelter. Soon he found himself standing at the door of the motel office, not certain how he had gotten there and not knowing what he should do next. The sand was stinging his eyes so badly he was crying. Wiping away the tears, he looked in through the glass. The office was empty. It occurred to him that he could go in and wait for the wind to subside and then run back to the room and let his father think he had had supper.

Lee pushed open the door, trying to make as little noise as he could. From somewhere in the back came the sound of voices, but they seemed to be far away. With the tides of the wind against the building he was sure he could go over to the armchair in the corner and leaf through a magazine without anyone's hearing him. His tennis shoes squeaked on the linoleum. Bending down, he took them off and tiptoed barefoot across the floor. He set them beside him, settled down in the armchair, and picked up a copy of *Field and Stream*. Before five minutes had passed he was asleep.

Sometime later he awoke. He stretched his legs out in front of him, wondering how much time had gone by. The wind had died. There was a strange stillness all around him, a complete absence of sound. No noise at all was coming from the back of the office, and even his own breathing was inaudible. He reached down and picked up his tennis shoes. As he put them on he asked himself again how long he had been asleep. His father, he was sure of it, was worried about him by now.

His shoes made a grating noise as he ran back across the pavement. When he stepped into the circle of light at the far end of the row of doors, he paused for a moment, catching his breath. Then, reaching for the doorknob, he turned it first to the left and then to the right. Nothing happened, so he pushed against the door with all his weight. Still it didn't open. For a moment he was terrified that his father had left without him, but then he saw that the truck was still parked where it had been earlier in the evening.

"Dad! Hey, Dad! Open up—it's me! Open the door, Dad!"

Lee banged on the door, but when there was no answer he stopped. Leaning his head against the door, he looked down at the mat with its letters yellow in the harsh light from overhead. Still there was no answer. All of a sudden a wild panic came over him. Opening a door of the truck, he felt for the parcel on the seat, ripped off the twine, and took one of the boots. Then he stepped up to the curtained window and pressed his face against the screen. The lights were off. The wind had loosened the screen so that he had no trouble yanking it off, but the window was bolted from inside. Lee paused just long enough to take a breath, and then, holding the boot by the toe, he smashed the glass. Some of it fell onto the pavement, making a dull, faraway sound. He paused for a moment, listening. Then, reaching in through the window, he unlocked it and raised it far enough to climb through. Inside, the room was completely dark.

When he turned on the light the first things that struck him were that his father's boots were twisted at a strange, unnatural angle and that the shotgun was lying on the floor. Then his eyes traveled to the wall above the bed, where a blot of color had spread out like an enormous open rose.

7

THE SUN WAS HOT on Beatrice's shoulders. She could feel it penetrating the thin cotton of her dress, causing the straps of her slip to stick to her skin. Across from her the preacher was reading from a crumpled sheet of paper. She had requested only a brief grave service, and for that reason she hadn't told the preacher anything about her husband. Yet somehow he had scraped together some insignificant facts, bits of information which on the right lips might have been words of love but which meant nothing from the mouth of a sweating stranger.

The cemetery was a typical desert-town tract: parched, treeless, with here and there a cluster of half-melted plastic flowers fastened to a gravestone. Beatrice glanced at the faces of the group of hired pallbearers. One of them was a Mexican who couldn't understand English. He was standing back from the coffin, his eyes turned toward the ground.

The preacher's halting voice lay heavily on the air. As she watched him glance down at the sheet of paper, she found herself wishing she hadn't asked for the service. It would have been less humiliating if she could simply have paid the burial fee, omitting entirely the mockery of ritual. But there had been Lee's feelings to consider, and, anyway, the indignities she had suffered in the marshal's office had been enough; she hadn't had the patience to argue with the undertaker.

Only she hadn't known the preacher would carry it to such

ludicrous length, and for no purpose, as in a dream. The sun was blinding. Readjusting her dark glasses, she looked over at Lee and saw that his face was white, except for a single flushed spot.

"Are you all right, darling?"

He nodded.

She took a handkerchief from her purse and began dabbing at his cheeks. "It'll be over soon."

She closed her eyes against the glare, pressing his hand into hers and fighting the impulse to cry out. . . . When her father had died, the little church on Pine Street had been filled to overflowing. It was a late-afternoon funeral, and the sky was overcast. At the cemetery she waited in the limousine, watching through a rain-streaked window as her mother bent to toss the first handful of earth. And then, on a November morning a few months later, her mother didn't wake up. Winter was in the air by then. At the funeral Beatrice wore a Neiman-Marcus suit which afterward she couldn't stand the sight of. . . . A buzzing rose to her ears. Opening her eyes, she realized it was the voice of the preacher.

"Please. Please, enough."

There was an awkward silence during which she gripped Lee's hand more tightly. Her head was aching from the heat, and Lee, she was sure of it, had a fever. The preacher put the sheet of paper inside his coat and brought the service to a finish with a few perfunctory words. The pallbearers stepped forward. The next moment the coffin had sunk beneath the level of the arid ground.

A great relief came over her with the sound of the first clods. As she led her son back across the cemetery she found herself listening for the scrape of the blades upon the piles of earth and the muffled sound of earth falling into the excavation. Quinn Lawrence was dead. He had put the barrel of a shotgun to his head and pulled the trigger—just a single clean motion of the finger and it had been over. That was all, except that death itself was far from clean. Once they were inside the limousine Beatrice pulled Lee close to her, terrified at the thought of what she knew he had seen. She didn't understand how any man could leave proof of his weakness dripping from the wall for his eleven-year-old son to see; there was something indecent about that.

As they left the cemetery in the distance Beatrice realized that she would have enjoyed throwing open the coffin and leaving the tortured remains to rot. Because Quinn had marked Lee's childhood with the memory of what should have been his own private hell. No one else, she told herself, should have had it thrust upon them.

The limousine pulled up at the marshal's office, and she and Lee got out. A group of Highway Patrolmen were standing around outside, and as Beatrice passed, two of them nodded. The one who had been first to arrive at the motel, a square-jawed man who had introduced himself earlier, pushed open the office door and held it as she stepped inside. For a long moment Beatrice stared at his face, wondering if his concerned expression gave her further cause for hatred.

"Beatrice, hon, reach over in my purse there and get me out another cigarette. And see if you can find me one that don't have a damp spot on it."

Alberta kept the comb going smoothly as Beatrice reached for the red plastic handbag beneath the mirror. Even with a cigarette in her mouth Alberta always managed to keep up a non-stop monologue, and whenever she thought Beatrice wasn't listening she would raise her voice to include the row of women beneath the dryers. It didn't seem to matter, Beatrice was thinking, that they had a thousand watts of hot air blowing about their heads and wads of Kleenex over their ears—their polite, deaf pantomimes were all the encouragement Alberta needed. Beatrice lit a cigarette and handed it over her shoulder, watching in the mirror as Alberta stuck it in the corner of her mouth. She was a big-boned woman with yellow curls and a voice like a cement-mixer going at full throttle, but she was a competent beautician who knew how Beatrice liked her hair.

"Thanks, hon. You remember that damned perfume I got through the mail earlier this summer? It leaked all out in my purse this morning. Not that I was sorry, mind you, because it was some of the stinkingest stuff I ever put my nose to. But to ruin my last pack of cigarettes—why, I'll be fit to be tied come eleven o'-clock!" She thrust the comb into the air for emphasis.

Beatrice turned her head to get a better view of the back. "No, I want it smoother, Alberta. And tease it out a little, please. There, that's better."

"Don't tell me what to do. I know how to make you look good for your aunt's dinner party this evening. And to think you've quit smoking—you shouldn't ought to have done that to me."

Alberta gave her a hand mirror and spun her around in the chair. There was something wrong with the cluster of waves at the nape of her neck. They were too high or not sculpted enough, she wasn't sure just what it was. But when she dressed for evening she demanded to know her profile was without a flaw.

"Nope," Alberta said, spinning her back around.

"You're going to make me seasick."

"Oh, hush up and let me get these bobby pins out again. If you're not the pickiest customer, Beatrice Lawrence. Though you always get your money's worth."

Beatrice leaned back and submitted to Alberta's knowing tugs, wondering how long she had been in there. Football tryouts were that afternoon, and she wanted to make sure Lee had a good lunch. He would be twelve not long after school started, old enough to play on the junior-high team—Beatrice winced as Alberta pushed a pin across her scalp. She was certain the coach would take him. All summer her uncle had been helping him with his passing and tackling, and, according to Milton, Lee had at last shown an interest in the game. Not that it had been easy to shake him out of his apathy. After the ordeal in West Texas there had been weeks when he hadn't been able to sleep at night, followed by days of silence when all he had done was sit and stare at the television. He had been so withdrawn and distant that Beatrice had sometimes wondered if he was the same child whose hair she had combed and whose bag she had packed, who had kissed her on the mouth and told her how much he would miss her. Just thinking about those awful weeks after she had brought Lee home made Beatrice angry all over again. How could Quinn have done that to him? Alberta pulled another pin out of the cluster of curls at her neck, interrupting the succession of her thoughts. But the next moment Lee's face was before her again, pale and expressionless as it had been during the early part of the summer. If only he could be successful at football, she thought, he might feel better about himself.

"There," Alberta said, going to work with a massive can of spray.

Beatrice picked up the hand mirror again. "Yes, that's fine. But I'd appreciate it if you wouldn't exterminate me."

She clacked her freshly lacquered fingernails against the arm of the chair. The clock on the shelf was almost hidden by a pyramid of lavender rollers, but she managed to get a glimpse of it as Alberta was spinning her around. Sometime before she drove Lee over to the football field she would have to stop in at the post office, and the cleaners had promised to have her dress ready for her by noon. Alberta unfastened the plastic drape, and she put on her sunglasses.

"I'll pay you for the month next time."

"All right, hon. You have a good time at your aunt's tonight. Oh, and ask Louise how her dandruff's doing. Tell her I still think she ought to switch to that new shampoo."

Beatrice waved to the women who were still, as Alberta called it, "cooking" beneath the dryers. Maybe, she thought half seriously, she really would mention her aunt's dandruff. The subject might liven up conversation around ten o'clock tonight when Louise's party had begun to be unbearable.

Beatrice stepped outside, leaving the air-conditioned cool along with the hum of the dryers and the shop's perfumed but ammoniac smell. The morning was still and humid. An end-of-summer calm had settled over Toombs Mill. The winds from the north hadn't yet begun to float among the pines, and the Sno-Kone man still had his sign out, yet the oppressive odor of chinaberries too long underfoot and the listless, sullen faces of the adolescent boys who hung around the filling stations were indications that summer had lost its hold—if not on the thermometer, at least on the imagination. Beatrice walked quickly toward the post office, hoping the heat wouldn't wilt her hair. As she passed

Hardy's Dry Goods she glanced in the windows, remembering how as a child she had loved to wander through the narrow aisles at the back where the rolls of fabric were stacked almost to the ceiling. It had been a long time, though, since she had bought anything there. Occasionally she would stop in for some notepaper or a button that had to be replaced, but since the shopping mall on the interstate had been completed, people rarely went to Hardy's. Beatrice went on down the street, passing the window of the barbershop where photographs of men's hair styles at least a decade behind the times were meant to display the skills of the town's oldest—and blindest—barber. Next door was the laundromat, the only place in Toombs Mill that was open at all hours, and farther on was the Town and Country Shop. Beatrice did her shopping on two-day trips to Dallas, but occasionally, when she was pressed for time, she would pick up a dress there. The salesgirl waved as she passed. Beatrice smiled and went into the post office.

"Why, if it isn't Beatrice Lawrence! I thought for sure you would have been spending the summer away somewhere. Eliot and I have been in the Caribbean."

The woman clasping her by the elbow was Ann Cramer. Ann had never been pretty, but she had always liked to believe she was; Beatrice glanced at the curly bangs that Ann still affected from her high-school days, noticing they looked no better on her now than when she had been sixteen. Then, murmuring a greeting, Beatrice stepped in line for stamps.

"You would have loved the Caribbean. The water was so blue and perfect, and everything was so green. Eliot and I spent the summer like real islanders—you would never have believed how exhilarating it was!"

"You mean to tell me you ran bare-breasted through the breakers?"

She couldn't help herself. It had just slipped out. Antagonizing Ann Cramer had grown dull over the years; Beatrice stepped up to the window and asked the clerk for a book of stamps—someone else could listen to Ann rhapsodize about her vacation.

Outside the post office again, Beatrice stopped in front of the Uncle Sam sign, trying to decide whether to walk to the cleaner's or go back to Alberta's for her car. Then in her mind she saw Ann sipping cocktails on the terrace of a tropical hotel, and an unexpected and long-suppressed feeling of resentment came over her. Even though Eliot Cramer was terrible in bed, there was something to be said for men who took their wives to the Caribbean.

As Beatrice walked toward the car she began to think back over the time which had passed since Quinn had left her. There had been a lot of men in the last five years, so many one-night stands that after a while she had no longer been able to gauge her boredom in terms of them, for somewhere along the line she had simply lost count. In a way it was all ludicrous, the insistence of two bodies on thrusting themselves together when the ultimate desire was always to free themselves from their mutual sloppiness and go their separate ways. But even though the Leon Pughs and the Eliot Cramers had aroused a feeling of physical disgust in her, she had been unable to overcome her compulsion to sleep with them. Confronting them in all their naked maleness seemed to satisfy a need, for men like that were never aware of how they were degrading themselves for her. There had been others, too, men who had lasted longer, who had managed to hold her interest for more than a single night. She had had several of what Toombs Mill ambiguously referred to as "relationships" in the past five years, though none of them had lasted more than a few months. Most of the summer she had been "seeing" Ron Prather. Before him there had been a red-haired executive who had gone back to Houston when she had refused to divorce Quinn.

"It would be absurd to divorce him," Beatrice had told her aunt when Louise had asked her why she didn't go ahead and do it. "We're as good as divorced as it is."

"But, goodness gracious, Beatrice, you can't get married again until you do!"

As she backed the car into the street, Beatrice asked herself whether or not what she had let her aunt think that day had been true. Yet she knew it hadn't been. Even if she had divorced Quinn and married another man, she would never have been able to crawl out from under the burden of the years she had spent with him. Those years had marked her too deeply, anchored her too far down inside herself. It would have been absurd to divorce him, not for the reason she had given her aunt but rather because she would still have been bound to him by something so intense that even his death hadn't freed her.

In the rear-view mirror she saw Ann Cramer leaving the post office. It occurred to Beatrice that as long as Ann got her trips to the Caribbean and a pretense of fidelity, she wouldn't care how many women her husband slept with. That was the way she herself had escaped the whispers of Toombs Mill—she had simply pretended that nothing was going on, even when it was obvious she wasn't spending her nights alone.

She stepped on the accelerator and sped down the street. After stopping at the cleaner's she headed toward home, hoping Lee hadn't run off without his lunch. As she was pushing open the back door the telephone rang. It was Louise, wanting to chat about the party.

"Tonight has me all excited, Bea. I've planned the guest list so that dinner will be both small enough to be intimate and large enough to be interesting. What do you think about that?"

"It sounds very nice," Beatrice answered, knowing her aunt had taken the phrase from Emily Post.

"Well, I hope so. You know I invited Rita Cobb, don't you?"

"Rita who?"

"Rita Cobb, the new English teacher who moved into the little house on Elm the other day. Not to be crass or anything, but divorcees often come in handy when you're making out your guest list."

"And widows?"

"Oh, Beatrice, don't upset me! You know I'm only trying to do what's best for you."

Beatrice glanced down at the telephone table, noticing a faint ring on the walnut finish.

"Louise, for the past two and a half months you've been trying to pair me off with any male specimen who has a five-figure income. What I'm really looking for is a man with a big bulge in the front of his pants."

"Beatrice! You embarrass me sometimes. Tonight I've invited

Martin Hunter Holt, the Dallas banker who's been buying all that land along the interstate. He's the one who's going to be building up the lake, you know, and so I imagine we'll be seeing more and more of him."

"Well?"

"Well, he's a widower!"

As Beatrice was hanging up the phone she heard Tony and his friends coming down the stairs.

"Hey, Mom! You said you were going to make some chocolate-chip cookies yesterday."

"Have you tried the cookie jar?" Beatrice asked when Tony stuck his head into the living room. "You might, you know, before you start scolding me for falling down on the job."

He came over and sat beside her on the sofa, seemingly oblivious of the glob of toothpaste on the visor of his baseball cap. Beatrice looked from the toothpaste to the water mark on the telephone table, trying to summon an appropriate maternal expression. Only she couldn't quite manage it. She was still thinking about her conversation with Louise, for what she had heard about the banker had aroused her curiosity.

"We had a fight in the bathroom," Tony said in a voice which indicated he wasn't afraid of trouble.

Beatrice watched him wrinkle his round nose. In the past two months she had become increasingly lenient with Lee and Tony. She she knew her relaxation of discipline was an attempt to spoil them into forgetfulness of the pain Quinn's death had brought them, but she also realized she wanted to make up for her growing awareness that she wasn't the best of mothers.

"What do you mean by a fight in the bathroom?"

Tony gave her a teasing look, as if daring her to challenge him. "Me and Jimmy had a tube of Pepsodent, and Hal and Ernest had the shaving cream."

He suddenly jumped up and ran after his friends. A moment later there came the squeal of tennis shoes on linoleum and then a series of Indian whoops as the lid of the cookie jar clanked against the counter. Going into the hall, Beatrice started up the stairs to see what sort of mess they had made in the second-floor

111

bathroom. As she pushed open the door she smelled the odor of artificial lime and saw that the walls and floor were oozing foam. Most of the toothpaste had hit the mirror, though there was a greenish smear across the shower curtain and another one on the window.

"Why don't you let Hattie clean it up?"

Beatrice whirled around. She hadn't heard Lee come up behind her.

"Darling, don't sneak up on me like that. Hattie doesn't come until Monday, so I'll have to get in here myself with a mop and brush sometime tomorrow. Alberta just did my nails, and I can't see ruining them before tonight."

Beatrice watched Lee shrug. She didn't know what to make of the gesture, whether it signified true indifference or was just a mannerism he had picked up somewhere. She managed to edge the thought out of her mind—the fact that Lee looked like Quinn didn't necessarily mean he shared his emotions.

"Lee, is something the matter? What have you been thinking about lately?"

"Nothing. I just wish you wouldn't make me try out for football, that's all."

"Nonsense, darling. You'll be the best one on the team. I can hardly wait until school starts and I can come and watch you play."

She watched the light in his eyes flicker and fade. He shrugged, more determinedly this time. Beatrice had an impulse to shake him and see if she could make the dark pupils come alive again, but something kept her from moving toward him. He was looking at the floor.

"Where did this can of shaving cream come from, Mother?"

"What?"

And then she remembered the night she had thrown Ron Prather out. She had told Lee and Tony she had a backache and had sent them over to her aunt's, but by the time Ron had arrived she hadn't been in the mood to put up with his romantic lovemaking and his phony Harvard accent. When she had told him to leave he had been so surprised he had hardly had time to collect his senses, much less all the grooming apparatus he had brought with him for the night. As Beatrice's eyes met Lee's she realized she was helpless to defend herself against his unspoken accusation. Never before had he confronted her like this. She looked down at the shaving cream again. Then she drew back her arm and slapped Lee with all her strength.

Instantly she was sorry. Reaching for his hands, she pulled him to her and pressed her face against his hair.

But there was nothing she could say to him. He had withdrawn into his own thoughts, and trying to talk to him would only make the matter worse. She let him go, watching as he hurried toward his room. After he had closed his door she stood for a moment on the landing before she started down the stairs. In the kitchen she picked up a pot and slammed it against the counter. It was perfectly obvious to her what had been going on in Lee's mind.

She wondered what other seeds of resentment Quinn had cultivated over the years.

8

SHE WORE WHITE because it suited her and because it gave her something to think about—there was something terribly ironic, she decided, about wearing a long white dress when you had on nothing underneath. A single strand of pearls was resting on her breasts. As the light from the candelabra flickered in patterns of shadowy gold, she could look in the mirror opposite the table and see the outlines of her nipples beneath the pearls' iridescent sheen. And when she reached for her glass or turned aside to talk, the thin white material stretched even tighter.

It was eleven o'clock. Louise had just had the remains of a gumbo whisked away from her guests, and now the black woman in the fluted apron and ridiculous doily of a cap—Louise always insisted she wear them for dinner parties—was setting the entré in front of them. Looking down, Beatrice caught the dead eye of the fish which had been unfortunate enough to end up on one of Louise's expensive floral plates, and inwardly she cringed. Louise had a passion for serving dishes which she referred to as "Southern French" and which she justified in terms of her "New Orleans heritage." Tonight, it seemed, she had outdone herself with fried trout amandine. Beatrice raised her napkin and coughed discreetly, wishing she had drunk enough to make a remark about ambiguous cuisine.

"Oh, how yummy it looks, Louise!"

Ann Cramer had had too many vodka collinses. Her face was

flushed, and drops of perspiration were glittering on her upper lip. The bangs, which semi-formal occasions always seemed to inspire her to curl more tightly than ever, had by now lost their necessary fullness and were straggling limply over her eyebrows. Every now and then Beatrice would watch her raise a ringed hand and push them over to the side of her face.

"I'm quite proud of it, I must say. *Truite amandine*—my mother used to serve it every other Sunday."

Louise smiled nervously. Her own hair was protected from the humidity by several coatings of Alberta's spray. Earlier in the evening, after the first round of cocktails, she had turned off the air-conditioning and rapturously thrown open the French doors and all the windows, explaining that summer breezes reminded her of her childhood. There had, however, been no breezes, and once the liquor's effects had worn off she had been too embarrassed to turn the air-conditioning on again. So everyone had had to endure the humidity until around ten thirty, when the air had begun to grow a little cooler.

The night was pouring in through the windows and open doors, bringing with it the heaviness of overripe peaches and a faint, familiar drift from the pine stand at the far end of the drive. Dinner had been served late because Martin Hunter Holt had called to say he would be detained. Louise, the model hostess, had simply continued serving cocktails; by the time they had sat down to dinner, all the guests were loaded with liquor, though no one except the schoolteacher had seemed to mind the lateness of the hour. Looking around the table, Beatrice let her eyes come to rest on Rita Cobb's face. All evening Beatrice had sensed that she wanted to make an early escape. For the past half-hour now Ron Prather had been talking to her, flashing his Phi Beta Kappa key along with his perfect teeth, and Rita had been listening, only occasionally putting in a word.

To Beatrice she looked bored. Bored and determined not to encourage Ron's obvious intentions, though it also occurred to her that there was something odd in Rita Cobb's expressions. It was as if she was nervous about something. Beatrice took a sip of wine. All evening she had watched the woman gaze at people with soft, defenseless eyes. Yet she had noticed a certain preoccupation in her manner, a constant straining inward. At times, too, she seemed almost ready to leap out at whomever she was talking with, for there was a breathless earnestness in the way she searched for words. Ron Prather leaned closer, and Beatrice was surprised to hear Rita laugh. As she studied the thin face with its longish nose and inexpertly made-up eyes, she tried to decide why the woman was attractive—for she was attractive, there was no denying it.

"Has your family lived in Toombs Mill long?"

Next to her, Martin Hunter Holt was finishing his trout. She had been talking to him off and on, but, despite Louise's intentions and her own curiosity, they hadn't gotten beyond an exchange of bare phrases. As soon as he had arrived everyone had been shuttled to the table, and all through the jellied chicken and the seafood gumbo he had been monopolized by her uncle. Beatrice had been forced to listen to Eliot Cramer talk about his trip to the Caribbean and afterward to the Episcopal minister's favorite fishing story. So it was with a feeling of relief that she turned again toward Martin Hunter Holt.

"Years. My maiden name is Toombs."

"So it was your father—"

"My grandfather. As I said, we've been here a long time. Too long."

Beatrice smiled and touched her pearls. In the mirror she could see the fabric of her dress pulled tight across her nipples, for she was arching her back a little as she leaned in the banker's direction. Martin Hunter Holt returned her smile, and she knew that the effect of her dress hadn't been lost on him. He was a soft-spoken, handsome man who had maybe just turned fifty. The candlelight was gleaming on a wing of steely hair, smoothed casually enough if it hadn't been for the mark of a comb which sculpted it back from the temple. As Beatrice watched him set down his fork and lift his napkin to his lips, she noticed the monogrammed cufflinks and the carefully buffed nails. All in all, she liked his looks. There was something compelling and quietly self-assured about him.

116

Leaning a little closer, she said again, "Too long."

"Well, maybe you won't feel that way after the lake area is developed into a resort. If the building goes as easily as the planning, the north shore should have a hotel and a dinner theater in just a little under two years. At the moment the projected completion date is the summer after next."

"A hotel and dinner theater? Toombs Mill is certainly coming up in the world."

"Give Holt Enterprises a chance and we'll even put you on the map."

He looked at her half seriously before he began to laugh. Once again the candlelight singled out the sweep of steely hair.

"I don't doubt you have the backing of the entire community. We've been crying out for some sort of resurrection, Mr. Holt, ever since the oil interests managed to squeeze the logging business from the top of the state's list of priorities. But you're a Dallas banker, so I'm sure you know all about the big money interests." She raised her wineglass and examined his profile over the rim. "So you're going to be the town's savior. You're going to save us from the Toombs."

She had succeeded in ruffling his composure, if only for a moment. In the pause which followed he emptied his glass and reached for the bottle on the wine stand behind her uncle's chair.

"Would you like a refill?"

"Of course."

From across the table Ann Cramer was staring at her with a look of open hostility. Beatrice gnashed her a smile and turned back to Martin Hunter Holt.

"Tell me what I should call you. 'Martin Hunter' is pretentious."

"Hunt," he returned, easing the bottle back into the ice. "And you?"

"Anything but 'Bea.' "

"Good enough."

The ruins of the trout were lifted away and a fruit compote was set in front of them. From across the table Eliot Cramer said her name. Beatrice looked up, hoping he wasn't going to start talking about the Caribbean again.

"Say, what do you call these little orange things in here?"

He motioned toward the crystal compote dish. She leaned back languidly in her chair, wondering whether or not Hunt was bored with her aunt's guests. If he was, she thought, he was tactful enough to hide it.

"What? Those are kumquats."

Eliot picked up his spoon and poked at the mysterious fruit.

"Kumquats," he repeated. "Sounds nasty."

Next to him, his wife said, "Oh, Eliot," and turned toward Louise again. Beatrice leaned forward, locking her hands over her forehead in an effort to stop an ache.

"Is something the matter?" she heard Hunt ask.

"I'll be all right in a minute."

It had just begun to dawn on her that she had had a lot to drink, and that the bubbles which she thought she saw in her glass were really in her head. It wasn't so much a pain as a light pricking sensation; if only people would finish their desserts, she was thinking, she might be able to step out onto the patio for some air.

"Coffee?"

The Episcopal minister was looking at her concernedly. At the far end of the table Louise was handing cups.

"Yes, thank you."

The minister passed her a cup and she managed a quick smile. Hunt's attention had been diverted by her uncle. She took a few bites of melon and set her spoon down beside her plate. Then, touching Hunt lightly on the arm, she waited for him to look at her.

"If my aunt wonders where I've run off to, you might tell her I've gone outside. Her Pouilly-Fuissé seems to have given me a headache."

"It's the heat," he answered. "The room is awfully close."

Beatrice pushed her chair back from the table.

"But I won't tell her a thing," he went on, "unless you promise to come back soon."

He looked up at her, one corner of his mouth lifted. No, she thought, the effect of her dress hadn't been lost on him at all. Especially now that she was standing up and every curve of her body was revealed.

"All right. You have your promise."

"But I never trust women who are beautiful in white."

"Have I asked you to trust me?"

"No. But it had occurred to me to try."

She left the table and went out through the French doors. A flurry of moths grazed her cheek as she passed between the carriage lamps, walking toward the far side of the patio where the camellia bushes thrust their fullness over the low wall. Pushing open the gate, she stepped onto the grass. Away from the house the windless night seemed lighter. All around her the air was luminous—fireflies, she realized, after a moment of surprise. The shape of a tree rose up ahead, and she guided her steps toward it. Smooth, almost cold leaves touched her face, and from far back in her past she recalled a summer evening she had spent with a boy beneath one of Louise's tulip trees. He was the only man, before Quinn, who had ever had sex with her, and for a long time she had worn his high-school ring. Now, though, she couldn't even remember his name.

For a while Beatrice stood beside the tree, watching the lights of cars far away on the interstate. At last her headache seemed to go away. Breathing deeply, she patted a few wisps of hair into place and began walking back to the house. As she approached the camellia bushes she saw Hunt step out onto the patio. Rita Cobb was with him, and the two of them were talking in low tones. Beatrice stopped in the shadows beside the wall, feeling a subtle anger snaking its way to consciousness. For a while she watched Hunt and Rita in the light of the carriage lamps. Then Hunt went back inside and Rita began walking in her direction.

"Oh, hello," Rita said when she reached the edge of the patio. "I almost didn't see you standing here."

"Are you enjoying yourself?"

"Very much."

Beatrice wondered if she was telling the truth. Moving closer to the woman, she said, "I'm glad to hear it."

"Everyone seems to be having a good time tonight."

"Why shouldn't they? It will give them something to feel guilty about tomorrow—and Protestant hangovers are always the worst kind."

For a few moments Rita was quiet.

"You have a son, don't you?" she said suddenly.

"I have two sons," Beatrice answered, hoping Hunt hadn't decided to leave. "One is nine and the other is almost twelve. Excuse me, but I really have to get back to the house."

The woman didn't seem to have heard her. Beatrice glanced at her face, trying to make out its expression as she turned her attention to the patio. Hunt had just stepped through the French doors again. She watched him take off his coat and look out across the lawn before he went back inside the house, where the lights were brighter now.

"And your husband?" Rita asked, almost too politely.

"My husband is dead."

"Dead?" she heard Rita gasp.

"Yes."

Beatrice was tired of sympathetic queries. She stepped past Rita and began walking toward the patio. There she saw the Episcopal minister sitting on one of Louise's wrought-iron benches.

"How are you feeling, Beatrice?"

"A little tired, Reverend. I think it's about time for me to go home."

Hunt was talking to the woman who had come with Ron, an affected blonde who couldn't have been more than twenty. Beatrice walked up to them and, without waiting for Hunt to finish talking, touched him on the arm for the second time that night.

"I wondered what had happened to you," he said.

"Were you worried?" she returned.

The blonde murmured a few polite words and left them to themselves. Hunt watched her go. Then he turned to Beatrice again.

"You're a beautiful woman. Something tells me I ought to get to know you better."

120

"Have you forgotten you don't trust me?"

"No," he said simply.

Beatrice looked into his gray eyes. The confidence she saw there made her want to ruffle him a little, and yet she felt drawn to him by that very quality. By some silent agreement the two of them began walking across the room. When they reached the hallway, where the light was dimmer and the rise and fall of voices seemed to be far away, he put his hand beneath her chin and turned her face up to him.

"No, I don't trust you. But it's hard to be reasonable when you keep getting more beautiful every time I look at you. That's quite a dress you're wearing."

With an almost imperceptible movement she freed her face from his hand.

"It's getting late. Why don't we go?"

"Good idea," he said.

As they were going back into the living room Eliot Cramer came toward them. His pudgy face was damp, and his movements were even less steady than they had been earlier.

"Say, Bea, don't you need another drink?"

"Beatrice has a headache," Hunt answered for her, taking her by the elbow and guiding her across the room.

"Who taught you to pick up your cues so well?" Beatrice murmured.

"My mother," he replied.

Outside, the crickets and cicadas were making their late-night sounds. She pressed close to Hunt as they walked down the driveway, wondering whether she would have to take the babysitter home or if the girl would call her boyfriend with the motorcycle. Louise's summer breeze had finally sprung up. Beatrice could feel the cool through her dress on her naked breasts and thighs.

"Can you leave your car here?" Hunt asked, brushing her hair with his lips.

"Of course. It's parked up there by the house."

"Good," he said. "That makes it simpler, doesn't it?"

She felt his hand on the nape of her neck.

"You drove up from Dallas?"

"No, I've got a rented car. I always fly in—I pilot my own plane."

They reached the end of the driveway, and Hunt guided her toward a Cadillac which, in the glow of the streetlamp, seemed to be a silvery color. He unlocked the door on her side and held it while she got in.

"So chivalry isn't dead?"

"Not dead at all."

Beatrice glanced over at him as he was turning the car around. For a man his age, she was thinking, he was in amazingly good shape.

"Where are we going, Hunt?"

They had turned onto a main street and were headed toward the interstate.

"To the Holiday Inn."

"Don't you have everything we need with you?" she asked him with a laugh.

In reply he reached over and drew her to him. The lights from an oncoming car caught him full in the face, and she watched him blink several times before he turned to kiss her, his eyes still on the road.

"We'll have a wreck if I'm not more careful."

"I wish you were drunk enough to just stop the car."

"I'd love to," he answered, more composedly than she had thought he would. "But good sense restrains me. Look, let's go to my room. Or to your place."

She glanced at his face again. Then, pulling away from him, she gave his hand a pat.

"My, how prudish we are. Turn around and make a left at the light."

Beatrice directed him down the wide, tree-lined street until they were in front of her house. As they got out of the car she saw that the upstairs lights were still on.

"It looks like the babysitter hasn't made the boys go to bed yet."

"Then let's go to my room at the Holiday Inn."

He caught her by the arm as they were going up the steps. She

122

swayed against his chest, letting him draw her closer.

"No. I don't like that idea."

"Why not?" he asked, kissing her. "Or we can find someplace else. But not here. Not with your kids."

The censorious note in his voice annoyed her. She reached into her purse for her keys, glancing at him over her shoulder as she led the way into the living room. When they passed the piano she stopped to lift two big, no longer perfect roses out of a vase. Their sticky stamens were bursting, and their scent was everywhere in the room. For a moment she leaned against the piano, gazing at the petals that had fallen on the mahogany top. Then she swept them into her hand and tossed them along with the flowers themselves into a wastebasket in the hall.

"Go on into the den where the boys are. I'll make us a couple of drinks, and then we can see if the babysitter needs a ride. Don't worry, the boys will love you. You're the picture of the—how shall I say it?—the father they never had."

She saw him wince at her display of bitterness. Something seemed to have come over her in the past few minutes, a vague sort of resentment which was directing itself toward Hunt.

"Beatrice, maybe I'd better go."

"What are you talking about?" she asked. Then, letting her fingers touch his thigh, she laughed. "We've already acknowledged the animal. So you have to stay—by natural law."

He opened and closed his mouth, reminding her absurdly of the fish that had stared back at her from Louise's floral plate. She found she couldn't keep herself from looking at Hunt, looking through him, it almost seemed.

Above their heads the clock began to strike.

"All right," he said at last.

She turned to go into the dining room, leaving him to find his way to the den alone.

Not that she needed anything else to drink. Her headache had come back again, and a million tiny bubbles were bursting against her skull. As she went into the dining room she pressed her palms to her temples, and for a moment the pricking sensation seemed to subside. Then it was there again, more insistent than before.

She poured an inch of brandy into each of two snifters and then went into the bathroom and swallowed several Valiums.

In the den the television was on. Lee was lying on the sofa and Tony was curled up snoring on the rug. The babysitter was talking on the telephone. As Beatrice set the glasses down, the girl hung up and announced that her boyfriend would be there soon.

"So what do I owe you, about four dollars? You should have put the boys to bed before midnight, you know." Beatrice looked at Hunt, who had sat down in a straight-backed chair. "Has Lee remembered to introduce himself?"

"We just met," Hunt replied.

"Well, did you tell Mr. Holt you made the football team today? You could have mentioned it, you know. Unless"—she flipped off the television and sat down beside Lee on the sofa—"you've decided you're going to sulk about it. Hunt, hand me one of Amy's cigarettes, will you? She's too young to be smoking, and I quit again last month."

Hunt seemed glad to get up out of the uncomfortable chair. Reaching for the pack of cigarettes, he took a lighter from the coffee table and moved closer to Beatrice.

"No, we didn't get around to talking about football. But congratulations, Lee. Your mother must be very proud of you."

"Yes, of course I'm proud of him," Beatrice said. Somehow, it seemed, she owed herself a cigarette, if for no other reason than that she had made it through Louise's party. "But that doesn't make any difference to him. Does it, darling?"

"I play football well enough. I'll make plenty of touchdowns for you."

"I'll bet you will," Hunt put in. "Say, have you ever been to see the Cowboys in the Cotton Bowl? When the season gets under way I'll take you to one of their games. But, as far as I'm concerned, it's baseball season till October."

"Can't you thank Mr. Holt, Lee?"

Lee looked at her. Then, tossing the *TV Guide* toward his sleeping brother, he stood up.

"Thanks, Mr. Holt. I'm glad I got the chance to meet you."

"Good night, Lee. Maybe next time we'll do some serious talking about your game."

Lee mumbled a hasty good night and started for the door. Beatrice drew in on the cigarette, wondering what was going through her son's mind.

Later on, as she was watching Hunt undress, it occurred to her that once there had been a time when she had wanted to give love. She had wanted it so desperately she had been willing to spend six months in the desert because Quinn had wanted to— it was what he had had to offer her. So she had endured his moods, waiting for a gratification which had only become real when she had stopped trying to will it. But by that time she had come to hate him, for something inside her had been used up by its own deliberate ruthlessness; after that there was always an element of violence in their lovemaking. She couldn't allow herself again that single moment of unconsciousness, because it frightened her to relinquish her hold upon her will. And that angered him, that drove him to extremes of love and denial, and whenever he succeeded in breaking through to her, she asserted herself more strongly against him the next time. . . . She felt the weight of Hunt's thighs on hers. He had been a little disturbed, earlier, by some of the remarks she had made to him in the car, but she knew that the subtle obscenity of her body beneath the white dress had fascinated him. She thought about that as she locked her legs around his waist, feeling the heat of his mouth against her face and neck. His hands beneath her hips were pressing her up to him. She heard his breath beginning to come faster, and suddenly she opened her eyes wide in the dark: afterward, when he was finished with her body, she would be safe and conscious and alone inside herself.

"Beatrice?" he said at last, his voice coming at her out of the stillness of the house.

"Yes," she answered. And then: "I hope you don't plan to stay all night."

"The children?"

"Yes," she lied. "The children."

9

SEVERAL MONTHS PASSED before Beatrice talked to Rita Cobb again. She hadn't seen her since Louise's party, when she had left her standing in the darkness next to the camellias with that strange, shocked note in her voice. At the party Beatrice had wondered about her, but as time had gone by she had all but forgotten the woman with the styleless clothes and the look of subdued intensity. So that when Beatrice saw Rita at the junior high school's Open House in the spring, she was surprised enough to lean toward the woman sitting next to her and make an inquisitive remark.

"The new English teacher has kept herself out of sight this year, hasn't she?"

"You're not the first person to notice," Liz Beale, the librarian, whispered back. "Several of us have been annoyed with her. Rita promised to be on the Open House committee, and at the last moment she changed her mind."

"Well, maybe she has better things to do than braid crepe paper," Beatrice said, settling back into her seat.

The auditorium became quiet as Ann Cramer stepped up to the microphone. Beatrice let her eyes wander across the rows of familiar faces, wondering why she had even bothered to attend Open House. Habit, she supposed. And, too, she was aware of the fact that she got a certain perverse satisfaction from mingling with people who knew the details of her relationship with Hunt

126

—and most of Toombs Mill did. Since September her trips to Dallas had provided the town with prime gossip material, for although in the past Beatrice had observed the unspoken proprieties which demanded she at least make an attempt to keep up appearances, in the last few months she hadn't cared what the town said about her. The hostility of people who had once claimed to be her friends was something she had learned to find flattering since she had begun her affair with Hunt. Not, of course, that anyone dared to be open about it. Just the week before, a group of women had yielded to the urgency of moral indignation—as to some violent rumbling of the bowels, or so it seemed to Beatrice—and hinted that she was obligated to withdraw her membership in the PTA. But they had been unable to respond to the icy grace with which she had reminded them that her grandfather had built their town, and nothing more had been insinuated.

After Ann Cramer had finished her speech in favor of "facts, and only facts, being taught in the American classroom," Beatrice saw Rita hurrying in her direction. It occurred to her then that she might have to endure another confrontation with small-town self-righteousness. Stepping in line for coffee, she armed herself for an attack.

"I'd like to talk to you, Mrs. Lawrence. Do you think we could take our coffee to the far table over there? That way we should have a little more privacy."

"Just as long as you aren't from the delegation that wants to tar-and-feather me. They've accused me of mule-fucking, or something of the sort."

To her amazement, the schoolteacher didn't seem to be offended. She unexpectedly found herself thinking that they were possibly more alike than any other two women in the auditorium, and she was willing, if only out of curiosity, to hear what she had to say.

"Actually, I wanted to talk to you about your son's work in my seventh-grade class."

"You're Lee's English teacher? I didn't know that. You see how little he tells me any more."

127

"It's the age," Rita replied.

She stepped into line behind Beatrice and didn't say anything else until the two of them reached the refreshment table, where Rita was drawn into conversation by a group of parents. It occurred to Beatrice that she didn't have the slightest idea what Rita wanted to talk to her about. As long as she could remember, Lee's grades had never fallen below average.

"Punch or coffee? And how about some cake? Mrs. Haley's is the best, though don't tell anyone I said so."

Beatrice looked at the Episcopal minister's wife over the top of an enormous punch fountain. "I'll have coffee, thank you."

"And a tiny slice of cake?"

Beatrice accepted the pink-iced cake and stepped aside to wait for Rita. The auditorium was full. The junior high school pressured parents to show up for Open House, and most of them felt obligated to. As they did every year, a committee of mothers and teachers had worked to hang the walls with student art and to make sure that the ceiling was generously festooned with crepe paper. This year the theme was "America the Beautiful." Beatrice had put in several hours helping make papier-maché miniatures of the Statue of Liberty, which Ann had decided should be placed on all the tables. She had even volunteered to stay around for the clean-up afterward, though she had agreed to it more from boredom than out of any sense of obligation; Hunt hadn't been able to fly in for the weekend, and she hadn't had time to make a new set of plans.

"So you've been Lee's English teacher all year?" she asked when she and Rita had found a quiet corner. They were sitting next to the stage, beneath an overhang of colored streamers.

"Yes. And I think he's an unusually bright student. That's the reason I wanted to talk to you, Mrs. Lawrence. You see, I have a special interest in Lee."

"That's fine, Miss Cobb. Now tell me what the problem is. Hasn't Lee always gotten reasonably good grades?"

The auditorium was chilly. Beatrice slipped on the lambskin jacket Hunt had given her at Christmas, and then, reaching for her coffee cup, she pushed Mrs. Haley's cake away.

"Yes, but it's not his grades so much as it's a kind of inattentiveness. He seems to be distracted all the time, so much so that I think it might be a good idea if he talked to one of the counselors. Do you care if I ask you a rather personal question?"

Beatrice waited a moment, wondering what was going through the schoolteacher's mind as she sat there with her head bent, seemingly studying the linoleum. There was something in the woman's expression which Beatrice was beginning to find annoying, a kind of concern which doubtless was no more than common nosiness. Unless, she thought, Lee had been talking to her.

"Miss Cobb, personal questions usually excite me to sarcasm, especially when they're directed at me by women. But if you think it's necessary."

She noticed Rita was tactful enough to ignore the tone of her voice. For a moment the two women simply looked at each other, and once again she found herself trying to figure out what it was that made the schoolteacher attractive. Her forehead was high, and her hazel eyes were prominent and well shaped, but her nose was much too angular for beauty. Her lips looked dry and slightly cracked, as if she had spent long hours out of doors, or as if, Beatrice thought, they had been bitten.

"Has it ever occurred to you that something in your family life might be upsetting Lee?"

"Like what?" Beatrice asked, holding the lambskin collar closer around her throat.

"I don't know. I wouldn't presume to guess."

"Miss Cobb, not only do I think you *would* presume to guess, but I also think you know something. What has Lee been telling you?"

"I've never spoken to Lee outside of class. And I don't think I have any business prying into my students' lives. It's just that I care very much what happens to Lee. Mrs. Lawrence, don't you understand that he needs to talk to someone? Haven't you ever noticed how distant he is? He seems to be frightened of expressing his feelings except out on that football field—and then he's all anger! I've watched him. It's frightening to see that much pent-up anger in a boy who's only twelve years old. You should encourage him to talk to one of the school counselors—even a minister would do. Or at least find someone who would be sympathetic enough to listen and to suggest some more creative way for him to spend his time than practicing sports five hours a day. Lee's terribly bright, Mrs. Lawrence. But for months now I've watched him. He isn't happy."

Beatrice felt anger rising to her throat. She realized she disliked this woman. There was something too personal in the way she spoke of Lee, and yet there was no touch of outrage or indignation in her manner. Unlike the women who had hinted Beatrice ought to resign from the PTA, this one obviously wouldn't be put off by a single well-aimed remark.

"Miss Cobb, let me remind you that as Lee's mother I have the right to demand that he be placed in another English class if I don't like the way you conduct yours. You're a stranger in Toombs Mill, and I think you're being more than a little presumptuous in making inquiries into families who have lived here much longer than you have. Obviously you've heard about Lee's father. And doubtless you haven't been deaf to all sorts of gossip —Toombs Mill, like most small towns, feeds on its own entrails, even if it won't admit it. But nevertheless I'd advise you to keep your concern to yourself. As I said, I have the right to demand that Lee be placed in another English class if I have reason to believe you're having some sort of influence on him. And let me also add that I have friends on the School Board."

She picked up her purse and walked hurriedly across the auditorium. The woman's assertiveness had angered her so much that she was almost blind to the crowd of people in her path. When Liz Beale called her name, she spun around impatiently.

"Beatrice, you aren't leaving, are you? You promised to help with the clean-up."

"Sorry, Liz. I just can't do it."

"But, Beatrice, you don't want to be irresponsible, do you? I mean—well, you know what I was saying about Rita."

"I have a headache. I'm going home."

"But you used to be so good about these things!"

Beatrice watched the librarian fume inside her badly fitting suit. Then, with no further apology, she stepped out into the foyer.

As she was walking toward the door the trophy case caught her eye. Hesitating, she went over to stand in front of the lighted glass. Toombs Mill had won the junior-league district football trophy that winter, and Beatrice couldn't help but feel proud of Lee. He had played so well the coach had given him a special commendation at the celebration dinner. She pressed her forehead to the glass. Her throat was throbbing not with anger now but with a mingling of pride and anguish which threatened almost to strangle her. She could see him again beneath the lights' unrelenting glare, running down the field with the wind sucking at his ankles, strangely deformed by the bulging of the uniform but nevertheless her son, and no longer just a child. How had they grown so far apart? she wondered. So far apart that a strange woman knew more than she did about his disappointments and his fears?

Beatrice felt the cold glass against her face. She had been twenty-one when Lee was born. Though it was hardly noticeable after all these years, the scar was still there where they had had to cut him out of her. Once—he couldn't have been more than four at the time—he had put out his hand and touched the scar, demanding with all a child's seriousness to know how it had gotten there. She had pushed his hand away, and he had stood there a moment before he had begun to cry. After that she let him come to her in the mornings while she dressed. He would put out his hand and touch the seam in her belly, wondering who had put it there and what it was and why. She never told him; listening in the silence for the padding of his feet, she would see him in her mind's eye as he walked with his toes curled because the floor in winter was so cold. She would wait until his small form appeared in the recess of the doorway, and then, moving quietly so as not to wake Quinn—who had come home dead drunk and couldn't have been waked anyway—she would slide out from the covers and take his hand, and then they would go on down the hall. Even in the dawn light she could make out his face. The next instant, in the sudden bright of the kitchen, she would watch him watching her. Through squinted eyes he would follow her as she spread the bread with butter and put the pan of milk on top of the stove to boil. Then she would duck into the bathroom to take her morning shower, while he would wait for her in one of the vinyl-backed kitchen chairs and flip through whatever book she was reading him that week. And finally he would hear it, their agreed-upon but unspoken signal—the sound of the shower's being turned off—and she knew he was setting the book back on the table and starting to pad across the floor. When the bathroom door opened she would be standing there naked and glistening, her hair made darker by the steam, her body firm-breasted and long-legged, her skin uniformly smooth and white except for the seam running lengthwise down from her navel. That would be the moment they had both been waiting for. Reaching out, he would trace the red line with the tips of his fingers, probing his own short past for that definitive something which would carry him beyond memory.

Afterward they would go once more into the kitchen. The toast would be ready, its fragrance sailing upward from the toaster. He would step to one side and wait for the crunching sound as she spread the toast with butter, though she knew what he was really waiting for was the delicate note of glassware which meant that the next moment the plate of toast would be in his hands. Finally, seated at one end of the table, he would begin to eat while she brought over two cups of hot chocolate and her own plate of toast.

They never talked until then. It was as if words would violate the secret ritual of their dawns, and only when they became mother and son at the breakfast table did either of them attempt to dispel the intimacy of silence. Often then she would begin to tell him of all the wonderful things he would do someday, imagining for him what it would be like to be running down a football field. And so the ashes of dawn would change into morning. He would scratch his ears at the sound of the crows and gaze out the window at the sunlight on the grass. Their napkins would be wadded. Only crumbs and cold dishes would remain on the table. Glancing up at the clock, she would take the dishes and run water in the sink. Then, sitting down again, she would open the book and begin to read. . . .

But she had never explained the meaning of the scar. Now, she knew, it was too late, for the words of love would become obscenities the very instant they left her mouth.

Outside, Beatrice stood on the steps and tried to steady herself against memory. The night was cloudy, chill with the spring air which had been drifting just the other side of the pines since late in February. She buttoned her jacket, shivering a little. Tucking her purse beneath her arm, she hugged the lambskin closer and began walking toward the parking lot, where rows of cars gleamed faintly in the haze from the overhead lights. The noise from the auditorium was in the distance. The only sound now was the staccato of her high heels against the blacktop and an indistinct ringing that could have been an echo in her ears. At last she reached the edge of the parking lot. Her car was in the block beyond, in front of the Episcopal church. Just as she was approaching it she saw someone coming out of the tangle of willows where the churchyard dipped down toward the creek. Instinctively she stepped into the shadows. The next moment there were footsteps, and then the streetlamp threw its glare on the minister's placid face.

"Reverend, you scared me!"

"Why, Beatrice, I didn't see you standing there."

Her immediate impulse was to grab his hand, to give in to the relief welling up inside. But she checked herself and stood there beneath the bluish downpour of light, beginning to feel her breath coming a little less frantically.

"Is the meeting over?" she heard him ask.

"Not yet. It's just that I don't have much enthusiasm for those things any more."

The minister made a noise which seemed to be a sigh. He was a small man, younger than he looked, with a receding hairline and an odd whine in his voice.

"I sneaked away early, too. But how are Lee and Tony? I

haven't seen them for a while." He took a handkerchief out of his pocket and began to blow his nose.

Beatrice waited, thinking about Lee. The ache of memory still hadn't left her. She found herself wanting to talk, but somehow words wouldn't come—she had never in her life asked a minister's advice about anything that mattered.

"The boys are fine, of course. Tony's all excited about his part in the fifth-grade play, and now that football season is over Lee's running track every afternoon."

"Tell them to come to Sunday school sometime. Well, I should get back over to the junior high before somebody misses me. Good night, Beatrice. Let me know if there's anything I can do."

"Good night."

As she got into the car she realized she didn't feel like going home. Louise was staying with Lee and Tony, and she had told her aunt she wouldn't be back until ten thirty. The clock on the dash said quarter to nine. Deciding she would just drive for a while, she turned at the next intersection and guided the car onto Main Street. Then she headed toward the outskirts of town. She passed the cluster of houses near the railroad yard and the Violet Crown with its shabby letters blinking purple against the night. Soon the reservoir and the sawmills were in the distance, and on either side of the road there was nothing but a jagged mass of pine. The only lights she could see were those of the town in the rear-view mirror until, nearing the interstate, she found herself in the path of another car. Veering to the right, she came within inches of the guard rail, and then she began going faster. Up the road was the curve onto the entrance ramp. As she approached it the reflectors winked warning and the signs told her to slow down, but the Chrysler took the turn at fifty, sailing onto the interstate with an open stretch of night ahead. Slipping out of her shoes, Beatrice forced the accelerator to the floor.

Toombs Mill was fifteen miles behind her when she saw the red lights. Easing off the gas, she took her time slowing down. The Highway Patrol car pulled up behind her on the damp clay of the shoulder, its lights slashing the darkness. Beatrice turned off the engine and rolled down the window. The scent of pine was like a tonic in the air.

"Good evening, officer. Was I going too fast?"

"Ma'am, you were speeding. I clocked you at a hundred and ten. Can I see your driver's license, please?"

Beatrice handed her license through the window, watching the officer's face as he studied it in the glow of a pocket flashlight. He was about her age, lean-jawed, his skin cratered from what she guessed had been a bad case of adolescent acne. When he asked her where she was coming from, she couldn't help but laugh.

"The Toombs Mill PTA Open House, officer."

"Is that the only place you've been, ma'am? I don't reckon the PTA spikes their punch."

"Well, after I left the junior high I stopped at the Episcopal church."

The officer peered at her. Then, motioning for her to get out, he led the way to a level piece of ground and put her through a series of movements. When she had balanced on one leg, bent backward, and walked in a straight line, he handed her her driver's license.

"Okay," he said as they walked back toward the cars. "You haven't been drinking. But I'm going to have to give you a ticket for exceeding the speed limit by fifty miles an hour. You were breaking the law, lady."

"Why shouldn't I if I can afford to?"

She looked at him teasingly. They were standing next to the patrol car, and in its inconstant light she could see him grimace.

"Because the law is the law. There's no two ways about it."

"Look, isn't there some other way we can settle this? Some way that would be a little more satisfactory to us both?"

At first he didn't seem to understand her offer. Then he grinned, wrenching his lips back so that his face became leaner.

"You talking about an informal settlement?"

"Certainly," she answered, pressing a little closer. "Unless breaking the law is something that undermines your manhood."

A strange, metallic taste was on her tongue, and yet she knew she wasn't frightened. She had been frightened in front of the church just before she had seen the minister step out of the willows, but it wasn't fear she was feeling now. It was something one notch up from fear, and much more rational. She put one hand on his neck and began to caress the little whorls of hair. A car passed. For a single instant she felt as though she had been turned to stone. Then the lights were gone and her limbs were transformed again. She was staring into a stranger's ugly, irregular face, despising him and yet asking him to touch her.

"Listen, lady. Just as long as everybody does what everybody wants, nobody's going to get in trouble."

Suspicion seemed to have made him determined to be rough with her. He pushed her back against the car, and for a moment she fought him. Then her hands were sliding down from his shoulders, down to the row of bullets on his hips, and she was holding on to him tightly as he began to kiss her. She felt his teeth on her lips and then the rasp of his hair against her throat. Unbuttoning her jacket, he pressed his mouth against her breasts. At that moment the lights of another car approached them.

"Let's go."

He opened the door and she got in. Making a U turn, he headed back in the opposite direction. For two or three miles neither of them said anything. Then she felt the car beginning to slow down and asked him whether he knew where he was going.

"There's a farm road up here. It leads out toward the lake, where all that construction's been going on. Never saw anyone out there at night, though."

They passed a cluster of darkened buildings as they turned off the interstate and onto a gravel road. Beatrice sat on her side of the car, listening to the pop of tires and watching the face of the man beside her. It reminded her of a wolf's; she turned away from him, wishing she had a cigarette. Hers had disappeared sometime during the Open House meeting.

Ahead of them was the lake. They drove past a wire enclosure, past the hulks of silent bulldozers, and out onto a promontory overlooking a rocky incline. A few yards beyond where they stopped was a sign that read HOLT ENTERPRISES: MILL LAKE DE-VELOPMENT. Beatrice read it aloud in the moment before the officer reached to turn out the headlights.

"Come here."

"Wait a moment. My dress."

She heard him breathe in, waiting. Taking off her jacket and then easing her dress over her head, she folded them and set them on the back seat. But before she finished undressing he pulled her to his lap, and she let him, helping him free himself from his pants. Disgust for his body didn't diminish her desire to drag him down inside her. She held his strange, exploratory hands and pressed them hard against her, and then, straddling him, she dug her nails into his neck.

"Bitch," he whispered. "Bitch."

He took her by the hips, and she felt his whole body straining. It seemed he would never let go of her, that she would never be able to get away from the rank smell of his sweat and from his labored, grunting breaths. But at last his hands loosed their hold and he began to relax away from her. Beatrice raised up off him, wanting nothing more than to free herself from a feeling of revulsion.

He drove her back to her car and let her off. She put the key in the ignition and stepped on the accelerator, cutting across the median and heading toward Toombs Mill. On the edge of town she stopped off in a gas-station bathroom to repair the damage done to her make-up. For a long time she stood over the wash-basin, studying her face in the dim mirror. She had aged in the past year, she told herself. She was thirty-three, and for the first time in her life she looked as old as she was.

It was after eleven when she got home. Louise was sitting by herself at the kitchen table, turning the pages of a cookbook as Beatrice opened the back door.

"Sorry I'm late. Cleaning up took forever."

"So how did everything go? Ann was worried that her speech might run over, and Mrs. Haley told me this afternoon that they might not have enough refreshments to go around."

"Oh, things were fine," Beatrice said. She hoped her aunt

didn't feel like staying to chat. What she wanted more than anything were a couple of Valiums and a long, hot soak in the tub, and after that to drop off like a stone into the farthest bottom of sleep; she was tired and frustrated, and the lines around her eyes depressed her. If her aunt stayed to talk, there was sure to be some kind of unpleasantness between them.

"Well, I guess I'd better be going. Tony went to sleep right after *Gunsmoke* was over, and Lee's somewhere upstairs. You ought to get to bed yourself, Beatrice. You don't look good."

"Thanks a lot," she answered shortly. "But I appreciate your coming over. I'll call you sometime tomorrow and we can plan our spring shopping trip."

Louise patted Beatrice's hand as she got up from the table.

"Oh, Hunt called. Beatrice, I'm sure he has intentions of marrying you. I can't understand why you don't push him just the tiniest little bit."

"Louise—"

"Well, people are talking!"

"I've told you a hundred times I'm not interested in getting married! Now please go on home. I'll call you tomorrow, all right?"

After Louise had gone Beatrice went into the bathroom and took a container of Valium from the shelf. Avoiding the mirror, she swallowed several tablets with a glass of water. Then, on an impulse, she swallowed two more. Never before had she had such an overpowering desire to sleep, to drop a curtain down over the vague tremors of apprehension which left her hands stony cold and her blood drumming against her skull.

After standing very still for a while, fingers pressed to her temples, Beatrice went upstairs to check on Lee and Tony. Tony was asleep on his face with his knees tucked under him and his bottom pointing straight up in the air. Beatrice smoothed the blankets around his shoulders, and then she went down the hall to Lee's room. His door was closed, but when she turned the knob and looked, she saw he wasn't there. Going in, she sat down on the edge of his bed and listened for him in the adjoining bathroom. At the sound of the tub's being turned on, she stood up

138

again. Suddenly her eyes were drawn to the corner of a manila envelope protruding from beneath the pillows. Curious, Beatrice reached for it. When she unfastened the clasp and emptied the contents onto the bed, she found a dozen glossy commercial snapshots of women in erotic poses.

For what seemed an eternity Beatrice gazed down at them. Then she looked around the room at Lee's sports equipment, his schoolbooks, his pennants on the walls—was she mistaken, or did all the snapshots seem to resemble her? The women with their shining buttocks and vulgar breasts were all dark-haired and slender. She put the pictures back into their envelope and rearranged the pillows. Then she noticed something else beneath a fold of the bedspread.

When she looked more closely she saw it was her wedding ring.

10

SOMETIMES, looking into night's wakeful mirror, he would make out his daytime self, all twisted and confused. At times like that —in the midst of restless sleep—it would come to him that the almost unrecognizable reflection in this pocked and grimy glass had, perhaps, an existence as real as the one he normally thought of as his own. Like the face in the silver coffee urn on top of the buffet, or in those distorting mirrors he had seen at tent shows, or in the backwash of disturbed water: it was much the same, a contortion of the familiar Lee which by the very fact of its presence made him question the face he knew.

The dreams came often now. He would lie with his head turned to the wall, eyes clenched tight against the darkness, as childhood fears returned to him with agonizing clarity, carrying him downward toward the center of his life. And often, afterward, as he lay there tasting the rank breath of sleep and counting the indrawn seconds in the wake of all that dreaming, he would ask himself what *was* the center of his life. But he couldn't say. Because once the tide had receded, that awareness seemed to slip away from him, and though the dreams would come back in snatches when he was running down the football field or sitting in his desk at school, they came back only as abstractions. They were empty then; they meant nothing. To try and recapture them was to circle something which wasn't there, to turn back on himself with an obstinate, fearful longing.

It was one of those mornings in early April when the grass was dripping and the sky was suffused with a mild, translucent blue. All up and down Main Street the chinaberry trees were budding, while on lawns and out across the hills the pines had lost their winter frailty. As Lee went down the stairs he remembered that tonight was the ninth-grade dance. He had been waiting apprehensively for it since the beginning of the spring semester, ever since he had gotten his learner's permit and his mother had begun letting him use the car. For a moment he paused, scraping the side of one foot against his calf in an effort to stop the itch of a bad gash which was nearly healed. He had had a motorscooter accident at the end of football season, and though the bruises on his face had disappeared in a couple of days, he had had to have forty stitches in his calf. His mother had forbidden him to get near the scooter again. To coax him into compliance she let him take the car sometimes, even though by law he lacked six months being old enough to drive alone. Tonight she had promised he could take it to the dance; Lee rubbed his foot against his calf again, half wondering whether she had changed her mind.

Tony was sitting at the table when Lee went into the kitchen. He was twelve and a half now, but he looked much younger. His sandy hair fell down over his round, smooth forehead, framing a face which still hadn't lost its babyish contours. Lee glanced at his brother and then, without saying anything, he went over to the pantry.

"Hi," Tony said. He had been reading the comic strips. The rest of the newspaper was scattered on the window seat. "I'm through if you want them now."

"Huh?"

"You can have the funnies."

Lee poured a bowl of cereal and headed for the refrigerator. As he reached for the milk he said absently, "No thanks."

"Dick Tracy captured the Cat Woman— Hey, don't use up all the sugar."

141

"You've already had breakfast," Lee answered, thrusting a spoonful of cereal into his mouth.

"No, I haven't. I was waiting to see if Mom was going to get up. She told me the other night she'd make milktoast on Saturday."

Lee took another bite of cereal. Tony was leaning on his elbow, looking at Lee across the table, a curious, expectant expression marking his freckled face. It occurred to Lee that if he had been able to give a name to the troubled promptings his brother's trust aroused in him, he might have been able to explain something to Tony. As it was, he could only fight to find any words at all.

"I wouldn't count on it, Tony. She was out pretty late last night."

"But she said—"

"Oh, come on."

Lee tossed down his spoon. Then, swallowing hard, he let his eyes stray past the windows beyond which, against the filmy blue of the sky, the tips of new-budding boughs were visible. What was it he had dreamed last night? He felt Tony watching him and picked up the spoon again with an abruptness which was almost violent.

"Why don't you go watch *Captain Kangaroo* or something?"

"I haven't watched *Captain Kangaroo* for three years," Tony returned. "You're just trying to get rid of me, aren't you? You're afraid I'll want to go uptown with you."

"I don't care if you come with me uptown. I'm not going to do anything but go over to the sawmill and see if Uncle Milton wants me to run the chipper this morning. After that I might see if Claude Earl needs the jail swept."

"What are you trying to earn all this money for? Ever since Christmas you've been talking about money."

Lee pushed the empty bowl away. Then, looking his brother straight in the face, he took a pack of cigarettes out of his shirt and lit one up. He took a long, deliberate draw. Already, if he didn't smoke a cigarette just after he got up, he could feel an annoying tickle far back in his throat.

"Hey, give me one," Tony pleaded. "Come on, Lee, just one."

"You going to keep quiet?"

Tony nodded. Lee handed him the pack.

"Mom knows you smoke. I heard her telling Aunt Louise about it."

"So what?"

Lee lit Tony's cigarette with his own. Tony inhaled timidly, his brows knitted in a serious expression which was a fair imitation of his brother's.

"You didn't tell me what it is you're trying to save money for."

"A car," Lee answered. "Now quit asking so many questions."

After a while Tony went outside. Lee lit another cigarette. When he had finished it he got up and wandered into the living room. Sunlight was straying through the drapes, warming the floor and causing pillars of airdust to rise. For some reason his neck was aching. Probably the way he had slept, he thought, tossing and turning until it had been almost light. He pushed his hair away from his neck and began to rub the sore spot, yawning, blinking, feeling the needles in his spine. It seemed he could almost recall what it was he had been dreaming about; the sun was smoking around the fringes of the shadows, and as Lee let his eyes follow its erratic path the dream seemed to come into clearer focus. For an instant, trapped on the edge of disappearance, it was before him. Then he lost it altogether again.

At the end of the hall he heard the shower running. His mother was up, but it would be close to an hour, he knew, before she finally came out of the bathroom. It occurred to him to wait and find out whether she still planned to let him take the car to the dance. Then he changed his mind. If she decided to drive to Dallas that afternoon he supposed he could always ask to borrow Claude Earl's.

It wasn't yet ten o'clock. As Lee walked down Main Street toward the Corner Café, where he usually found his uncle on Saturday mornings, he thought about how much he wanted to get out of Toombs Mill. There was something stifling about the place, something which seemed to give everyone license for petty probing into everyone else's life. At least, he thought, there was one good thing you could say about West Texas: in towns out there no one really cared what you did. People had such a hard time keeping the sand and caliche dust from burying them alive that they didn't have any energy left for backbiting. They were harder, more self-contained people, but there was something you could trust about them. Lee kicked at a pebble, telling himself he wasn't going to forget that. As he neared the café he stopped and looked around him. Across the street, in the window of Hardy's Dry Goods, the rolls of fabric were bright and fixed, and the sun was solid, like a sheet across the glass. Next door in the barbershop he could see old half-blind Mr. Haley giving old Mr. Tibbs his Saturday shave. All up and down the sidewalks people were window-shopping or talking or wandering in and out of stores. For a few moments Lee watched them, thinking with a kind of flat detachment that he was looking at his life.

As he opened the door of the café he heard Buck Jonas yelling. Buck had one fist upraised, ready to pound the counter in front of him.

"Goddamn it, Brenda, there's legs in my eggs!"

"What do you mean?" Brenda Dew returned. She set down the pitcher she was carrying and looked impatiently at Buck. "Who ever heard of such a thing—legs in your eggs."

"I mean there's the locomotive parts of a cockroach over easy in my breakfast! Get over here and see for yourself—see there, right next to the grits."

Brenda bent over the counter and examined the plate of eggs. Then, sniffing, she snatched the plate away.

"All right, you'll get another one."

"And this time cut the cockroach!"

It only took Lee a second to see that his uncle wasn't there. Going over to the counter, he sat down next to Buck, who was muttering and stabbing a paper napkin with his fork.

"Hi, Buck."

"Hi yourself. I'd buy you some breakfast, but that yellow, wall-eyed Ubangi they got cooking here likes to salt his eggs with cockroach. And cockroach before eleven in the morning just ain't to my likes."

"Oh, come on, Buck, he's not as bad as all that."

144

"Well, he's a sight better than that ole boy from California they had running the kitchen last year—goddamn Yankee interloper." Buck gave the napkin one final stab and then, grinning, he leaned toward Lee. "Say, you know the difference between a damn Yankee and a goddamn Yankee?"

Lee looked down at the big red hand which still held the fork. On the back of it, against the redness of the skin, even the coarse, burnished hairs looked pale.

"Nope," he answered, knowing that was what Buck wanted him to say.

"I'll tell you. A damn Yankee is one who comes down here and goes away. A goddamn Yankee stays!"

Buck burst into a raucous laugh. Lee laughed, too, even though he could have predicted what the joke would be. As Buck became quiet again, Lee found himself studying his friend's face. It was a full-fleshed face, but the flesh couldn't conceal the long, heavy skull beneath it, beneath the blood that seemed to flow too close to the surface of the tough, too-thin skin.

"Well, what'll you have?" Buck said.

"I thought you weren't buying."

"Buying, hell. We're gonna get this one free—hey, Brenda, bring Lee something that won't rot his guts out. And tell that Ubangi if he kills me, I aim to come back and haint him."

Brenda Dew came over and took Lee's order. She had become a heavy woman in the past few years. Her face, no longer a mask of make-up, was stark and puffy, and she wore a wedding band on one hand. Lee watched her shout the order to the cook and then fill three cups of coffee with a single movement of the wrist.

"Well, what's been going on with you, Buck?" Lee asked.

"Same as usual. Trying to scrape a living off a place that's ever God's inch mortgaged."

"How'd your Christmas-tree gamble come out?"

Buck picked up his coffee and dumped some in the saucer. Then, before he took a drink he began to blow.

"You know, you asking that makes me realize I ain't talked to you in a while. What you been up to, anyhow?"

"Football," Lee told him. "I was captain this past season. And when football season was over I went out for basketball, only I got in a motorscooter accident and bunged up my leg."

"Shit," Buck answered, hunching over the counter to cool his coffee again. "You couldn't get me near a football field or a basketball court either one. God never put a passel of boys together to run after a pig bladder that ninety-nine percent of them didn't turn out to be sons-of-bitches. And basketball ain't no different."

Brenda set another plate in front of Buck. He grunted, poking at the eggs with his fork. Just as he was ready to take a bite she returned with Lee's pancakes. There was a silence as both of them began to eat.

"Well, so how did the Christmas trees go?"

"Terrible as I expected. I run a load down to Dallas and sold about half. Say, what'd you do to your leg, anyhow?"

Lee swallowed a mouthful of pancake. Then, bending down, he rolled up his pants leg to expose a long, shiny scar that was still bright pink.

"Goddamn if that ain't ugly. How'd you do it?"

"I was riding up a steep embankment and the scooter kicked back on me. If I'd jumped off in time I would have saved myself from getting hurt, but my scooter would have slid down and gotten torn all to pieces."

"So it was okay for the scooter and tough tiddy for you."

"Pretty much," Lee agreed, turning back to his pancakes.

Buck finished eating and signaled for another cup of coffee. Lee watched as he began to slurp from the saucer again, the drops of dark liquid clinging to his mustache.

The café was quiet for a Saturday. There were a few boys playing pinball in the back, and the usual group of old men were trading lies at a booth by the windows. Otherwise the place was empty. Lee looked around at the rickety chairs and scarred wooden tables, and then he let his eyes wander to the snapshots that had been hung on the walls to cover the spots where the boards had begun to splinter. Most of them showed men in plaid shirts posing beside the carcasses of deer or fowl, or bare-bellied men holding fish on stringers and grinning at the camera past

146

upraised beer bottles. His favorite one was just above the cash register. It showed Buck and his father leaning against the hood of a truck. Buck was clowning with a bird dog, while his father was showing off a brace of pheasants. Quinn's face was dark and smiling and his head was thrown back a little.

Buck noticed what Lee was looking at.

"Yeah, the birds were thick as leaves that season. We got a little of everything, me and Quinn."

Lee turned to him, trying to make out the expression on his face. As he looked into one blue, fixed eye he realized with a start that it was Buck's good one—for the space of a single instant it might easily have been glass.

"He always liked to hunt," Lee said.

"Yeah," Buck answered subduedly. "Yeah, he shore-God did."

As they were leaving the café Lee paused on the steps.

"What's the matter?"

"Nothing. It's just that sometimes I sure do hate it here. Has it always been like this? Has Toombs Mill always been the same?"

"Pretty much," Buck said, pulling a key out of his pocket and beginning to clean his ear. " 'Course, it's gotten bigger by two or three thousand, and them tracts of crackerboxes have been built. Seems there's something conducive to breeding in the smell of pine—though more likely it's the boredom. Three blamed fourths of this town goes to the Baptist church, and what else can a Baptist do for fun except breed more Baptists?"

Lee watched Buck wipe the key on the seat of his pants before putting it back in his pocket. Then, bending to pick up a rock, he practiced his fast ball at a street sign.

"Well, I'm going to get out of here before too long. The older I get, the more I can't see any reasons for staying."

"You got to be dumb or senile to stay around this place. Me —well, I expect I'm just plumb lazy."

They walked down the street without saying anything. Lee was wondering where his uncle was, whether he had already gone over to the sawmill. When they reached the intersection of Main and Pecan, Lee turned to Buck.

"See you. I'm going over to ask Uncle Milton if he wants me

to run the chipper today. And thanks a lot for the breakfast."

"It didn't cost me nothing. Say, why don't we drown some worms before the weather gets too hot? Go up toward the mouth of Sulphur Creek and catch us a mess of bass."

"I'm going to be pretty busy working on the weekends. And then there's going to be baseball practice—"

Buck stepped in front of Lee and seized him by the shoulder. "You come out to my place before too long. You come out and spend the night."

Lee nodded slowly, but Buck didn't release him. For several seconds the blue eyes regarded him with the same fixed intensity Lee had felt when the two of them had shared their thoughts about the snapshot. It occurred to him that Buck was going to say something else about his father. He didn't, though. When Buck finally freed his shoulder and they went their separate ways, Lee felt himself in the grip of a confused, insistent sadness. There was much that was too painful for him to think about, much that even now he couldn't bring into the light.

It was five o'clock when Lee finally turned off the chipping machine. The men at the far end of the conveyor belt had stopped feeding him the logs, and once he had guided the last batch into the saws he flipped the switch to off. It had been a steady five hours of work, and he was glad of it. When he had to concentrate on keeping the logs in line he didn't really have time to think about things that were bothering him. And this afternoon a lot of things were bothering him. Like what had been left unsaid between Buck and him. And his mother—Lee had a feeling she wasn't going to let him take the car after all.

Leaving the scream of the saws behind, Lee crossed the main area of the mill and went down the hall to his uncle's office. As he opened the door Milton looked up from a stack of ledgers.

"Going home?"

"Yeah, I guess so. I've put in five hours today."

"Getting rich, huh?" his uncle said abstractedly, adjusting his glasses on his nose as he squinted down at the books again.

"Not exactly. Hey, did my mother call?"

"What? Oh, you're right. She called a couple hours ago—wants you to call her back as soon as you're off work. Which means now, I take it."

Lee reached for the telephone on the desk.

"We're expecting you and Tony for supper. You know how Louise is. She gets upset that Bea lets you boys stay alone now."

Lee felt a quick pang of anger. Tautly, tonelessly, he said, "So she's doing it again."

Milton rubbed his bald spot, trying to avoid Lee's gaze. "Well, yes. If you mean she's spending a few days in Dallas. But Hunt's good to her, Lee. He'd make you a fine stepfather."

Lee let the receiver slip back onto the hook. Then, without thinking, he picked up a sheaf of papers, wadded them, and hurled them against the wall. His uncle looked up so abruptly that his glasses flew off his nose.

"Now don't get personal, Lee, don't get personal. All I was doing was—"

Lee slammed the door behind him as he left his uncle's office. Once again his mother had told him something and then gone back on her word. Once again she had acted without taking his feelings into account, making him feel stupid for ever having believed that wouldn't happen. Like the time a few weeks before when she had promised to leave him alone if he brought a girl over after school. The girl was someone he really liked, and he had pleaded with his mother not to embarrass him by insisting they have milk and cookies. Lee recalled how the two of them had been sitting on the sofa, doing nothing but talking and occasionally touching hands, when his mother had walked in, flicked at an invisible speck on top of the piano, and then let out a comment about the pair of dirty socks he had left on the kitchen table. No, he thought, she hadn't embarrassed him in the way she had agreed not to. But she had done it nevertheless—just a comment in passing, yet it had been aimed at making him uncomfortable with the girl. So not only had she ruined his afternoon, she had gone back on her word. She had lied to him. It was as if, he thought, she had been trying to force a confrontation in order to see how much he could take. And tonight was no different—she had told him more than once he could take the car to the school dance.

The afternoon was beginning to ebb. Lee walked through the millyard, past the stacks of pine, which looked peculiarly white and naked in the long, level light. On the slight rise of ground at the end of the yard the men were unhitching the trailers, getting ready to go home. Lee walked past without so much as waving. He was deep in his own thoughts, not even aware that the close, rapt air filtering toward him through the tree-lined streets was the first breath of summer, come early again this year. When he reached the gate he hurried toward the center of town. Walking directly across the square, which was almost empty now, he headed for the Sheriff's office; Claude Earl was on duty till six on Saturdays, and Lee hoped that with a little coaxing he could get him to loan out his car.

But when he pushed open the side door he was disappointed to find out that Claude Earl had already gone.

"Naw, he left early this evening," Johnny Kingman said. "Taken his paycheck and buggered out."

"Where do you think he went?" Lee asked.

Kingman cocked his chair back farther. Then, in the insinuating tone of voice which had always made Lee dislike him, he said, "You might try the nearest buckberry bush."

Lee moved closer to the desk, looking into one of the faces he had seen around Toombs Mill for years. Kingman's small, bloodshot eyes were set deep in the puckered flesh on either side of a veiny, heavy nose. To Lee, all his features, all his gestures, seemed to express contempt.

"Do you know where Claude Earl went?"

"Well, maybe I do and maybe I don't. But he likes to get laid a right smart on Saturdays."

"You're a lot of help," Lee declared, moving toward the door.

"I wasn't aiming to be."

Lee heard the chair creak as Kingman put his feet up. Impulsively he turned toward Kingman again, disliking him even more when he saw the way he was sprawled behind the desk.

150

"I don't know what Sheriff Mac ever hired you for. You're the most no-count son-of-a-bitch I ever laid eyes on."

Kingman spat, a thin, hissing stream that flickered brightly in the brass spittoon. "I figger he needed him someone to beat on the drunks and niggermeat."

Outside again, Lee walked aimlessly through the streets. A gauzy dusk was beginning to fall. The sky appeared to have moved closer, and only a faint streak of violet marked the position of the sun. For some reason Lee couldn't comprehend, he began to feel a longing amounting almost to nostalgia, and soon he was thinking back over the seasons he had spent in Toombs Mill: the autumn mornings he had stood at his bedroom window watching the live oaks flare in the steady but not oppressive sunlight; the winter afternoons when a norther had blown down from the distant plains, when the snow, polished hard under the wind, had glimmered in the dark across the river bottom when he had come home late from practice; the summer middays, swollen with the scent of roses and with the odor of bruised peaches throbbing and falling through the leaves; the spring nights like this one which hadn't yet completely descended, when the air was still fresh from the rich, damp daylight hours. Yet the moment he realized where his thoughts had taken him, he began to feel uneasy. It was too long, he told himself, to have lived here. There was something cloying about Toombs Mill, something that always seemed to be closing in on him.

He walked on for a few more blocks, feeling his mingled emotions slowly draining away. At last, stretching out on a low stone wall a few blocks from the school, he lay with his chin in his hands and watched the cars go by. Though it was too early yet for people to be going to the dance, the Saturday-night traffic was starting. A group of his friends, boys a year or two older than he was, drove by in a pick-up, but the dusk kept them from seeing him. Soon the Sheriff's car cruised past, and after that he recognized Mrs. Haley's. As it got darker the katydids began tuning up; Lee listened to the high, constant humming which seemed to grow louder with every passing moment. Suddenly, out of the tail of his eye, he saw the streetlights blink on. He also saw his mother's

Chrysler make a right turn off of Elm Street and disappear down the block.

Once again anger touched him, only this time, more than anger, it was a sense of loss, of deep and blatant betrayal. The class dance no longer mattered. The fact that his friends would be driving their parents' cars made absolutely no difference to him, and he was ashamed for his outburst in front of his uncle. For the whole thing about the car was trivial. What really mattered was this sense of having been deceived, this loss which seemed to well up from some half-concealed truth which was only slowly becoming clear to him.

After a while Lee began walking again. Headed nowhere in particular, he turned onto a side street, from time to time glancing up at the globes of light visible through parted curtains or at the massy shadows of lamplit shrubbery. At the school the dance was beginning. He could hear the band, faintly, above the sound of his own footsteps, and though he knew he had time to go home, change clothes, and make it over to the gym, he also knew he didn't want to. The excitement was gone for him now. What he really felt like doing was taking his motorscooter out of the garage and riding out the dirt road along the bar pit.

The windows of his house were dark. Lee guessed Tony was having supper with his aunt and uncle and they probably supposed he was at the dance by now. His mother had no doubt been worried when he hadn't called her after work. He didn't care, though. As he opened the garage door it occurred to him that maybe his mother didn't care either. Maybe, driving toward Dallas at eighty miles an hour, she was thinking about the good time she was going to have with Hunt in Europe the coming summer. Or maybe she was planning what to wear tonight. But ten to one she wasn't worrying about him.

Lee's fingers found the light switch just inside the door. His scooter, dusty from three months of disuse, was parked in a far corner of the garage. He went over to it and examined the back fender, which was dented but not so badly that it rubbed against the tire. Satisfied the fender wouldn't give him any trouble, Lee began to wheel the machine toward the door. That was when he remembered his mother had hidden the key to the ignition. She had taken it away from him after he had had his accident and refused to tell him where it was.

Lee stood very still, looking down at the scooter. His mother's absence, marked by the space where the parked car should have been, had no more meaning than it would have had if she had been standing right beside him. He could stay here all night, he thought, listening as the katydids chirped time away into silence, and she would still be with him, her half-hysterical questions echoing in the empty garage. Because she had been worried that time. When he had been in the emergency room having his leg sewn up she had been so worried she had almost cried.

There was a pair of pliers on a shelf next to the door. Lee reached for them and began yanking at the battery wires. One of his friends had shown him how to cross wires on a car, and he hoped he would be able to do it on his scooter. At first nothing seemed to be happening. He put one set of wires back in place and tried another. A flurry of sparks flew upward. After a few false starts the machine came to life.

As Lee sped along a dirt road on the far edge of town he felt the air damp and chill against his cheeks, and excitement ran all through him. Recklessly he pressed the accelerator, leaning forward until his face was almost even with the handlebars. The dirt road was gradually giving way to a trail which he had often traveled, though he had never tried it in the dark. Here weeds grew in patches, concealing old ruts. On each side the trees reached out toward one another, so that the darkness was close and narrow between them. Lee rode on, from time to time imagining that the darkness was that of a hall or corridor. Ahead of him, where the trees ended and the treacherous bulldozed embankment along the bar pit began, the sky was hazy with light. Diffuse grayish clouds were drifting on the southern horizon. He thought of the wind rising off the surface of the water and anticipated the moment when he would leave the narrow lane behind.

The ground broke away toward the bar pit. Lee slowed down a little when he felt loose dirt beneath the wheels. To the right of him the embankment shelved down toward blackness. Some ten yards below, he knew, it disappeared into the water, water which was filled with all sorts of submerged debris and which was as much as fifty feet deep in places. A single slip of the wheel could send him hurtling over the lip of the embankment—Lee thought about this as he guided the scooter across the open space. And when he hit a rough spot and found himself suspended, strangely motionless, in the moment before he plunged toward the water, the same impotent self-warning flashed across his brain.

He went under, came up again, swallowed. The cold, oily water rushed down into the cavities of his body, filling him with fear. It was hideous, this unwilled and empty privacy. He was cut off from everyone, from everything but his fear. Once again the water closed over him. When he surfaced this time the pressure on his chest seemed to be less intense and the sky had lightened a little. A star winked in the west. He had the impulse to stop flailing at the water, to simply let himself bob and float there on the surface, to let his arms, which were outstretched, sink slowly to his sides. But he mastered it. He fixed his gaze on a point in the distance where the still water converged with the stiller shadow of the embankment, trying to delude his senses once again into fear. The next moment the water, colder and more inimical than before, began to force its way into his lungs and stomach. He struggled, kicked, cried out against it. He focused all his awareness on that line of shadow which, with each exhausted effort, appeared to be coming closer. Soon he felt an upsurge of something solid, and with the last of his strength he pulled himself to safety.

There was not a sound. There was nothing in the gape of space before him: the water was undisturbed. It was as though he had never fought it, as though he had never been there.

With a choking noise he began to breathe again.

11

LEE SPENT A WEEK in the hospital with his left arm in traction. During that time Rita Cobb came to see him twice, and each time she brought him a book. The first time it was a collection of poetry. The second time it was a short novel by Conrad, which he surprised himself by reading. When he had finished it he lay in the narrow bed and thought about Rita Cobb. She was a funny woman, he decided, funny in the sense that he didn't know what to make of her. There was something in her manner which confessed its own ineffectuality, but at the same time there was an odd spontaneity about her. He thought back to the year she had been his English teacher. Her lectures had been long and often painfully pedantic, but sometimes, he recalled, she had been capable of infusing him with excitement. On certain mornings she had walked into the classroom and been overcome by a kind of breathlessness. Lee had always expected her words to lurch out, sticking somewhere in the back of her throat when she opened her mouth to talk—and on mornings like that her words *had* lurched out. Yet despite her uncertain manner she had been able, on those rare occasions, to interest him in the poem or story she had assigned.

And there was something else about her, something which it was much harder for him to figure out. He had an inexplicable sense of having known her at some other time in his life. Yet whenever he tried to capture her face and fit it into the puzzle of dreams and memories, he was never certain where to place it or even that it belonged. More than once he had dreamed about a woman who reminded him of her. And in some lost place of memory the two of them were walking across a stretch of sand to look at a cactus blossom while the scentless air of the desert flowed up along their bodies and dried the dampness beneath their clothes.

So Lee was unsure when it all began with her. Maybe it had been years before or maybe it had been when he was in the seventh grade. Maybe, too, it hadn't been until that second afternoon she came to see him in the hospital. Rita—she had asked him then not to call her Miss Cobb any more—was going out of the room, her floppy school satchel flung over one shoulder, just as Buck was coming in. They had exchanged greetings in the doorway, Buck in the embarrassed voice he was often afflicted with around women, Rita in that quiet tone which always made it seem as though she was thinking about something else. Afterward Buck dragged a chair over to the bed, giving Lee a quizzical look.

"That's one woman going to wear herself out before her span. She won't even be around to catch her second wind if she don't get at whatever it is that's eating her."

"What do you mean?" Lee asked.

"I can't explain it exactly. But I bet my ragged ass she got the rug pulled out from under her. She's one of them women that got that look—sold her soul to some man for two bits and a shinplaster."

"Who do you think it was? Someone here in town?"

"Beats me. But I'll tell you something else. She's got the eye on you, Lee."

"Come on, Buck, you're—"

"No, I swear it. I swear I know what I seen on that woman's face."

As the summer came and went and the next school year began, Lee often found himself thinking back to what Buck had said. By then he was seeing Rita two or three times a week, going over to her house after school to talk about the books she loaned him. He

156

had developed an appetite for reading after she had brought him the Conrad novel. Because his weak arm kept him out of sports, he found himself reading more and more. Novels, plays, poetry —he read quickly, eagerly, taking anything she handed him. Literature became almost like a drug; to read was to escape from the peculiarly bitter discontents of adolescence, to leave fears and nightmares and disappointments far behind.

On a rainy afternoon in the middle of his tenth-grade year Lee was sitting in his English class listening to Mrs. Davitt talk about sentence diagrams. A restless feeling had come over him. Bored with Mrs. Davitt, bored with the class, he turned toward the windows to watch the flight of the dim rain. The windows were swimming with reflections, for the room was unnaturally bright with the lights from overhead. Moment by moment he felt himself drawing away. Something was coming back to him, provoked by the sound of the rain, one of those half-lit memories which were always promising to come clear. How old had he been that first summer after his father had left? Seven? And hadn't there been a night sometime during his brief visit in the desert when he had lain awake until almost dawn, listening to the dry, sterile thunder and watching the sheet lightning illumine the shotgun on the rack above his head? When at last it began to rain it was a violent rain which threatened to tear the door off its hinges and lift the panes of glass right out of the dusty stucco. Even then the thunder didn't stop. He lay on the sofa, tense with waiting, and listened to the sound echoing in the distant mountains. All of a sudden the thunder came louder than before. Lightning turned the room a fleeting white, and in that split second he saw the bedroom door open. It was the woman who was staying with his father, the woman whose name he could no longer remember but whose face sometimes returned to him in dreams. She came over to him and knelt down and asked if the thunder frightened him. At that moment he heard his father calling from the other room.

"For God's sake, dry bones can't hurt anyone!"

The woman had gone back into the bedroom then.

By the time class was over, the rain had become a torrent. Lee looked out the window at the waterlogged sods that had once been climbing roses. The rain was bursting against the building to sluice along the branches, and he could see how shiny and distinct the thorns had become. English was his last class of the day. Because of the weather, football practice had been canceled. Though he couldn't play, he sometimes went to watch. Now the remainder of the afternoon stretched ahead of him with nothing definite in sight. Gathering his books, he joined a noisy group of students in the hall.

"Hey, you want to go to the café for a hamburger?" Eddy Haley shouted to him above the banging of locker doors.

"Sure!" Lee shouted back. "Just let me get these books out!"

The afternoon dissolved into the rain's darkening screen. Lee spent two hours playing pinball with Eddy. By the time they were leaving the café the regular supper crowd was beginning to come in. They hurried across the pavement and got into Eddy's car. Eddy flipped the radio on. Both boys lit up cigarettes.

"Well, I guess I better be getting home, Lee. My grandmother gets mad when I don't show up by six. Where do you want me to take you?"

Lee thought for a moment. Then, shrugging, he said, "Just let me off at Rita Cobb's."

"Say, do you have a thing about her or something? I mean, you're always going over there."

"She loans me books," Lee said flatly. "She loans me books and that's all there is to it. Shit, Eddy, she's my mother's age."

Eddy laughed. As he was starting the car a popular song came on the radio, and neither boy said anything else.

At first Lee thought she wasn't home. Huddling beneath the protective overhang of the porch, he pulled his jacket closer and knocked again. Just as he was ready to go back down the steps he heard her call, "Come in." He pushed open the door and stepped into the living room then. She was standing by the windows, one hand on the glass curtains, the other fingering her long braid.

"Didn't you hear me knocking?"

"What?" She let the glass curtain fall to. "I must have thought it was the wind."

Lee walked past her and put the volumes he had borrowed back

158

in place. The room was comfortably warm. It was a large room, but the ponderous glass-fronted bookcases rising to the ceiling, the crewel-embroidered loveseats, the bric-a-brac and the painted screens, the heavy carpets, the china vases—these objects crowded in on one another. Lee stood in the midst of them, aware of her gaze and of his own excited heartbeat, breathing the dusty odor which always invaded his nostrils in this room.

"You didn't see me standing there?"

"No," she said.

He watched her go over to the sofa and bend toward the heap of sleeping cat fur. She picked up a big, mottled calico, one of the half-dozen cats she kept.

"How could you have missed me if you were right there at the window?"

"Take off your jacket," she said. And then: "I guess I was thinking about something. A few minutes before you knocked I saw someone go by—the Mexican boy who works nights at the funeral home, you know who I mean. I had him in my third-period class last year and he was always falling asleep. Isn't that a depressing way for a twelve-year-old boy to have to earn money?"

She sat down on the sofa, curled up with the cats. Lee watched as she stroked them, aware of a confusion between Rita and himself. It was in the air, it seemed, a kind of mutual awkwardness. He turned back to the bookshelves and picked up another volume. They exchanged a few remarks, but he was certain neither of them was listening. When he finally sat down beside her on the sofa she reached for his hand, something she had never done before.

"A long, broad hand," she told him, spreading the fingers one by one. "Not a boy's hand."

She leaned toward him then. Gently, deliberately, she kissed him. But he felt himself holding back from her.

"Are you frightened?"

"No," he said, though fear was running like a current through his body, electrifying his fingers into a kind of tenuous life. He wanted to touch her, but blindly, unthinkingly, the way he

159

touched women's bodies in his dreams. And he was frightened because he sensed that wasn't what she wanted.

She led him into the bedroom and they sat down on the edge of the bed. The room was dark, but in the rain's luminescence he could see that she was watching him, her hands clasping the coverlet in what seemed to be painful stillness. Lee closed his eyes. She kissed him again, but then, with a soft click, their teeth met, and he turned his face away.

Her bed smelled of wet cats and talcum powder. Lee lay back against the pillows, every muscle tense. Still she sat there and looked at him. He wondered if she was going to tell him that maybe, after all, he ought to go. Out in the street a car was passing. As its lights shone into the room, creating rain-blurred shadows among the moving pockets of glare, Lee saw Rita raise one hand and put it to her face.

"Do you want me to go or what?"

"No."

She stood up and took off her clothes. Naked, she bent over him as he began to undress. Then she was lying beside him and his fingers had found her breasts. Tentatively he touched them, unable to control his trembling.

"Don't be frightened, Lee," she said.

It was impossible for him not to be. This wasn't the way he had imagined it, the way it had been in dreams. He had never thought he would be expected to acknowledge her as complete and individual, the center of a universe as significant as the one he understood concentric to himself. If he could forget her, if he could obliterate what he knew as truth—then, maybe, his body might obey him.

"Relax, Lee. Try to relax a little."

She pressed him closer to her, but he was wild inside with fear. Even after he stopped responding she kept up her slow caresses, touching him in ways he had never been touched before. Yet her hands, he knew, were charmless. For always, in the half-light, her eyes were there.

After a while she moved away from him.

"Lee. Lee, listen to the sound the rain makes. It's let up a little,

160

hasn't it? But that rattling, clacking sound—like teeth chattering —must be the drops falling onto the sidewalk from the upper branches of the pines."

He was afraid she was going to smooth her hand across his hair or try and comfort him with some other nameless maternal action. Instead, she pulled the covers up around them and let several moments go by before she spoke again. All the while Lee lay there listening to his own breathing and to the slowing of the rain. The past half-hour had left him feeling absurdly like a child; he felt ashamed, wanting only to crawl into himself.

"One of the cats is on the bed. It's Gogol. Poor Gogol, he must have gotten lonely."

Lee felt the weight of the cat as it settled itself between them. Almost involuntarily he reached out and began to stroke its fur. Then he felt Rita's hand brush his.

"They're such independent creatures. You can go away for weeks and they never seem to have missed you. Not that I've gone away and left them often. I've always wanted to travel, but somehow I've never done it."

"My mother's going to Europe this summer."

Almost immediately he felt ridiculous for having said that. But she didn't seem to notice, or if she did she didn't let on.

"Is she? I'd love to go to Europe, though I guess I've always been more fascinated by exotic places. When I was a child I used to dream of going to dead cities with names like Tarquinia, Persepolis, and Palmyra. You see, I believed names ought to be charms and that simply by saying them I should be able to evoke reality. So, in a way, reading about them has always been as good as going there."

There was a silence as both of them continued to stroke the cat. Lee felt his fear dissolving, though he still couldn't stop thinking about what had gone on between them.

"Let's go into the kitchen and make some tea," she said. "Or if you want, you can stay in bed and I'll bring it in here."

"No. I'll come with you."

She put on an antique-looking dressing gown, and he slipped into his pants. They went into the kitchen. He watched as she

161

took the bright-colored tea set from its shelf and filled the kettle with water. Though her tea-making ritual was familiar to him, as he sat at the table listening to her chatter about her cats it occurred to him that something, this time, was different. She no longer moved in the same way. Even the quick, automatic motions of her hands from kettle to pot to cup had a changed quality about them. Or was it all in his way of seeing her? He forced himself to imagine her the way he had seen her before tonight, but the image kept slipping away from him. It was difficult even to picture in his mind all the evenings they had spent together, she talking excitedly about Eliot or Conrad or Lawrence, he listening in fascination as the dream world became graspable, transformed into ideas. When the tea was ready she carried their cups into the living room. Lee followed, still trying to recall that other image.

He sat down at the far end of the sofa. Though he wanted to be near her, he was too self-conscious to let her know. As they drank their tea she became oddly quiet. He looked over and saw she was biting one corner of her underlip, obviously thinking about something which took her deep into herself. Her fine brown-gold hair, freed from the braid, hung over her shoulders almost to her waist. It occurred to Lee that he had never really noticed her hair before, and that with it down like this she seemed almost pretty. Only she wasn't pretty like many women were. There was that austerity about her features which kept her from being pretty in the usual ways.

As he was thinking these things she said his name in a low tone, almost a whisper.

"What?"

"There's something I should tell you."

Lee watched, as she picked up her teacup and began toying with the handle, wondering at the note of urgency in her voice.

"Lee, don't you remember me?"

She was speaking so softly that if he had really wanted to hear he would have had to move closer to her, much closer.

"What are you talking about?"

"Think back to the summer you were seven."

Something which he could only call fear seemed to roll out from her in waves. Yet if he had had to say whether or not it was in her voice he would have said no, it was just there, like the fear a cat can smell or like the apprehension he himself was feeling and could only identify now as anger. He moved toward her and took her by the shoulders, feeling the lightness of her bones beneath his hands. She reached up and touched his cheek. That angered him even more, but he let her fingers stay there, let them explore the curves of his face. Because he knew with sudden certainty that this face wasn't his own.

"You brought me desert flowers and little bits of colored rock. Once you left an arrowhead on my suitcase where it would have been impossible for me to miss it—you were such a strange, dark child, Lee, so much like your father. Did you know that I came to this awful town because of him? No, of course you didn't, but it's true, I actually packed my world and got a job here, and Quinn was the reason why. And after I found out I was too late, I couldn't do anything but recede further and further into myself. I couldn't do anything. My life was a vacuum of lost possibilities, and it seemed that the only logical outcome would be complete stasis, day after day of staring into nothing. I thought I was going crazy. I was sure I was. But then, sometime in the spring of that first year, something happened. You became real to me. Until then I had, of course, known who you were, but even so you were never in any true sense there. After that I began to watch you, to wait for you to walk into class each morning. I realized that just being in sight of you made me happy, though there were times when I longed to take you aside and talk to you, to share the sense of purpose you had created in my life. Because of you I was able to take an interest in things again, just little things, books and curios and walks across the hills, but those have always been the things that, added together, are my life.

"So it was after I discovered you that I rediscovered something vital inside. You were only twelve, though, much too young to understand, and for that reason I had to keep everything to myself. I had to watch in secret as you grew older, wondering how long I was going to have to wait for you. And then, last year, you began to come and see me, and things seemed to be falling into place of their own accord. When you turned fifteen I realized we could begin to share things. How I loved to watch your eyes grow bright as you hunted for words to convey something of the magic you found in the books I gave you! I loved it, too, when you listened and stared down at the floor, because I knew then that I'd drawn you closer. Lee? Why are you looking at me like that?"

What happened next he wouldn't let himself think about until afterward, and then only as a series of detached and discontinuous moments. There was the shattering of china as her cup fell to the floor, the surprised yowl of a cat, the warmth of her breasts beneath the dressing gown. And then, his face rammed against the sofa among the loose-flowing eddies of her hair, he was inside her, and all his fear and shame were gone.

She lay very still beneath him. It seemed to Lee that no time had passed at all. Through half-closed eyes he was aware of the books and bric-a-brac, the embroidered loveseats, the objects of her life.

"Your skin smells like talcum powder," he said when his breath had begun to come more evenly.

She took his face in her hands. "I want to talk some more. We have to talk."

He shook his head free and laid it against her hair again. "I don't want to hear about you and Quinn. I don't ever want to know anything."

"All right. We won't talk about it, then."

It was late when he left her house. The rain had stopped, and a blurry, pale moon was visible through the trees. As Lee walked slowly through the drifts of light the houses on either side of the street seemed very far away from him, and the branches that bent and trembled as he slipped beneath them seemed to have faded into nothing once he stopped and turned to look. He touched the wet curl of a leaf and it slid out of his grasp. Even the pavement seemed to be gliding out from under him. But by the time he reached his doorstep he had grown quite comfortable with the night. Its formlessness seemed to be proof of something, though he couldn't have said exactly what.

12

Buck Jonas had been in her kitchen for thirty minutes now, slurping coffee out of a saucer and gesturing with his big, knotty hands as he kept up his incessant talk. If she had answered the door he would never have gotten in, but Louise had been there. Louise had let him in, Louise with her strained and uninterested politeness and her inability to be forceful except in some rabbit-like way. Foot-thumping, Beatrice was thinking, that was all her aunt was capable of. She couldn't even defend her own arbitrary ethics, she was so obsessed with niceness, with appearing to do things right.

"Well, like I was saying, it was when me and Quinn was working for the phone company. We was supposed to lay a cable through some property that joined Mrs. Battle's—God rest her soul, I hope she's hanging on a Christmas tree for orphan kids in hell—that joined the ole lady's yard. Well, Quinn didn't cotton to her hollering at us, so he hollers back at her, 'You goddamnned bitch, we got orders from the phone company!' Mrs. Battle goes inside and about two minutes later we get a call on the line from the supervisor. 'Quinn,' he says, 'we can't have our employees talking to people like that. You got to go and apologize to Mrs. Battle.' So Quinn goes and knocks on her front door. 'Sorry I talked so ugly, ma'am,' he tells her. 'But I thought you was a fucking bush!' "

165

Buck burst into raucous laughter. Louise turned bright pink and stared down into her coffee cup.

"Buck," Beatrice said, "would you do me the kindness of waiting out on the back porch?"

She stood up and was going to open the door when she saw Lee and Tony coming up the steps. At least, she thought, she would be rid of him now, though she didn't like the idea of his taking her sons fishing.

"It took you two long enough to locate your rods," she said as Lee and Tony came into the kitchen.

"We had to dig through a lot of junk in the garage," Tony answered, flopping down on the window seat to examine his tangled line. "All those cardboard boxes of stuff you're giving to Goodwill."

"What stuff?" Louise asked. "You know, Bea, it's not a good idea to get rid of too much."

"Why not? After they're married he'll buy it all for her again." Lee looked at Beatrice and gave her a flippant smile.

She decided to ignore the comment. Turning back to her aunt, she said, "But the house will be overflowing after Hunt moves in. Anyway, there were three closets still full of Mother and Daddy's things."

"But not of Quinn's," Lee said. "You threw all of his things out."

Buck pushed back his chair and touched Lee lightly on the arm. "Come on. Them bass are waiting on us. Thanks for the coffee, Bea. And I guess I ought to congratulate you."

After he and the boys had left, Louise got up to make more coffee. Beatrice had hardly touched hers. Listening to Buck's obsessive reminiscing had made her nervous. And he was so dirty, she was thinking, and not just in his talk.

"Shall I heat up those sweet rolls, Bea?"

"Not for me," she answered. "One gust of Buck was enough to take my appetite away."

"Yes, I agree. It's awful to have to be around him."

Beatrice was about to ask Louise what she had let him in for, but she didn't feel like fighting a battle already lost. Turning toward the window, she looked out at the lawn, which was beginning to wither in patches. The summer had been an intensely hot one. Even the pines seemed to have lost their brilliant, constant freshness, though possibly, she thought, after having seen the Black Forest she simply didn't appreciate them the way she once had. But no, it was more than the recent dry spell and more than her trip to Europe. It was her whole way of seeing East Texas, and that had been changing over many years. Her girlhood vision of a lush and fertile country was one which was almost completely alien to her now. She thought back to the times she had saddled her father's gelding and ridden northward across the hills, over land that was clay-red beneath the pine needles, between stands of spruce and always pine, out past the lake and on to the upper branches of the river. What had she been thinking on those mornings when the light was green beneath the trees, when the sun shone down translucent through the dew on the high, still needles? Even the memories had paled for her. It occurred to her that soon there wouldn't be anything but a memory of memories, an eternal present without any light or color. She took a sip of coffee. It was cold. She pushed the cup away.

"Have you decided what sort of announcements you'll want to send out?"

Louise came back to the table and set down a fresh pot of coffee. She had a plate of sweet rolls in one hand.

"No," Beatrice answered. "I haven't thought about that at all."

"Well, sooner or later you will. I guess you've been so busy sorting through your closets you haven't had time to think about annnouncements. Have you decided on the date yet?"

"September."

"September!" Louise exclaimed. She gawked at Beatrice. "But that's next month! That's ten days from now!"

Beatrice was aware of a tightening sensation around her mouth, as though, involuntarily, the muscles which controlled her facial expressions were going haywire. She reached for a cigarette from the pack beside her cup.

"You're smoking too much these days, Bea."

"I know it."

167

"Then why don't you stop?"

"I don't want to, Louise. It's as simple as that, okay?"

"You know you're ruining your health and yet you go ahead and do it?"

"True. Correct. Right on the mark."

Beatrice narrowed her eyes, letting her gaze blur momentarily. Yes, she thought, sometimes her aunt looked amazingly like a rabbit.

"Well, is it going to be early or late September?"

"Mid."

"Mid? Before or after Lee's birthday?"

"What difference does that make?"

"Well, because I know Hunt wants to buy Lee a car, and it wouldn't be right, somehow, before he was really in the family."

Beatrice inhaled, slowly this time. Louise watched her over the rim of her upraised coffee cup. When Beatrice let out a breath of smoke her aunt gestured in her direction as if she was about to make another attempt at scolding. But no words came. The gesture hung absurdly on the air.

"The wedding will be the eighteenth," Beatrice said.

Louise looked relieved. "Everything should work out, then. I just didn't want there to be any incongruities. That *is* a word, isn't it—incongruities? But have you arranged things with the Reverend? The eighteenth is a—yes, it's a Saturday, and you know Saints and Sinners goes on until three o'clock. Oh, I imagine he'll be—"

"Louise." Once again she felt the muscles around her mouth begin to tighten. "We're getting married in Dallas. And we're going to a Justice of the Peace."

As Beatrice had expected, it took a moment or two for her words to sink in. Louise seemed puzzled at first. Then, reaching across the table, she patted Beatrice's hand.

"Of course. You don't want to make a fuss about it, do you? Second marriages are always a little awkward—so many things are involved. You know, in my opinion, Bea, it's a good thing Hunt doesn't have a family. There are less complications than there would be if he did, though it's a shame I can't give a nice dinner

168

for new nieces or nephews or whatever. That would be so much fun. Doesn't he have anyone, Bea?"

"A ninety-eight-year-old grandmother who's a vegetable in a nursing home."

"Well, couldn't we invite her—"

"I'm sure she drools," Beatrice said, cutting her aunt short. She glanced up at the clock. It was almost time for her appointment with Alberta.

"Well, how does Hunt feel about living in Toombs Mill?"

"With the lake development expanding he should stay busy for a year or two. After that there's every chance we'll move to Dallas. Now please, Louise, don't keep interrogating me like this. I don't want to think about things any more than I have to."

After Louise had gone Beatrice emptied the coffee pot into the sink. She took the cups and set them on the counter, feeling herself moving as awkwardly as if the weight of her thoughts had settled in her limbs. It was a heaviness, a bloodlessness, the sensation which had come over her. She stubbed her cigarette out among the coffee grounds in the sink, thinking about the remnants of her parents' lives which she had stuffed in cardboard boxes and put in the garage for Goodwill. They had been useless personal things, things that had done nothing but clutter the upstairs closets, so she knew it wasn't a surge of sentiment over old golf clubs and knitting needles which had left her feeling this way. And though she had asked herself a thousand times why she had finally agreed to marry Hunt, she had come to realize that one way or the other it was all the same to her. Married or unmarried, it didn't really make that much difference.

So it wasn't the marriage business either, she told herself. It was something else, something which Lee's taunting had called up in her. How was it that when she looked at him most intently, into the very depths of his eyes, he always seemed to be withdrawing from her, willfully, into an ambiguous distance?

Letting cold water run, she scraped the coffee grounds into the disposal. All of a sudden she found herself wishing she were prone to nightmares. Because soon, she knew, the day would come when she would wake and find her world altered to fit one.

"Nervous?" Hunt asked, nodding his approval as Beatrice turned toward him. She was wearing the dress she had bought especially for the occasion, a V-necked green linen one which heightened her coloring and called attention to the long, elegant line of her throat. As Hunt watched, obviously pleased with the way she looked, she took a hairbrush from her make-up kit and went over to the dresser.

"Of course I'm nervous. I've smoked a pack and a half of cigarettes since we got here last night."

Hunt laughed and touched her shoulder. She went on brushing her hair, his resonant laughter lingering in her ears. Hunt's laugh had many times been described to her as pleasant. People said it was a spontaneous sound, a sound full of tolerance for the little annoyances and importunities that were part of his busy life. It was a confident laugh, they said, one which inspired belief in an ability to make everything work out. Yet as Beatrice listened to it now she was conscious of a desire to tell him to get away from her.

"What is it you're nervous about, Beatrice?"

She looked at him in the mirror. For all his good looks, his was the face of a man who was fifty-five.

"When I'm seventy-two you'll be ninety," she said matter-of-factly, setting the hairbrush down.

Hunt bent and kissed her neck. "When you're seventy-two you'll still be beautiful."

"Yes, but what will I do with a ninety-year-old husband?"

"Hide his crutches if you don't want him chasing you around."

She reached for an earring, but Hunt caught her hand and turned her toward him.

"Anything you want, Beatrice. The best restaurants, the best hotel—we're going to make this a weekend to remember."

"Anything I want?"

"Anything."

"I'll think about that," she answered.

He drew her to him. She could smell his cologne and the champagne they had had with breakfast, and she wished he would let her go. But when he finally did, it was only to hold her slightly away from him and gaze at her with a puzzled expression in his eyes.

"Sometimes you really do make me feel old," Hunt said.

The telephone saved her from replying.

She was thinking about Quinn, she realized as she watched Hunt talk. She was remembering how different she and Quinn had been from the couple in this hotel room. Quinn had been thirty when she had married him. His moody, reckless laughter had had nothing to do with happiness, and he had smelled of sweat and whiskey instead of cologne and good champagne. Those were the only things she, on that other day, had wanted to give herself up to, the only things she had ever imagined could evoke love in her for a man. But she herself had been much younger then, too naïve to comprehend the ruthlessness with which she had gone about finding someone who could make her love him for the very qualities she was bound, in the end, to deny. And now, it seemed, she was incapable of giving a man anything. Hunt's kisses, the almost tangible affection in his laughter, made her want to turn him wrong side up, like a fish, in order to expose the shocking, vulnerable flesh of the underbelly.

She continued to dress, listening without interest to Hunt's end of the conversation. At last he put down the telephone.

"That was the Porsche dealer. I think we'll be able to get just what we're looking for. The man says he has a loaded orange one ready to be driven off the showroom floor. That *is* what you think he'll want, isn't it?"

"Lee's always liked orange," Beatrice answered.

"How would you like to drive it home on Monday?"

"I'd love to."

"I'll call the dealer back." Hunt picked up the receiver again, smiling at her across the room.

"It will be quite a surprise," she murmured, looking down at her hands. In the light from her make-up mirror the nails shone bright as brass.

"What's that?"

"I said it will be quite a surprise, that's all."

The manicurist at Neiman-Marcus had done all right, she

thought. Frost pink with just a hint of deeper color. And the dress was perfect, and her hairset still looked fresh—she couldn't understand what was the matter that she wasn't enjoying herself. The night before, during dinner, she had tried to get very drunk. The idea of getting married had suddenly seemed ludicrous, and she had had to focus her attention on something in order not to laugh. So there she had been, carefully dressed and flawlessly made up, sitting in an expensive restaurant reciting the alphabet to herself. When the alphabet hadn't worked she had concentrated on the names of presidents, and when that hadn't worked she had decided to get drunk. Drunkenness hadn't come, though, not even after liqueurs, and she had spent the entire evening holding back hysterical laughter.

What had set her off was a little scene, almost a pantomime, between the waiter and Hunt. It had been nothing out of the ordinary, but somehow the seriousness with which the two men performed a ritual from which she, as a woman, was automatically excluded struck her as comic. It also struck her as symbolic of the fact that her life had begun to seem out of her control.

"Your wine," the waiter said.

He opened the bottle and set the cork on the table. Hunt lifted the cork to his nostrils.

"No," Hunt said, shaking his head almost imperceptibly.

"Sir?" The waiter's voice was soft, incredulous.

"Smell that."

The waiter sniffed. Then Hunt sniffed again. They looked at one another and in the pale, shaded light their noses were identical. Their solemn expressions, too, were exactly alike. Tweedledum and Tweedledee, she thought. The Bobbsey twins. Then the waiter went out apologizing and came back with another bottle. As he was pouring she had to keep saying the name of the restaurant over and over in her mind to make sure she didn't laugh at them. After that she had started on the alphabet and then on the presidents, and finally she had downed her wine so quickly Hunt had looked at her amazed.

"It's all set. We can pick the car up early Monday."

Hunt came toward her and put his arms around her again. This time she closed her eyes, trying not to think.

"Is something the matter, Beatrice?"

"No," she said.

He lifted her face to his. "Let's go get married, then."

"Yes. It's what we came here for."

On the way down she mentioned casually that he might have some trouble persuading Lee to take the car.

"Trouble? What do you mean?"

"He's been saving money for almost two years to buy a car. In fact, I'm certain he already has one picked out."

She glanced at his face as they got off the elevator. It showed hurt and surprise, the mouth hanging open a little, the creases above his eyebrows beginning to gather themselves together. He raised both hands and swept them through the sides of his hair, and then he stopped and looked down at the carpet in the middle of the crowded lobby.

"Beatrice. Why didn't you tell me?"

"I didn't think you'd want to know."

"My God," Hunt said slowly, without fervor.

The rush of the elevator had left a strange feeling in her stomach. She began to hurry in the direction of the street.

"Beatrice, I don't understand you," Hunt said as they stepped through the glass doors. "Why didn't you tell me that?"

"Maybe you can persuade him to take it anyway. Louise seems to think you can."

"No," Hunt said. "The last thing I want is to make Lee resent me. That's a long time for a boy to work for something. And Lee's stubborn. He's got a lot of pride."

"Just like his father."

Hunt didn't seem to have heard her. "No, I don't want him to resent me. Can't you understand that?"

The morning was bright and windless. Beatrice reached into her purse and put on her dark glasses, for in the store windows and on the sidewalks everything seemed to glitter.

173

At first it seemed as though things were working out. Her life in Toombs Mill hadn't changed much after she had become Mrs. Martin Hunter Holt, and Hunt seemed to be happy. She still went to the Women's League meetings and the bridge-club parties with the same amount of boredom, though people like Ann Cramer and Liz Beale had dropped the note of insinuation in their voices and consequently Beatrice could no longer take satisfaction in acknowledging disapproval. For the way she led her life now was acceptable to Toombs Mill. That, if anything, was what had changed; it was as though the years since Quinn had left had been erased from people's minds, as though they had never whispered about Ron Prather, or the Houston executive, or Hunt. Or Leon Pugh, she recalled wryly, letting her thoughts wander back to that September afternoon. Over nine years had passed since she had taken those hundred-dollar bills in exchange for an hour at the Violet Crown. And what would have happened if she had refused that offer, if she had been properly shocked when Leon Pugh had let his hand crawl up her leg? Maybe Quinn wouldn't have left her. Maybe the unnamable urge that had made him lift the shotgun and press the trigger would never have been realized. Maybe Lee wouldn't have learned to hate her. Maybe a lot of things, she thought. But the afternoon with Leon Pugh remained, irreversible in whatever consequences it had had. It couldn't be undone either now or in the future. Yet the odd thing was that the purpose, the desire, had gone. Now that she had married Hunt and her life had become acceptable, the nine preceding years were exhausted in their fulfillment, so that it was hard even to guess what the original impulse had been.

Beatrice stopped flipping the pages of the magazine in her lap. To hell with it all, she told herself. Nothing was so simple. She couldn't trace nine years back to a single act. Maybe if she hadn't had children or married Quinn or been born in Toombs Mill or been born at all. Maybe if the whole world were different. But it was absurd even to think like this—she had done what she had done and that was that. None of it mattered anyway, because it was all behind her. The only thing that mattered now was keeping

Tony from hating her as Lee did. And keeping her life in order, as much as that was possible.

She got up and went into the den, where Tony was watching television. At fourteen he was lanky and still freckled, and his sandy hair was perpetually a mess. Beatrice sat down next to him on the sofa, looking closely at his face.

"Hi, Mom. What's for supper?"

"I don't know yet. Maybe when Hattie finishes ironing I can get her to make chicken and dumplings. Would you like that, darling?"

"And lemon meringue pie. And coleslaw."

Tony turned back to the television. Beatrice studied his expressions as he pushed the remote-control button and tried to make up his mind which channel he wanted to watch. At least, she thought, he wasn't moody. At least she could count on that.

"Have you done your homework this weekend?"

"Nope. I'm stuck."

"Stuck? Is it algebra? Maybe Hunt can help you."

"It's English. I have to write a theme, and I can't think of anything to write about. Lee said he'd help me, though. He gets ideas from all those books he reads."

"Yes, he's been reading a lot ever since he had his accident. Does he talk to you much, Tony?"

"Huh? Wait a second. . . . Never mind, there's nothing good on anyhow." He punched the button again and the television picture went off. "Sure, he talks to me all the time."

"But I mean does he talk to you about anything important? What does he think about these days?"

She hadn't intended to ask that. But it was on her mind. Lee was on her mind. It bothered her that he was so secretive. These days, when he wasn't shut up in his room reading, he was never at home, and she had no idea where he spent his time. He no longer practiced sports. He rarely ran the chipping machine for her uncle any more. And on more than one occasion she had seen him talking to Rita Cobb, who—she had no doubt about it—had influenced him.

"Oh, I guess he thinks about books. And now that he's bought his car I guess he thinks about it a lot. I don't know, Mom. Why don't you ask him?"

Beatrice found herself recoiling from Tony's question. She didn't want him to know how difficult it was for her to answer him, and, more than that, she didn't want her curiosity to create a gap between Tony and herself. Because even though Tony and Lee were very different, Beatrice recognized a powerful bond between them, the bond of children whose parents' life together had never made their own lives easy. When she finally answered him it was with a lightness she didn't feel.

"Oh, he doesn't want to talk to me."

"Maybe Hunt knows what he thinks about."

"I doubt it, darling. Hunt hasn't had much time to spend with either of you recently. But that eccentric English teacher—"

"She's the one he gets his books from. Miss Cobb, you mean."

"Yes. Miss Cobb."

Tony got up and stepped out into the hallway. Beatrice noticed how tall he was getting. He would be taller than Quinn had been, she thought, taller than his brother.

"Hey, I hear Hattie in the kitchen."

"I'll ask her to make chicken and dumplings and coleslaw for tonight."

"And a pie."

"Yes. A pie."

Tony went into the kitchen. Beatrice watched him go, wondering whether she had seen something communicative in his face or whether it had been nothing more than ambivalence.

As the fall passed, Beatrice began to pay more attention to Lee's comings and goings in the house. Sometimes, late at night, she would go quietly up the stairs and find him asleep with the light on, an open book beside him on the bed. Other times, when he walked in the back door after spending an evening out, she would be waiting for him in the kitchen with a cup of hot chocolate ready on the back of the stove. Yet she didn't question him. She merely watched and waited and fought against the moments when some accident of light and shadow would seem to blur his features and single out his fine, dark eyes. It was the eyes that

176

reminded her of Quinn. For, like his father's, Lee's eyes revealed a self-absorption which made her think he was preoccupied with some frighteningly private irony.

"You worry too much," Hunt would say, trying to reassure her.

"You don't understand," was her usual answer. Or often she would ignore him. Because more and more Hunt seemed to be receding to the periphery of her life. She ate with him, slept with him, lived with him, yet when she really let herself acknowledge his presence, it was only with annoyance.

"No, you don't understand at all."

Her words hurt him, and she knew it. Nevertheless, she told herself, it was the truth. Hunt would never be able to understand what she had suffered for Lee, just as he would never be able to understand what she had been through with Quinn. And there was no explaining it, no possibility of making him understand. She and Hunt, it seemed, belonged to two entirely different ways of seeing, two separate streams which could never be united. They couldn't even be reconciled, because there was no bridge from one to the other, no canal of connection. And Hunt's way of seeing was as fatal to her as her own had been for Quinn. For Lee, too, Beatrice thought. Though it had taken her a long time to realize it, she knew now that there was a gulf between Lee and herself which could never be crossed without some sort of fatal wrenching of the vision.

Yet she had to try to reach him. She had to. On those nights when she waited up for him to come home she often found herself tense with anticipation. If only she could strip away the past, strip away the future, and leave the naked presence of the moment disentangled. For the moment was sharp and stark, unfettered, and completely without consciousness—what would the two of them have to tell each other if they found themselves stripped down to the razor edge of oblivion? Would there be nothing but hate and more hate? Would the love, the only spark of real exchange, have long since exhausted itself, plunged into the vortex of its own consuming flame?

That was what she was afraid of. Yet until she confronted Lee she couldn't quite bring herself to give in to the certainty of what she knew.

It was mid-December when Beatrice found out about Rita Cobb. The night was cold, and there was a hint of snow in the twilight sky, although as evening turned to darkness it became evident to Beatrice that the snow wouldn't come until far into the night.

"What do you think, Mom?" Tony asked, pressing his face anxiously against the window. "Are we going to get some snow? Those big clouds over the river look like a sure sign of it."

"Probably not until later," Beatrice answered. She went to stand beside Tony. He was still looking out into the street.

"What makes you think that?"

"When I was a girl my father taught me how to read the sky."

"You've never told *me* things like that," Hunt said from across the room. He and Tony had brought home a Christmas tree, and Hunt was in the process of tightening the screws on the metal stand. "I always imagine you as a girl sitting over there at the piano, with a white dress on and pink ribbons in your hair."

Hunt laughed as he said it. But the teasing note in his voice had left her completely cold, and she felt no impulse at all to turn around to him. The smell of pine seemed to pervade every inch of air. Without thinking, Beatrice let herself be carried backward to the moment when she had stood beside her father watching a norther blow in across the hills. Beyond the pine trees the blue had gotten thinner. Then there had come an indiscernible vagueness, as of too much wind and light descending on the spot where she had stood. . . .

"What do you think of the tree, Beatrice?"

"The tree? Oh, it's fine. It smells good, at any rate."

"Where are those decorations you told me you'd dig out of the closet?"

With Tony right behind her, Beatrice crossed the room and began walking down the hall. When she came to the closet where she stored a collection of odds and ends, she jerked open the door and reached for a cardboard box. Then, handing it to Tony, she told him, "I'm going out for a while, darling. Take the decorations in to Hunt for me, will you?"

"Aren't you going to help us trim the tree?"

Beatrice looked into Tony's face. She could see the disappointment written there.

"Later, Tony. Right now I just have to get out for a while."

"Are you coming back soon?"

"Of course. And will you tell Hunt I'm going?"

Tony took the box. Beatrice went quickly into her bedroom, picked up her coat, and went out into the night.

Powdery flakes fell and melted on the windshield as she drove along Main Street, not sure where she was going. Turning on the wipers, she watched the errant snow smear and then appear again, seeming less like snow than bits of dirt detaching themselves from the sky. No, she thought, the storm wouldn't come until later; this was just the beginning of what doubtless would be a full-fledged blizzard.

As she drove she found herself looking for Lee's car. He had told her he was going out with friends, but he hadn't mentioned where. And as usual she hadn't questioned him. If she let herself seem too curious he almost always clammed up, and sometimes he would simply tell her that what he did was none of her concern. So, keeping her eyes open, wondering, Beatrice drove around for a while. Cars full of teen-agers passed her, the headlights tracing shafts of yellow, but she didn't see Lee's car among those cruising aimlessly through the streets. At last, after circling the courthouse for the fifth or sixth time, she pulled over beneath a streetlamp and turned off the engine. After a few moments she began to get cold. The snow, though still sporadic, was falling a little more thickly, in flakes that no longer melted as soon as they touched the glass. Beatrice reached for the ignition again. It was then that she saw the patrol car pull up in front of her and Johnny Kingman step out into the light.

Beatrice waited, one hand on the key. When Kingman tapped on the glass and shone a flashlight in her face, she rolled down the window to ask him what he wanted.

"Nothing much." He stabbed the air with the light, letting the beam play across the dashboard. "I just saw your car and taken a mind to find out how you was getting along. What are you out on a night like this for anyhow?"

The flakes of snow were beginning to dampen her cheeks. Tense, impatient, she started to roll up the window, but Kingman stuck the flashlight in.

"Would you get that thing out of my face!"

"I reckon you better ought to move over, Mrs. Lawrence. We got a few little things to discuss here."

It outraged her that she could do nothing to stop him from getting into the car. Nothing, she thought, unless by a sudden surge of will she turned the key and stomped on the accelerator. And then, of course, he would be after her.

"What do you want?"

Kingman opened the door and Beatrice slid over in the seat. In the light the streetlamp cast through the intermittent snow, she saw Kingman's pocked, heavy features come together in a squint.

"Like I said, we got things to discuss."

"To my knowledge, I have nothing to discuss with you."

Kingman let out a kind of laugh. "You know, you look real sharp-faced, Mrs. Lawrence. Like a she rat that catches the smell of a trap."

"Would you come to the point?"

"All right." He switched the flashlight off and then on again, directing the beam around the car. "I'm aiming to make me a little pocket money."

"That's no surprise. But what do you think you're going to hold over me?"

"I know something about that boy of yours." At the sound of his words rasped out in the darkness, an irrepressible contempt began to twist a knot inside her. But she was frightened as well, and for a moment her nerve almost failed her. Then, collecting herself, she told him to go on.

"It could be real bad for you, Mrs. Lawrence. Folks finding out about him and Rita Cobb, the way they've been going on ever since your boy was fifteen. Why, just think what would happen if the whole town was to know Lee Lawrence had been humping that skinny schoolteacher. He ain't even legal yet, and she's more than twice his age. It could even get into the courtroom if the law was to take an interest."

Kingman looked over at her, his eyes narrowed, his downturning mouth ready to wrench itself into whatever expression Beatrice's reaction might demand. But she was incapable of responding. Even though his words seemed, momentarily, to be the anchor of her awareness, reducing whatever thoughts she had to their furtive, insistent cadence, they were meaningless, nothing but undifferentiated sound. She looked out at the street, where the flakes were beginning to stick now. The lamplight was rapidly becoming hazier, beginning to suffuse the dark silhouette of the courthouse with a whitish, unreal light. Yet beyond the town, she knew, in the stillness of the pine stands, that same unreal light was bringing the features of the landscape into startling clarity.

Kingman moved in the seat, flicking the flashlight off. Beatrice could feel his anticipation. It was almost tangible, as tangible as her fear.

"You can pick up a check tomorrow. Now get out of my car."

He reached for the door handle. Then he said in a tone of dispassionate evenness, as though delivering a memorized set of lines, "Money's the devil's promise, ain't it? But I knew a woman like you would understand. You see, I never did forget about you and Leon."

13

THE HIGH WHINE of the branches followed Lee along the trail.

He could feel the needles beneath his feet as he ran steadily on, keeping the pace his body knew and could sustain, it seemed, forever. The constant rush of cold and pine, that influx which left him confused but uncaring whether he was hearing or smelling or feeling, seemed to lift him beyond himself. He felt as though he was being carried on by nothing but a pure, visceral joy, as though his running was setting up a centripetal motion that let him take in the night at every breath: out there, dimensionless as night on the front of a Christmas card, the world was silent, while inside in some whirlpool of the senses the cold, the stars, and the smell of pine were raging.

The trail stretched on. Buck's house was on a strip of uncleared land along the creek, and in winter when the rains came the low-water bridge was often flooded, making it impossible to get in and out by car. This year the rains had turned the creek into a river; Lee had parked along the highway and taken the trail across the hills.

The ground was dark and sloping, the trail gashed by a gulley whose sides weren't unfamiliar to Lee even in the darkness, for he had come this way on countless winter evenings in the past. He located the black opening up ahead of him, calculating how long it would take to reach it, and then without breaking stride he followed the trail as it disappeared over the edge and reappeared on the other side. When it was only another quarter of a mile to Buck's house he stopped. He leaned one hand against the trunk of a pine and let his body droop, exhaling at last the night's three dimensions. After a moment he began to breathe more quietly.

Ahead of him through the pines the lights were on. He began walking toward them across the frozen ground. The hulk of the house came nearer. He hurried across the clearing and climbed the steps to the porch. As he reached the door and lifted his hand to knock he heard Buck calling out to him.

"Who's there?"

"It's me, Buck."

The door was jerked open.

"I ain't seen you in a coon's age. Well, don't just stand there, get your ass inside!"

Buck led the way into the kitchen. The tiny room, as always, smelled of gun oil and bacon grease. Lee sat down at the table, glad to see his friend but uncertain how to tell him what was going through his mind.

"You should come out to the house more often. You ain't been here all fall."

"I know."

Buck nodded. Then he got up and lit a match beneath the coffee can on the stove. Lee guessed the coffee was a day old and bitter, but when he was handed a cup he took it, grateful for its warmth.

"Go on. Drink it. It ain't got no eggshells in it."

Lee sipped the coffee slowly, leaning on his elbows. Outside, beyond the circle of the clearing, the pines were scraping their boughs into the wind. He listened to the sound they made, conscious of its nearness and its almost devouring insistence. The next moment he was wondering why things always seemed to be what they were when, even as you looked or listened, they were becoming something other.

"Something's eating you," Buck said, picking up a sliver of wood and sticking it between his teeth.

Lee didn't answer. Buck looked directly at him, contemplating him with the same detached intensity as he had the wood sliver the moment before.

"I said there's something eating you."

Buck's eyes were pinpoints of blue light. Lee found himself staring hard at him, half believing that simply by willing it he could make those eyes tell him everything. How was it hate could grow in you like the budding leaves in spring, tender and unobtrusive, until finally it burst forth full-blown? How was it you could look, day after day, out your window and be sure of what you were seeing, and then suddenly, one afternoon, you could see nothing because those same leaves blotted out everything? And even though you had known it would happen, you were as surprised as though it had happened overnight?

"Yeah," Lee said, looking away at last. "Yeah, there's something eating me, all right."

Buck waited. Then he reached to turn up the gas heater in the corner. Lee had begun to shiver; even with his jacket on, the room seemed cold.

"That better?"

"Thanks."

"Come on. You came here to talk."

The low, sibilant sound of the gas was all Lee could hear. He strained to catch the wind outside in the pines, but it had died momentarily. Then, shrugging, he looked down at the ring his cup had left on the rough wood of the table.

"I'm going to leave Toombs Mill."

When Buck didn't respond Lee pushed back his chair and stood up.

"Well, what do you think of that? Why don't you tell me what you think? I could go down to the gulf and get work on a fishing boat. I could head up to the panhandle and see if I could find a job on a ranch. There's all kinds of things I could do. Hell, I could even go out to the oil fields. They'd take me. I know they'd take me. They can always use another roustabout, and it's not like I've never spent any time around a drilling rig. Well, what do you think, Buck? What do you think of me going out to the desert?"

"A man's got to act according to his lights. My lights ain't your

184

lights. Your lights ain't my lights. You want to be wrong-gaited, don't act according to your lights."

"What kind of an answer is that?" Lee cried at him.

Buck stood up slowly, facing Lee across the table. "It ain't. But if you think I'm mistaken, you can tell yourself I'm getting senile."

"Shit!"

"Listen to me. Quinn had his own reasons, but you ain't him. If you're set on going to the desert, I hope you've sat down and figgered out why. Because if you think standing on the same sand will tell you why he put that shotgun to his head, you're wrong. It don't take a desert for a man to lose hisself in distances. And it don't take that kind of endlessness to teach a man to hate. So you ought to ask yourself what your reasons are for being there. Figger that out—and then go your own gait."

Lee fumbled with the sleeve of his jacket. "I'm leaving. I'm going out to the oil fields."

"Then I got nothing else to say about it. You know you're welcome to stay the night. It's late to be burning sleep."

He reached for the switch and the bulb above the table blinked off. Lee was left by himself in the light of the gas fire as Buck began moving toward the hall.

"I'm leaving here tonight!"

His friend's broad back disappeared around the corner. Lee stared for a moment at where it had been in the doorway, trying to comprehend Buck's absence and yet at the same time wanting not to. At last he took a step toward the doorway. There was no sound coming from the hall, nothing but that absence which with each passing second deepened his sense of self-awareness so that once again he seemed to be breathing in a vacuum. The world outside him was a universe with no dimensions, while inside his senses churned; for a long time Lee stood with one hand against the doorjamb, trying to slow his roaring insides. He found himself becoming dizzy and had to lean against the wall and tilt his body forward so that he would manage to keep on breathing until the room, the cold flowed out of him. Then he heard the floorboards creak.

"Buck?"

He wanted to run, but his body wouldn't obey the impulse. His hands seemed a long way out in front of him in the darkness. At last he managed to push away from the doorjamb, and his fingers found the coarse boards of the wall. He let them guide him until he sensed he had gone far enough. Then he reached forward, giving the door a jerk. It flew open, and he felt the bitter inrush of the wind.

Not that she wouldn't let him put his head in her lap and cry until the crying had exhausted him. Not that she couldn't comfort him. But he knew it could never be the way it had been before something definitive had occurred inside him and he had come to know that her hands weren't to be trusted. He could no longer even imagine the way it had been then, before her touch had become coercive and her love something other than what it seemed. He had been torn from that time too long ago for memory to even matter.

"Lee?"

Her voice startled him. He had known she was there in the split second before he heard her say his name, but the sound of it confused him. As she turned to go into the kitchen he let the back door slam shut. A moment later he followed her. She went over to the stove, opened the oven, and turned to him again, but he walked quickly past her.

"I've kept your supper warm. Would you like hot chocolate?"

"I'm going to bed."

Lee felt her watching him as he went up the stairs.

It wasn't until he was in his room, surrounded by his books and his sports equipment, that he could let himself feel safe. Closing the door, he lay down on the bed and breathed the room's familiar smell, wondering how much cash he had on hand. The next moment he jumped up and began to rummage among the clothes on the closet floor. Pushing a pile of camping gear aside, he located his metal lockbox and dialed the combination. Inside were two twenties and some ones. Lee stuffed the bills into his pocket and was about to close the closet door when his eyes fell on the rifle Quinn had given him when he was ten. For a brief moment he hesitated. He hadn't touched the gun in years. Then, lifting it out of its corner, he unzipped the cover and took the rifle in his hands.

On the shelf above he found a half-filled box of bullets. With the blood pounding in his ears he reached for them and filled the chamber. Afterward he put the box in his athletic bag, along with a shirt and a pair of Levi's.

When the house was quiet Lee stepped into the hall to see if the lights were out downstairs. As he leaned over the banister and peered into the darkened dining room he saw a faint glow coming from somewhere at the back of the house. Automatically he began to listen for the almost inaudible contact between his mother's slippers and the hardwood floor. It was a sound he had grown accustomed to listening for, the soft tread which would a moment later become her eyes peering in through a crack in his bedroom door. But everything was quiet. Unless she, too, was listening somewhere in the house.

The clock below him chimed eleven. At last he went back into his room, picked up his bag and rifle, and turned out the light above his bed. He made his way softly down the stairs, stopping in the dining room to listen for his mother again. Nothing. He waited a moment longer. As he began to move toward the hall the butt of the rifle knocked against the table, and he heard the door of his mother's room open. Then the dining-room light came on and she was standing in the doorway, while everywhere he looked the room's reflecting surfaces were throwing her image back and forth. The polished panels, the mirrors, the rows of punch cups and hurricane glasses glittering like ice—he couldn't get away from her.

"I was going to make us some hot chocolate."

She said it in that ruthlessly even, curiously repressed tone of voice, her eyes fastened on the bag and gun. Lee looked at her standing there in her robe with her hair curling down around the white skin of her throat. Without surprise he realized she was mocking him.

"I told you I didn't want any."

"Why not? You always liked hot chocolate. Surely you aren't keeping secrets from your mother, are you?"

"I've kept secrets from you ever since I can remember. But you'd tear me up just to find out what's going on inside me, wouldn't you? No, I've never told you anything. I don't have to tell you anything now."

"Who ever said you had to tell me everything? You don't have to tell me anything you don't want to. But I'll find out. I always find out. Like that business with Rita Cobb—didn't it ever occur to you I'd find out you've been fucking her?"

Lee felt his fingers tighten on the gun. The mockery in her voice made him want to hurt her, yet he was surprised at how calmly he managed to reply.

"Nothing you can say is going to get to me. You're a whore, Mother, and everyone in Toombs Mill knows it. Don't think marrying Hunt has made a difference, either—all you've done is confirm what people already knew. Anyway, you're getting older. You'll need that contract if you plan to keep trading on your cunt."

He watched as she drew her lips together in such a way that her face became ugly. Then, catching sight of her reflection, she relaxed into a momentary smile.

"You seem to forget my father left me with an income."

"Yeah, but it's never been enough for you, has it? And it hasn't always been money you've sold yourself for, either. You know how to whore in other ways."

"Why do you want to hurt me, Lee? My God, how I've loved you!"

"You call that crap you've forced on me love?"

"Don't you remember those dawns we used to spend together? And all the nights I stayed up holding you, keeping you from nightmares? After Quinn's death all I wanted was for you to be like other boys your age, the boys who hadn't seen what you had seen, who played football in the afternoons and came home tired and hungry so their mothers could feed them and tuck them into the clean sheets on their beds. Later on, of course, you brought

188

home trophies and ribbons and gave them to me with your kisses, but there was never any joy in it for you. You did it only to appease me. You didn't love me, Lee. Or maybe you did, how am I to know? Didn't I once find my wedding ring among a stack of erotic pictures?"

She was laughing at him. Almost before he realized what he was doing he had cocked the rifle and aimed it in her direction. She opened her mouth to scream as the gun went off, the bullet shattering a row of crystal punch cups on top of the buffet.

"You're lucky I didn't kill you," he said, resisting himself as if he was slamming a door against a storm. But the still, fixed look in her eyes was fascinating. He had never seen her so frightened before. "So you found out about Rita. Well, here's something else for you. Before she was with me she was with Quinn for a long time, too."

His mother's face seemed to crack open. Lee felt the drops of sweat on his forehead. He wanted to say more, but the sound of tires on the driveway cut him short. It was Hunt, he could tell by the slamming of the car door.

"Go let him in," his mother said. "The chain is on."

"Go let him in yourself."

Lee watched the panels of her robe swirl around her thighs as she turned and hurried down the hall. He went into her room then. Sitting down in a wicker rocking chair, he began, slowly, to rock. Not that he had intended to tell her. It had just come out, because except for killing her it was the only defense she had left him.

"Lee, put that gun down."

When he looked up he saw that Hunt wasn't wearing his usual careful expression. The gaze which had always struck Lee as an attempt to appear both sympathetic and noncommittal was gone, and the line of his mouth had lost its promise of amiability. All of a sudden he felt sorry for Hunt. He stopped rocking, keeping the gun balanced on his knees.

"Stay out of this, Hunt."

"Hand the gun to me."

"For your own sake, stay out of this. In just a minute I'm going

189

to get up and walk out of this house and you won't ever have to see me again."

"You leave here and your mother and I will have the State Police after you within two minutes. Now give me the gun."

"Don't waste your breath on him," his mother said. She was just beyond the doorway. Hunt was between them and so Lee couldn't see her, but he imagined she was just standing there, absorbed in her own unwillingness to accept what he had told her and yet somehow managing to reconcile herself without surrendering anything. "If he's going to shoot me, he'll do it anyway. Just like he shot his father."

For a single moment Lee wasn't sure what was happening. He jumped up. The rocker turned over with a violent crash. All words, all thoughts had dissolved and fallen away from him, and there remained only a small, fiercely burning particle which relied on nothing but hatred for its strength.

"You bitch! How can you say that?"

"Because he failed you. Your father failed you."

She backed away from him and leaned against the wall. Lee could see the rise and fall of her breasts and the play of shadows on her hair.

"What you mean to say is he failed *you*. And you were glad about it, weren't you? You always wanted him to believe he was a failure."

His mother didn't answer. Hunt crossed the room and came toward them, looking angrily at Lee.

"Beatrice, why don't you let me talk to him quietly and reasonably, without all this accusation?"

"Because you haven't the faintest idea what it's all about," she answered, turning on him. "So you might as well keep your rationality to yourself. This family never understood anything but accusation anyway. His father made sure of that. Not a day passed that he didn't come up with something to accuse me for, something dredged up out of the pit of his own bitterness. Because of him our lives have been hell, and if you can't understand what hell is, Hunt, you might as well get out of here. You, too, Lee. I think you're right about leaving—I want you to leave. No, maybe what

190

I really want you to do is blow your brains out. It would give me a chance to feel sorry—this time I might even cry."

"Beatrice!" Hunt shouted.

He put a hand on her shoulder, but she pulled away from him. Even from where he was standing Lee could see the vein throbbing in the center of his mother's forehead. Her breath began to come faster. Then, clenching both fists, she screamed.

"Take her other arm and let's get her to the bed!"

"No," Lee said slowly. "She doesn't want anyone to touch her."

Hunt stared at him as he picked up his belongings and started down the hall. Pausing only long enough to make certain his keys were in his pocket, Lee opened the back door and hurried down the steps.

He pulled up in front of Rita's house and turned off the engine. Lighting a cigarette, he slid down in the seat. It was almost midnight, and though he was jittery with nervous energy, a subtle exhaustion was overtaking him; he was beginning to feel like a swimmer who in spite of his most determined efforts is drawn continually backward by the tide. Nevertheless, after a moment Lee mashed out the cigarette, got out of the car, and went quietly into the house. Going straight to her bedroom, he entered and closed the door behind him. She was lying in bed with her back to him. Next to her on the nightstand the lamp was on.

"Rita?"

She mumbled something, turning toward him and pressing her face into the pillow. He hesitated. Then, slipping out of his clothes, he got into bed beside her.

He found her strange, not as he remembered her. The days which had passed since they had last been together seemed to have left her small and childlike, while he had always thought of her as womanly. It was bewildering the way she clung to him, tightening her arms around his neck with a kind of willful sightlessness. As she lay curled against his chest it seemed to Lee that all she wanted was to make herself small, to feel his arms around her and the rhythms of his breath. And when, after a long sleep, he awoke and came fully to himself, realizing that hours had gone by and the windows were gaping with gray, she stirred, looking at him with wide, uncomprehending eyes. He could hardly bring himself to kiss her, she seemed so strange to him.

"You've never stayed all night before."

"No," he said, looking past her toward the windows.

It was the dawn's palest hour, when the first light was falling. The pines were still, their black-green limbs misted here and there with gray. As Lee looked at them it occurred to him that he must seem strange to her, too: an odd distance had arisen between their bodies. He suddenly wanted to be gone from her, to get away from the tangle of hair upon his shoulders, away from the clinging which only seemed to drive them farther apart. Pushing back the covers, he got out of bed.

"Are you going?"

"Yes."

"Will I see you again this week?"

"I've decided to leave Toombs Mill, Rita. I don't know when I'll be back. Maybe never." He shrugged, beginning to get dressed. "We couldn't have kept on anyway."

He tugged at his socks, thinking how brutal that had sounded. And yet he sensed that voicing what he knew was less brutal than keeping quiet.

She reached for his wrist, forcing him to look at her. "So you know your mother found out."

There was a long pause. At last Lee pulled away from her and began searching for his shoes among the clutter of female clothes on the floor beside the bed.

"Yeah," he said.

"She went to the School Board. They requested my resignation two days ago."

"She knows about you and Quinn, too. I told her."

"When?"

"Last night."

"I guess it doesn't matter now."

"No," he said.

She sank back onto the bed, curling up as she always did. Lee recalled the times how, after they had made love, she had gone to sleep like that with her head on his arm. When he had slept as long as he had dared he had always been careful to withdraw his arm gently. Invariably, though, he had waked her, and as he had dressed she had lain there watching him, her knees drawn up, her hands beneath her chin. Like now. Only before he had never found this attitude disturbing.

"You're really leaving?"

"Yes," he said, glancing at her once and continuing to dress.

"Because she found out?"

"No. For lots of reasons."

When he was bending over her to say goodbye she locked her arms around him.

"Wait. Don't go yet."

"I have to."

He disengaged himself as gently as he could. But she grabbed his wrist, so he sat looking at her from the edge of the bed.

"Where are you going?"

"To work in the oil fields."

"Oh, Lee." She moved her head against the pillow, and a tangle of hair fell over her eyes. "You know, sometimes I wonder if I was ever able to get beyond myself and my own illusions about him. I remember once I thought I understood who he was. I told myself he was spiritually isolated, and that that was the reason he was fascinated by the desert, because he found his own situation taken for granted in every rock and bit of sand. But I didn't know how much that was my myth about him and how much it was the truth."

"I told you I never wanted to talk about you and Quinn."

"You were part of it all," she went on, as if she hadn't heard him. "Part of what I sometimes admitted was only myth-making. I was looking for Quinn in you. And now you're going to the desert, too."

"So?"

"It makes me wonder, that's all."

He pulled away from her. Then he headed for the dresser to

get his jacket. Halfway there he stopped and turned toward the bed again.

"What are you going to do now that you won't be teaching here any more?"

She pushed her hair out of her face. Only then did he see that the spark of whatever it was that drove her had withdrawn completely inward.

"Oh, I don't know. Stay in Toombs Mill for a while. Visit those exotic places I told you about, the ones that don't exist."

He took his jacket, quickly, and went out of the house.

As Lee drove through the empty streets it occurred to him that he had eaten nothing since lunch the day before. The Corner Café was just ahead of him. He pulled up next to the steps and hurried in to the counter.

"Toast and coffee. And, Brenda, could you make me a couple egg sandwiches to go?"

"You're up early," she said curiously.

"Yeah, I am, I guess."

He ate quickly, thinking only of leaving Toombs Mill behind. It would be a relief to get out on the interstate. Driving alone, smoking cigarettes, listening to the radio—yes, he told himself, it would be good to be on the road. He finished the toast and took a last long drink of coffee. When Brenda set a sack beside him he laid a dollar on the counter and left.

The morning was cold and tranquil, without a touch of wind. Along the streets yesterday's ice was grayish in the low places, where the week's rain had collected and not yet turned to mud. Today, though, promised to be sunny. It would be a heatless, brassy sun, Lee knew, but nevertheless he was glad the sky was clear. Driving would be easier, and he wanted to be the other side of the Pecos River before dark. He huddled down into his jacket as he headed toward the interstate. He wished he had thought to bring his gloves. The heater wasn't working properly, and even the defroster didn't seem to be doing much. When he reached the access road he pulled the car over to the shoulder and scraped the film of ice from the windows. Then, warming his stiff fingers in his sleeves, he got back behind the wheel and turned west onto the entrance ramp.

For the first fifty miles he sped along at seventy, his jacket pulled over his fingers to keep them from going numb. Brenda's coffee had jolted the sleep out of him, and he had the egg sandwiches to chase the remnants of hunger away; he put a cigarette in his mouth, trying clumsily to light it while he kept his hands inside his sleeves. At last it took fire. He leaned back in the seat, concentrating on the road and wondering how far he was from Dallas. The farther from Toombs Mill he got, the darker the land became, and after an hour of driving the stands of pine along the interstate had disappeared. There were more farms now, more fences, and it occurred to him that the countryside was more uniform and anonymous than he remembered its having been when he had driven west with his father years before. Lee recalled how he had sat up on his knees in the seat of the truck, staring out at the houses of people he didn't know and imagining what it was like to live other, different lives. Unwrapping an egg sandwich, he ate it quickly; Brenda had put too much catsup on it, and the soaked bread was falling apart.

Halfway to Dallas, Lee stopped for gas. The attendant, a tow-headed boy a few years younger than he was, gazed at him vacantly when he told him to fill up the tank.

"Better not," the boy said.

He rolled the window down a little farther. "What do you mean?"

"Your rear end smells like gas."

The boy stepped out of the way and Lee opened the car door. He too could smell gas. Going around to the back, he checked the cap on the gas tank, and then he bent and peered beneath the car.

"A leak in the fuel line. I must have hit a rock on that stretch of gravel where they were working on the road a few miles back. Is there someone else around—someone who could get me some copper tubing?"

The boy rubbed his nose with the rough back of his hand. "We don't stock no parts. And Daddy ain't here anyhow."

"Is there someone who could tow me, then?"

"There's a Shell station up the road a piece. They'll tow you into town to a mechanic for a dollar a mile—cost you about twenty dollars plus the service charge."

The boy rubbed his nose again. Lee watched him, exasperated by what seemed to be a display of nonchalance.

"Twenty dollars is a lot of money. You mean there's nobody else around? You're here all by yourself?"

"Yep."

A camper had driven up and was honking for him to get out of the way. Jerking open the car door, Lee got inside and pulled the car over to the garage. As he was getting out again, trying to decide what to do, he heard a female voice shouting at him from the camper.

"Hey, you! Yeah, I mean you!"

Lee looked at the woman leaning out the window. Her hair was in pigtails, and as she waved at him the sunlight reflected off her rings. Curious, Lee crossed the driveway and approached the camper. A fat man in a fancy leather jacket was showing the towheaded boy where the gas tank was.

"You having problems?" the woman asked, leaning on her elbows and smiling down at him. "If you need help, you know, all you have to do is ask."

"I don't know what you could do unless you happen to have eight feet of copper tubing handy."

"You making whiskey or something?" the woman said, giggling and tossing her pigtails.

"I'm having car trouble. A ruptured fuel line." He thought for a moment, letting his eyes roam over the camper. "Say, is there any chance you could tow me up the highway? That kid says the nearest town is about twenty miles."

"I don't see why we can't. This baby pulls our T-bird, so it ought to pull your little Chevy. Yell around to my husband there. Wait, here he is—hey, come over here, sugar."

The fat man came around the side of the camper. "What's the trouble?"

"He says his fuel pipe's got a hole in it—wasn't that what you said?—and that he needs someone to tow him into Greenville. We can do it, can't we?"

"Sure thing. We got a hitch on here and everything, so just roll her over and we'll get you all set up."

When they had secured his car to the back of the camper the fat man opened the door and ushered Lee inside. The interior was elaborately decorated, equipped with a bar and oversized stereo speakers.

"Well," the man went on as he slid behind the wheel. "We ought to get to know each other. This here's Toots, I'm Slick, and back there's Mrs. Weatherall."

"Slick's granny," Toots explained, giving Lee a wink.

He turned around to see a thin old lady lying on the berth beneath a mound of quilts.

"I'm Lee Lawrence."

"Welcome aboard, Lee," Slick said. He grinned and touched his fingers to his hat. "There's beer in the cooler if it's not too early in the day for you. And I hope you like music, because Toots and Granny and me have our hearts set on listening to some tunes —isn't that right, girls? Say, where did you tell me you were headed?"

"Calvary. Out past Fort Stockton."

"What a godawful part of the state that is."

The music came on, a blaring of steel-edged strings which made all attempts at conversation impossible. For twenty miles the sound kept up. Though Lee was glad he wasn't expected to make small talk, he felt as though he had had a corrosive poured into his veins when the speakers suddenly went silent and all he could hear was the ringing in his ears. It was then that he realized he had been thinking about something, though he couldn't remember exactly what it was.

The woman was talking to him.

"—no point in leaving you off at Greenville when you have to go through Dallas anyhow. And the garage is just off Stemmons, isn't it, sugar?"

"Sure thing. You come on to Dallas with us, Lee."

He thanked them and settled back into the seat as the stereo came on again, louder than before.

By mid-morning they were approaching Dallas. Lee watched the buildings on the horizon grow from toy blocks into skyscrapers, aware of new smells and the glint of sun on steel. Traffic was moving at a measured, mindless pace. Slick guided the camper into the exit lane and sped around an embankment. The next moment they were swooping toward an underpass, and Lee recognized the stretch of road where Kennedy had been assassinated. Beyond it was the textbook depository, a dirty brick building with rows of darkened windows.

"Oswald was on the fifth floor," Slick said, turning the stereo off. "See the red circle on that window? That's where he aimed the rifle from."

"You can buy a picture postcard of it if you want to," Toots put in.

Slick slowed down as they passed, and Lee obliged them by feigning interest. Yet something inside him was revolted by the ease with which these people seemed to let themselves forget that a man had died here. He found the acceptance on their faces more disturbing even than the curious fascination in the eyes of the old woman, who had raised up on one scrawny elbow beneath the quilts.

"I don't think I'd want a postcard, thanks."

They left the assassination site behind and began weaving through the downtown traffic. Lee kept his eyes out for the garage. He was anxious to be on the road again, and without the burden of strangers' company.

"There it is, sugar. Isn't that tan building it?"

"Yep. Well, Lee, looks like this is the end of the line. Though you're welcome to come home with us and watch the SMU-Baylor game."

"Thanks," Lee said as the camper came to a stop. "You've been a lot of help, but I really have to get going."

"Well, what do you think the odds are?"

"I'd put my money on SMU."

Slick grinned, leaning over to give his wife a light punch in the

198

ribs. "You hear that, Toots? Me and Granny are going to win some money. Say, you ought to come on home with us, Lee."

"I appreciate the offer, but, like I said, I've got to go."

"You aren't really heading out to West Texas, are you?"

Lee looked impatiently at the man. "What's the matter with that?"

"Nothing. It's just that except for the desert there's not a goddamned thing out there."

14

LEE WATCHED THE GREYHOUND BUS lumber into the terminal. Stuffing the remainder of a stale candy bar into the nearest trash container, he waited for his departure to be announced before he pushed open the doors and went to stand behind the yellow line. It was almost midnight. Cold air was blowing through the terminal, while in the street beyond a fine drizzle was dampening the pavement. Lee felt in his pocket for his ticket, mentally counting how much money he had. Then he saw that the driver was signaling passengers to board. Lee picked up his athletic bag and hurried over to the bus.

"Sorry, sonny, but you'll have to check that." The driver was looking at him stubbornly from beneath the visor of his cap.

Lee hesitated. Then, realizing it would be futile to argue with the man, he turned around and went back into the station. The clerk at the ticket counter urged him to hurry as he handed him his claim stub.

"This near Christmas you may not find a seat. And you won't be pulling into Calvary until eight o'clock in the morning."

The bus was crowded, but Lee managed to find an empty seat. He slid all the way over, turning up the collar of his jacket and thrusting his hands inside the sleeves. Beyond the window people were coming and going with nervous movements, grappling with luggage and hurrying to avoid the cold. Inside the station, he knew, the drone of massed voices continued, while somewhere

200

behind the bus a man was shouting obscenities in hoarse tones. Lee turned abruptly away from the window, noticing the trace of fog his breath had left on the glass.

So far things hadn't gone the way he had expected. In his eagerness to leave Toombs Mill he hadn't stopped to think beyond his own hasty fantasies—the possibility of having car trouble hadn't entered his mind, and it had never occurred to him that he would spend the afternoon wandering in and out of pawnshops trying to come up with enough money on his rifle to have the necessary repair work done. It was with a feeling of relief that he had gotten rid of the rifle. Yet by the time he had gone back to the garage the mechanic had upped his price. Angry and frustrated, Lee had offered to sell the car to the garage owner, and when the man had quoted a price he had agreed immediately, even though his better judgment had warned against it.

But at least, he told himself, he was on his way again.

The bus ground into gear and lurched toward the street. Reaching into his bag, Lee took out an apple, soft in places from having been in a bus-station vending machine too long. As he bit into it he realized he didn't want it. Yet he ate it anyway, looking out the window as the bus took him past blocks of hazy neon and into the backside of the warehouse district. Soon it was crossing the Trinity River, headed almost directly west. Lee glanced at the faces of the couple across the aisle from him. They were young people, not much older than he was, and on their entwined fingers he could see identical wedding bands. He found himself staring curiously at the girl, whose eyes were unblinking and whose rosy underlip was held firmly between her teeth. From time to time the boy would lean over and whisper something in her ear; at last a hand reached up and turned out the overhead light, leaving Lee to himself on the opposite side of the aisle. And so, breathing slowly, dreaming, falling through sleep only to wake once more, he watched the succession of city and darkness.

After Fort Worth the intervals between stations grew longer. As the lights of nameless towns slipped away into the night, claimed by the rolling, bare-hilled land only to become visible in miniature a few miles farther on, Lee realized he was in prairie country. If it were day, he knew, he would see cattle grazing on the long brown slopes, and windmills thrusting themselves skyward from ridges or shadows, from stark, grassy swells or from some broken feature of the land. For here—for the first time—the countryside gave warning of the regions that lay ahead. Neat plowed fields were behind him, far in the eastern distance, and even farther away were the pine forests and the tangled, clay-red river bottoms. Miles and miles would pass and there would be nothing now but prairie, its billowy openness framed at every turning by a continually shifting backdrop of mesa or divide or hill. Farther on, past the one-hundredth meridian—that landmark whose invisibility had been a mystery to him as a child—the prairie would flatten out. Horsehead pumpjacks would appear on every horizon, and the sky would begin to tilt away from view. Except for mesquite and salt cedar, trees would vanish altogether. The landscape would become more rugged, shelving down toward the Permian Basin in a series of bluffs and washes, and it would be impossible to escape the feeling that the disorder on the surface was a dim but powerful shadow of the chaos that lay below. For the Permian Basin marked the heart of oil country; the breaks and folds, the slabs and shelves, the violent, frozen rhythms of faulty lime and sandstone—the signature of an inland ocean was carved larger beneath the surface, in an ancient, unread hand.

And so his mind carried him on, past the lights of Abilene dancing a line from north to south, past the twin cities, Midland and Odessa, where the lines of unwinking lights on the drilling rigs illumined the horizon from one end of its arc to the other. Soon he could visualize the sand flats of the trans-Pecos country, still as remote as he remembered, as fire-licked and as washed out. Here there were fewer boundaries for the eye to achieve. Here distance was less real because it seemed to be all around you, exploding everything that promised to contain sight. The bluish mountains could as easily disappear in a haze of dust as a mirage could break into reality with a range of dream peaks, and the solid-seeming clouds that passed over, trailing shadows, often split open without warning. It was a glaring, windy place, this corner of the earth beyond the Pecos River. A sun so bright it forced you to squint and a wind harsh enough to turn your neck raw through your collar—you didn't come here unless you wanted to be exposed, for sun and wind followed you everywhere. Soft, hidden things were alien, were things that couldn't last; the elements forced them into the open, there to die or become real, to shrivel and blow away or to learn new ways of surviving.

All of this passed through Lee's mind as, awake or dreaming, he looked out at darkness or at the bright outlines of cities or at the sudden, confused fluorescence of near-empty bus-station waiting rooms. Once he opened his eyes to find they had come to a standstill on the side of the highway. Fighting to keep his disordered awareness from slipping back toward sleep, he rubbed his eyes and leaned into the aisle.

"What's going on?" he asked the boy across from him.

"Police roadblock. A trailer jack-knifed up ahead."

"Did the driver say how long we can expect to wait?"

"Not much longer. They've almost got the road cleared now."

Lee let his head drop back onto his chest. After a few minutes he heard the sound of the engine, and then the bus began to vibrate. For several hundred feet they proceeded slowly, scarcely seeming to be moving. Lee opened his eyes and looked out again. Police flares were penetrating the dark with their reddish fires. A ring of men was gathered around the truck, the cab of which was partway over the embankment. But soon the bus was picking up speed again; Lee let himself be lulled by the rhythm of the highway, and the next time he opened his eyes it was morning. Across from him the boy and girl were sleeping, folded into each other's coats. Colorless sunshine was slanting across their faces. Lee noticed that both of them looked dulled and tired, and he wondered how much farther they were going.

"Next station Fort Stockton," the driver called. "Your only rest stop before El Paso."

When the bus had come to a stop he got slowly to his feet. The hours of cramped half-sleep had left him hardly rested, but he knew he would feel better after he had stretched his legs and gotten something to eat. A blast of chill air hit him in the face as he stepped off the bus. It pierced the wool of his jacket and seemed to cut him to the bone, and, turning his face away from the wind, he hurried inside the station.

While the other passengers crowded into the cafeteria, Lee walked up and down in the drab waiting room, trying to make up his mind whether to eat there or to wait until he got to Calvary. Finally he decided to go in. As he approached the glass partition he saw there was only one place left, at a table where the busboy, a Mexican, was drinking coffee. Although hunger was turning his stomach inside out, he wasn't sure he wanted to share a table with someone and be forced into conversation. Yet even while he thought this some part of him was protesting: he was lonely, and it might be good just to talk. So, going into the cafeteria, Lee loaded his tray with toast, milk, and two orders of chicken-fried steak. Then he crossed the room and sat down next to the Mexican.

"Say, could you hand me the salt and pepper?"

The man turned toward him, his face drained of expression. It was then that Lee realized they didn't speak the same language, and he saw himself as this man must see him—as a stranger, an alien here where he had wanted for so long to come.

So this time, pointing, he tried to recall some of the Spanish his father had taught him.

"Dame, por favor."

The Mexican pushed the salt and pepper shakers in his direction. "Hablas español?"

"Solamente un poco."

"Tengo que trabajar como un negro para vivir como blanco. Nunca tengo un día libre."

He got up, leaving Lee to his breakfast. It occurred to Lee then that for the first time in his life he was on his own.

Even with the clatter of silverware and the rise and fall of voices, Lee felt as though a silence had opened around him once he found himself sitting at the table alone. Now there was no possibility of conversation to keep him from his thoughts, from apprehensions of what the day might bring. The first thing he would have to do when he got to Calvary was get a room in a hotel, and after that he would have to ask around for work;

finishing his steak, he tore a piece of toast in half and sopped it in what was left of the gravy. All of a sudden he remembered how, when he had been younger, his mother had warned him against doing that in public, and almost involuntarily he set the toast back on the plate. His thoughts wouldn't let go of him then, for a kind of duplicity seemed to be revealing itself in even his most insignificant actions. He felt a loathing for everything his mother had taught him; picking up the toast again, he crammed it into his mouth. It was as if nothing belonged to him, nothing was his own —as if he was infected with her emptiness. Or as if her emptiness had revealed to him an empty space inside himself.

Lee pushed his plate away and sat very still for a while. If only someone would walk up and say something, ask for a light or even for the time, the enormities of self wouldn't seem so limitless. But no one approached him; he stood up and began to walk back toward the bus.

He pressed his face to the glass. The bus began to lurch through the streets of Fort Stockton, past weathered storefronts and blocks of unpainted houses. As they turned onto the interstate, leaving the few strips of hoarded greenery in the distance, Lee looked out at the dingy and tenacious varieties of scrub which were the only living obstacles to the sweep of naked space. Here and there mesas rose, geometrical as temples. Ribbed inclines of sand, culminating in knolls or hillocks, presented shifting surfaces to the wind. The bunchgrass, the cactus, the groping fingers of yucca and mesquite—beyond them the land merged into a sky whose gray light wasn't caused so much by cloud as by a hazy glare across the sun.

It was when an arroyo flashed by him, and next to it a furiously spinning windmill, that he realized where he was. Just up the highway was the old gas station where he had spent four Christmases and almost as many summers; soon he could see it, the stark, colorless stucco making the building appear to be something that had sprung up out of the salts of the desert floor. As it came closer Lee could make out the overhang sagging toward the pumps as well as the squares of boarded windows. The bus passed the driveway, and Lee turned in his seat, gazing behind him at the open door. It was swinging back and forth in the wind, which was whipping the sand into miniature cyclones on all sides of the building.

Twenty miles up the highway the bus slowed for the turn-off to Calvary. Lee let himself look briefly at the sign that read SUNDOWN MOTEL. Then, realizing he was near the end of his journey, he sat up straight and felt in his pocket for his claim stub.

It was cold mid-afternoon outside the hotel window. As Lee looked down through the parted curtains at the still streets and the low, squat warehouses beyond the railroad tracks, it occurred to him that somewhere out there his father was buried. His eyes searched the rows of houses on the far edge of Calvary, the collection of roofs and fronts whose gaunt aspects seemed to insinuate the leanness of the lives they sheltered. The cemetery, he recalled, had been nothing more than a few parched acres wedged in between the highway and a line of barbed-wire fencing which marked the point where the town ended and the sand began again. Exactly where it had been, though, he couldn't say; turning away from the window, he went over to the bed and lay down with his hands behind his head.

A feeling of uncertainty had come over him as he had stood looking out. There was something about Calvary which wasn't the way he remembered, something frighteningly anonymous about the town. A sense of countless repetitions in other, uncounted places—the drafty buildings, cracked sidewalks, and silent, crumpled faces gazing in denial at the sky—left him with the suspicion that there was no mystic significance to place. His father was buried just down the road, but what did that have to do with him? Why had he come back here? For, like the hotel room in which he found himself, this West Texas town belonged neither to him nor to the next person. It was reproduced in a hundred thousand other towns, and not even the surrounding landscape could convince him that, as his father once had told him, place was something you couldn't scrub off your soul.

It was a new thought, and Lee wasn't sure what to make of it.

Because what had he come all this way for if there was really nothing for him here?

He looked at his watch. It was two thirty. Though the sun's glare was still gray-tinged, the veil of the sky seemed to be less dense. He got up, stretching, and reached for his jacket. Then he opened the door and made his way down two flights of stairs, not meeting anyone until he reached the lobby. There he saw the desk clerk, a hawk-nosed man of indeterminate age, shelling a sack of Spanish peanuts.

"Afternoon," the clerk said without stopping what he was doing.

"Afternoon," Lee replied.

"Staying long?"

"I haven't decided yet."

Lee watched the man empty a handful of peanuts into his mouth.

"Raw goobers. Good for the stomach."

Lee nodded. The man's hand disappeared inside the sack.

"I might stay awhile and then I might not. It depends. Say, where's the cemetery in this town?"

"You got kin?"

"Nope."

"Dead, then?"

Lee nodded again.

The clerk cracked a shell and laid the nuts out on the counter. "It's back toward the highway."

"What's the fastest way to get there?"

"Cut through the wrecking yard and keep on walking."

Outside, Lee realized the wind was blowing harder than it had been earlier in the day. He felt its pull and toss, like the movement of an insistent hand continually grabbing at his clothing, as he walked along the main street in the direction of a sheet-iron structure. He had seen the building from the hotel window and, recalling that it housed a wrecking yard, had headed for it as soon as the desk clerk had finished his peremptory direction-giving. Its metallic roof gleamed dully beyond the wood and stucco storefronts, deflecting the light that penetrated the vague cirrus clouds above; he kept on walking, one hand pressed to his forehead to shield his eyes from the blowing dust, the other crammed into his jacket pocket. From time to time he had to stop and wait, his head ducked down into his collar, as a gust caught him in its vortex and threatened to lift him off balance before it released its hold. At last he reached the wrecking yard, where a Texas flag was flapping wildly on a wire hung from a window. Lee glanced up at it as he passed by, wondering if that flapping was the town's only continuing activity. For all around him the streets were empty. There wasn't a moving vehicle anywhere in sight, and in none of the windows along the street had he seen even a single face.

He cut across the back lot of the wrecking yard, skirting the jagged piles of parts as well as the acres of car carcasses rusting beneath the years. The ground was loose here, seeming to slide out from under him in wave on sandy wave. Lee felt his feet sinking and the cold air creeping beneath his clothes, and for a moment he almost turned around and ran back toward the hotel. In the street, at least, the buildings offered some protection from the wind; beyond the line of barbed wire that marked the edge of town there was nothing but open space.

He found the cemetery before he had walked much farther. It was an unidentified plot enclosed by strands of wire that sagged to the ground where no posts were supporting them. As he made his way among the graves whose names and dates were sad reminders of an inevitability which even they couldn't explain, he felt his knees go tense. Death itself seemed almost tangible. He could sense it, he thought, in the oblique, dark rise of the derricks above the symmetry of their shadows, in the broken bits of liquor bottles, in a shell placed on a grave. And yet he knew that none of these things was death, or even the image of it; death was nothing but itself, its own universe and meaning, and any sign by which it spoke to him was guaranteed to be false.

When he came to his father's grave he stopped and looked down. The stone was leaning slightly forward. Though it had gone gray from rains and freezes, the lettering was still clear. The granite itself seemed ironically hard and weighty, surrounded as it was by other, older markers, slabs of sandstone whose lettering had sloughed off. Lee gazed at the patch of ground where no grass had ever grown, wondering what significance it held for him. A kind of throbbing was beginning in his throat. He swallowed, closing his eyes against memory, and when he opened them again the pain had gone. The wind was tugging at his jacket, making him shiver a little. He jammed his hands down farther in his pockets. Then he turned and walked back toward the opening in the wire.

Before he knew it he had reached the highway. Looking up, he saw the Sundown Motel just ahead, and without letting himself stop to think he began walking toward it. A flatbed truck passed by him on its way to the oil fields. It stirred the air to violence on both sides of the highway, leaving it perceptibly thicker in its wake. Lee coughed and rubbed the grit from his eyes. Then he hurried on toward the motel parking lot, where a handful of cars was parked in front of the line of doors. As he passed the coffee shop he felt someone watching him. Turning around, he saw a boy peering out through the big plate-glass window, beneath a sign telling him he could get a gizzard platter for a dollar and fifty cents. For a moment he paused, returning the child's stare. Then it crossed his mind that maybe the room on the end was occupied, and he turned his thoughts to what he was about to do. But there was no car parked in front, he could see that at a glance. Going over to the last door, he put his hand on the knob and gave it a sudden twist.

What struck Lee first was the utter blankness of the room: its furniture was clean and dustless, its carpeting functional, its walls painted a nondescript cream color. The bathroom, too, was so uniform and sterile that he had a fleeting sense of no one's ever having used it. But gradually, as he looked around him, he began to realize that this room was a minimum world, deliberately put together to keep the mind from response. Hundreds of people had come and gone, though not one had left his mark. And if it hadn't been for the lamps whose bases were replicas of covered wagons and the plaster-of-paris cactus, painted green, on the wall above the nightstand, there would have been nothing about this room which he would have recalled at all; he went over to the bed, where the smell of freshly laundered chenille met his nostrils, along with a faint odor of furniture wax. No, he told himself, there was nothing he recognized here.

As he was turning to go he saw a movement just beyond the open door. Then the boy whose face he had seen through the coffee-shop window stepped away from the side of the building and came into the room.

"You ain't supposed to be here," the boy said.

"Go on. Get out of here."

"I'm going to tell."

Lee took a step in his direction and the child began to run. Lee watched him disappear inside the coffee shop, and then, closing the door behind him, he went back out to the highway.

Another flatbed truck was approaching. Lee stood on the shoulder with his thumb out, and a hundred feet past him it came to a rattling stop. He ran toward it. When he reached the cab the driver rolled down the window.

"How far you going?" Lee shouted.

"All the way to Fort Stockton!"

"Can I ride with you up the road?"

"Climb on back—just don't ruin my day by falling off!"

He hoisted himself up onto the empty bed of the truck, holding on as best he could as the driver stepped on the accelerator. The man riding shotgun waved, and he waved uncertainly back. The truck gained speed quickly. From time to time the driver seemed to be playing some sort of perverse joke, for the wheels would veer dangerously near the shoulder when they approached an arroyo or a ragged upthrust of sandstone. Once, gripping a steel crossbar, Lee braced himself against the icy wind and half stood in order to bang on the rear window. The driver waved at him, and the other man turned around and laughed, but the truck neither slowed down nor moved closer to the middle of the road. The next moment it began to zigzag across the white line, and Lee was thrown over on his side. Cold and angry, he crawled back toward the cab and didn't try to stand up again for the next fifteen miles. It was only when he saw the gas station flash by him that he clutched the crossbar and pulled himself cautiously to his feet.

210

When he began to beat on the glass this time the man who had laughed at him tried to wave him down, but he kept on pounding. Soon the truck slowed. When it came to a stop he jumped off.

"You hung on real good!" the men whooped. "We thought for sure we'd lose you!"

But Lee was already running down the embankment, scattering sand and loose stones.

The gas station was completely deserted. As he approached the pumps he saw that they had long been out of order. On both of them the glass was broken, and one looked as though its sides had been smashed with a sledgehammer. Lee stared at the rusty dents, wondering who had put them there. Then he went around to the far side of the building, where the heads of giant thistles were nodding into the wind. They were dry and colorless, but even though winter had blasted the life out of them, there was something intentional in the motion of the heads. As Lee began to poke among the oil drums and the remnants of machinery and tires, he stayed away from the thistles and their grotesque pantomine. They made him feel uneasy, as if he were being spied on. Yet after a while the thistles ceased to bother him; he pushed his way among them and continued to probe the sand, looking for something, though he couldn't have said exactly what. Broken glass, the handle of a jack hammer, bits of rusty tin, bent nails— at last, not knowing what else to do, he lashed out at the thistles with a stick. The heads swayed and nodded, and at the same moment two tumbleweeds began a halting dance on top of the rotted tire pile. Lee watched in fascination as the spiny fingers caught and loosed, until the wind lifted them roofward and finally out of his sight.

Going back around to the pumps, he propped the door open with a cinder block. Inside, the building was dim. Light was tunneling in through an opening in the boards, but not enough that he could see anything more than the vague outlines of boxes. As he felt his way around the cramped room that had once been both store and office, it occurred to Lee that someone had been using it for a storage area. He couldn't remember his mother's ever having mentioned that the property had been sold, but when he knelt and struck a match it occurred to him that it had been. The name HUMBLE and a serial number were stamped on the sides of the boxes. Standing up again, he lit a second match. This time he held it above his head and surveyed the stacks along the walls. The boxes seemed to contain grease or parts for drilling rigs; the match went out and he struck another. Its flames bounced off the low ceiling, illuminating the lettering on a box of explosives. Lee backed away, almost stumbling as a rat ran beneath his feet. Once again the room went dim. He began to feel for a light switch, but when he found it nothing happened. The next moment his fingers were brushing against a pile of magazines. In the flickering of another match he saw they were covered with powdery dust, and when he picked one up and held it to the flame, it took fire easily. Taking another magazine, he lit it, too, and then he lit another one, until he had a makeshift torch. Just beyond the pile of magazines was the door leading to the back. Holding the flames carefully, Lee put one hand on the knob.

At first there was nothing. Then he saw the trash and rags and smelled the thin, acrid odor of dust. The magazines were scorching his fingers. Stepping back through the doorway, he lit three more, and then he stomped the others out on the concrete.

Not that he had expected to open the door and find the room as he remembered it. Yet it was startling to find it so uninhabitable, so close and so heavy with the years; he gazed around him at the gray, peeling walls where the remains of spiders' catches, mummified by the desert air, were dangling. A slow dread began to crawl through him. All his impulses directed him to turn around and go back outside, but at the same time he felt divided against himself. At last he hurried into the bedroom, where he let the torchlight play along the floor and walls. Here, too, trash was strewn around. A jar, unbroken, was sitting on a window sill. As the light struck dully through the stains on the glass, he could see at the bottom an accumulation of unidentifiable filth, and he felt his stomach turn. He shone the torch in the other direction. An assortment of pipe wrenches caught his attention then. When he took a step toward them he noticed a huddle of clothing against the wall. It seemed to be lying as it had dropped there, and on an impulse he bent to pick it up. A flat black beetle, shiny as a button, crawled from the spot where it had been hiding and disappeared into a crack. Lee held up the piece of clothing. It was a Levi jacket, faded almost white now. The fabric was stiff and wooden between his fingers, and it had long since lost the suggestion of any human shape. He let the jacket fall, listening to the dry sound it made against the concrete. Then he closed the bedroom door and went back to the pile of magazines.

If he could only pry the boards off the windows and let the wind scatter the dust and send the spider webs sailing—his father had always told him that close, confined spaces made him feel like death. Suddenly Lee shut his eyes, imagining the whisper of strange wings against his cheek and feeling the soft, deceptive darkness settling down around him. No, he thought, his father hadn't wanted to die. There had been too many nights spent under a sky brilliant with stars, their blankets tossed down on the top of a mesa, while below them the desert was spread out like an enormous empty room. And even though they had been no more than two blots in all that immensity, Lee couldn't believe his father had accepted willingly the bitter omnipresence death offered.

When he breathed in again, the air was dry. Remnants of nightmare were unraveling and beginning to drift through his mind. Though his fear was without a name, it clung to him, so that he was forced to acknowledge its presence. And then in a single instant his mind, split into two, recognized and refused what he saw, the reasonable, coherent self watching the consuming frenzy of the other and teetering on the edge of admitting the truth of the other's fear. Yet, searching among memories of words, that self could come up with nothing, and in spite of what it willed it let the other have its way. Only what Lee felt was more like waves breaking in accord with their own rhythms than a deluge of whatever it was reason had been unable to name. Kneeling beside the magazines, Lee took them one at a time, set fire to them, and tossed them into the back room.

The trash on the floor began to send up yellow tentacles. Lee kept on tossing the magazines, watching in fascination as the flames shot toward the dry walls. Though the stucco itself refused to catch, the paint flared and crackled, peeling off the walls in long, floating streamers which the fire fanned outward in the moment before they turned to smoke. As Lee gazed into the room, he watched his shadow grow. Soon it was enormous, black and undulating on the wall. With an effort he kept himself from crying out. He felt light and giddy, excited by the irrevocability of what he had done in that instant outside of will, and certain he had been right in doing it. For at the center of the fire there seemed to be a perfect calm. It was as though the flames touched on some constant depth far below the roaring surface, a place where everything was clear as glass and he could see into himself. On the opposite side of the room a mound of newspapers burst into life. Lee was drawn out of his thoughts, and though the smoke was like a drug in its power to make him want to lie down and enter a phase of pain in which there was no consciousness, he began to back away. By now the entire room was filled with fire. Through a half-world of smoke and shapes he could see that the flames had found the bedroom and that the boards on the windows were beginning to blaze. For a moment longer he continued to stand in the doorway, his eyes fastened on the fire as it writhed upward to make new finds. And then a shattering of sparks began at his elbow, and he turned and ran through the strange light of the other room.

Once outside he headed for the knoll a hundred yards behind the gas station. As the land sloped upward, his breath began to come faster and his feet were less sure on the sliding surface of the sand. But he kept on going, stumbling over rocks and cactus, while on all sides of him sky and earth seemed to be a continuum of sun. At last he reached the top of the incline. Below him he could see the building, flames shooting from the back windows and sending volumes of confused smoke to be gathered by the wind. He tried to follow its erratic path as it floated toward the mesas, but suddenly his eyes were drawn back to the scene below.

With a violent drumroll the building exploded. Dark, bleeding flames were thrown high into the air and the smoke billowed skyward in clouds of oily black. Behind Lee's eyelids the water

shimmered. His mind was a jumble of stabbing colors and apprehensions, for it seemed it was summer once again. The desert
glare was parching the little islands of sweat which had collected
on his forehead. The wind had become still. Beneath him he
could feel the insidious vibration of the sand shifting into itself,
but he refused to be absorbed by it. Because though that vibration
was a kind of life, it was life reduced to its most sterile rhythm,
the ticking of the dry land among hot rocks, in the breathless air.